Beneath the Law

Stewart Hutchison

Polygon

Polygon
An imprint of Edinburgh University Press Ltd
22 George Square, Edinburgh

Typeset in Galliard
by Hewer Text Ltd, Edinburgh, and
printed and bound in Great Britain by
Creative Print and Design, Ebbw Vale, Wales

A CIP Record for this book is
available from the British Library

ISBN 0 7486 6286 3 (paperback)

Beneath the Law

In memory of
Max Begg
who introduced me to Scoresby

Chapter 1

YOU FOUND your way. Sorry to make you climb through the garden. Louise, my wife, felt the back door was best. We're used to journalists here, but eyebrows rise when they camp on the doorstep. It's not done. Not in West Ferry. Of course it has almost blown over. When I last looked, there was just one dreary soul sitting with a thermos flask in a Montego. He's been here every day. Heaven knows which editor he has annoyed. And don't mind my tin walking stick. I'm a wee bit slow on the pins. At first they thought I might lose some toes, but the circulation's coming back. It's just a matter of time I'm told by the lassie who comes to massage my feet.

Quite right. The house is Arts and Crafts; the early period with decadent additions. You have an eye for architecture. I dare say you would, working on *Tempo*. I have an eye for a bargain, or so Forbes said when I bought the place more years ago than I care to remember. Louise has left coffee in our decadent conservatory. Just say if you'd rather have tea. And push those papers out of the way. I'm amusing myself with my defence, though as I said on the phone, they haven't brought a charge and time is running out. Whatever else you may think, I know the law.

I see you prefer a tape recorder. Incontrovertible evidence. Forbes was seldom without one. Latterly he took to producing a video camera at the drop of a hat, but Forbes was always state of the art. At the leading edge. I've become quite familiar with video myself recently. We'll come to that later. On you go. Here's an ashtray. We've given up, but I know how it helps you relax. Young women are particularly vulnerable, I hear. Now, when you said you wanted the inside story, I told you I'd give you all the facts provided I tell them in my own way. You see, the Forbes I knew was not the person who appeared on television and filled the arts pages of magazines and weekend papers. Or rather I saw a different side of the man. Though I'm a solicitor whose business rarely takes me a step out of the city and Forbes was known all over the world, we are second cousins. I've known him all my life, or rather all his life as I was born a few years before he appeared on the scene. And we kept in touch, as people say. I hope to let you see why things turned out as they did. You can add the London galleries and New York salerooms yourself. You know more about them than I ever will. But I know where Forbes Wedderburn came from. So press the button and I'll begin. Of course you may ask questions, but I don't guarantee an answer. You can draw your own conclusions.

Picture fine, slanting rain drifting from a November sky and falling evenly on the city. It falls on mansions and tenements, gardens and mills, on cobbled streets turning them to silver and on dirt roads turning them to mud. It is just cold enough to sting burning cheeks. It is just wet enough to dilute salt tears on maidenly lips. Mary Philp and Harriet Todd are running through the rain. Despite the mud, despite the puddles in the cart track they care nothing for high-buttoned boots or the hems of their petticoats. Their smocks are already a disgrace.

What's that? A word of introduction. If you insist, but please don't spoil my train of thought. My name is Gilbert Dow, Bachelor of Law, senior partner in the firm of Scrymgeour, Dow and Chalmers, Writers to the Signet. I am well past fifty. My wife, whom I married late in life, is considerably younger. We have no children, though Louise, I suspect, has not entirely discounted the possibility. Like most people, I lead a humdrum existence. In fact the only characteristic that sets me apart from you or anyone else, except for a passion you may well share for objects made of bone, is a fear of doubt. I have an overwhelming desire to get to the bottom of things, to balance the books, to set the record straight. A mystery, particularly if it concerns my family, nags me like toothache. When I have finished my story, the evidence will be there to be weighed. But who can judge events which ran their course so many years ago?

The girls' breath is coming faster. Tears of excitement fight back tears of fright. Harriet Todd would like to touch her salt tears with her tongue. Harriet's tongue can reach the end of her nose, but she is running too fast. Her teeth are on edge. We can't risk a bitten tongue. Sixteen-year-old lips part, gasp, pucker ready to scream or giggle. Sixteen-year-old bosoms heave. The track meets the main road at the station. Someone's sure to be there.

And so, my dear, let me set the scene. A scene which hasn't changed much to this day, and with which old Paton, who built this house, would have been quite familiar as he stood in that wee glazed gazebo watching for jute ships crossing the bar. Let me build an encampment of tarpaulin shelters, fill the damp air with fine limestone dust that refuses to be laid and introduce Miss Ethel Wilkie, who stood under the tarpaulins to avoid the rain on the second last Saturday of the second last month of the last year of the nineteenth century.

Chapter 2

DESPITE HER fur-trimmed coat with hussar frogging, despite her kid gloves and Paisley handbag full of schoolbooks, Ethel Wilkie was quite at home under the dripping tarpaulins among dust and limestone chippings. Her father was the master mason in charge of the half-dozen tradesmen and journeymen who stood behind her attacking limestone and facing stone with cold-chisels, etching-chisels and stone saws. Engineering operations were in progress. A road bridge was being built across the cutting that then, as now, divided the communities of West Ferry and Stannergate and spewed forth the Caledonian Railway and North British Railway joint line to run straight as a die along the slate-grey shore of the Firth of Tay. Ethel was proud her father had been chosen to supervise such an undertaking. She had gladly offered to carry his enamelled dinner pail out from the city when her mother, who was at a difficult time of life, had said she didn't feel up to the trek that day. But now Ethel's pride was giving way to annoyance. She had an appointment to keep in Crescent Street and was already behind. It had occurred to her that precious minutes could be saved by asking her father to let her cross the track in the Blondin Car. But he was away at the quarry. His dinner would get cold and the car was on the other side of the cutting, where two labourers were slowly unloading pieces of timber.

Let me take a moment to describe this unorthodox and significant mode of transport. Like Blondin, whose feats had been the talk of the music halls, it crossed chasms on wires. In place of a tightrope, cables had been slung across the cutting from short wooden towers. Suspended from the cables by a pulley and an iron framework was a wooden carriage like a little, open, wheel-less railway wagon. A guide rope passed through rings at either end, and, by pulling at one end or the other, the carriage could be moved back and forth above the railway line with whatever stones, cement or scaffold poles were needed to build the piers of the bridge. Ethel had travelled this way before. Very sensibly, she had stood in the centre of the carriage and not looked down. But then Ethel was a sensible young woman in her twenty-seventh year who taught junior classes at Baxter's Half-time School and who, despite her auburn hair and thoroughly buxom figure, took life seriously and could never be described as giddy or light headed. Ethel watched the navvies remove the last baton from the carriage. She considered shouting to them to pull the Blondin Car over to her side of the track, but in the rain and with the wind from the river she doubted her voice would carry across the cutting. A young mason was sharpening a chisel a few paces behind her, but when she spoke, her words had no effect. He stood open mouthed, staring out from beneath the tarpaulin to where the black embankment met the pale-grey sky that already had the purplish tinge of evening. The grindstone revolved more and more slowly. Ethel Wilkie followed the young man's gaze. One by one, the masons under the tarpaulin, the builders on the scaffolding and the labourers at the Blondin Car straightened up, rubbed their eyes and looked due west. Someone was running down the railway track. Someone thin and lanky with long legs that took a leap every four or five strides. Someone who wore an Ulster or an Inverness cape. For the time being, Ethel forgot her appointment and adjusted her position to get a better view. The grindstone paused, turned back on itself and stopped. A second figure had appeared followed by a third. The second figure could not catch the first, which was now almost under the scaffold. The second figure was bare-headed and broad-shouldered. His legs were too short. He stumbled along waving his arms in a long-sleeved waistcoat and an apron which

Ethel and all the bridge builders knew was the property of the North British Railway. Jimmy Ritchie, the porter at Stannergate Station, was running along the Dundee and Arbroath Joint Line, stopping every now and then to pick up a stone and throw it in the direction of the first figure, which was now past the site of the new bridge and receding with flying coat-tails in the direction of West Ferry. And following the porter through the cutting came another figure, as tall as the first but not as thin, an imposing figure in a high-buttoned greatcoat who held on to his cap as he ran. It was Lieutenant Glass of the City Police. He was running fast, in more of a hurry than the porter and quite contemptuous of the police burgh boundary he was about to cross beneath the bridge.

One or even two people running along a railway line arouses curiosity. When a lieutenant of police takes to stumbling over sleepers, when a normally peaceable porter repeatedly and before witnesses attempts common assault with fist-sized pieces of the permanent way, something must be done. The masons and builders scotched the idea of an Inverness cape or an Ulster coat. In their eyes, the first figure was wearing the devil's cloak. Beneath them on the railway track, leaping between earth and air was the Craigie Ghost. Hadn't she heard? Didn't she know the stories? The Craigie Ghost frightened women and girls and made children sleep with their heads beneath the bedclothes. It pounced at night, laughed, touched, sighed but never spoke and made its escape on spring-heeled boots. The bridge builders clambered down the wooden scaffold and ran up the dripping, muddy cutting after the lieutenant. The masons rubbed their eyes with dusty fingers, snatched up mells and chisels that might prove useful in an encounter with the supernatural and set off along the rim of the cutting to intercept the ghost where the railway met the shore.

Of course Ethel Wilkie had heard of the Craigie Ghost. For six months or more, gossip in Dundee and Broughty Ferry and even in Monifieth had consisted of little else. The Craigie Ghost lurked in the woods near Craigie House. The Craigie Ghost had surprised two women in West Ferry. One had been touched.

The other had fallen and bumped her knee. Stockings had been ruined. The Craigie Ghost had appeared at Stannergate and startled Doctor Fraser's horse on the Dundee road. The good doctor had struck the ghost with his whip, but he had been unable to stop his gig until it reached the horse-trough beside the gas works. He had been considerably shaken, though he said it himself. The ghost was no respecter of power or position. The wife of Baillie Williamson, found by her maid lying in dishabille behind the French windows, laid the blame for her swoon on the Craigie Ghost, which had appeared in the garden and grinned through the glass at an embarrassingly indelicate moment.

Meetings had been held. Activity had taken place in both the city and county police forces. Likely suspects had been questioned in the nearby orphan institution and even on the *Mars*, which swung darkly on its mooring in the tideway with its cargo of unruly boys bound for a life at sea. There had been talk of organising patrols on the lonelier byways, and gangs of eager youths had ranged without success as far inland as Barnhill. But that was months ago. In September and October nothing had been seen of the Craigie Ghost. Questions from Ethel's pupils had become less and less frequent. The children knew the Craigie Ghost wore a horrid black cloak. They knew all about his spring-heeled boots, but they also believed he was a summer ghost who hated cold and rain and fog. For weeks past, even the youngest had been brave enough to poke their heads from beneath the blankets at night, even though their ears got cold.

What did you say? Be patient, lass. It's part of the same story, and we agreed I'd tell it in my own way. Unless you understand the beginning, you'll never know what led to the tragic end your readers are so keen to hear about. Where was I?

Yes. Ethel Wilkie was alone under the tarpaulin amidst the stones and dust and damp. Maybe she gave a wee shudder and pushed her hands deeper into the pockets of her coat. Hunting ghosts was all very well, but it took time. She was still on the wrong side of the cutting and no closer to her appointment at the schoolhouse where Mr Meiklejohn would introduce her to the personable young man so keen to improve his English. The ghost and his pursuers were by now silhouetted against the water. There was more interesting work afoot than dressing and hauling stones. The builders would not come back. So Miss Ethel Wilkie, who could tell a solid footfall from a ghostly one, shrugged and picked her way to the little wooden gallery built on the edge of the cutting that served as the northern terminal of the Blondin Car. Yes, of course she could have scrambled down the bank and crossed the line at the bottom of the cutting. She might even have found her way through the builder's debris to the path which led to the Dundee road, but this would have taken time; and in those days no young woman, however high-spirited, would have scrambled down a muddy, precipitous embankment in ankle-length skirts.

The rain was easing. Carefully Ethel removed her gloves. The guide rope had only to be untied and, hand over hand, she could pull the carriage towards her along the cable. Don't imagine Ethel was daunted by the prospect. I've seen photographs. The era of the Gibson Girl was about to dawn and Ethel had anticipated the fashion. All of five feet six inches tall, her hair piled high beneath a black straw hat and her bosom thrust above a corseted waist, she had all the majesty of a ship's figurehead, quite equal to any task involving rope. She was half way to the southern side of the cutting when things went wrong. Her thoughts were on the student waiting to meet her when her handbag slipped from the ledge on which she had placed it. She sprang forward to save it from the mucky floor but too late. Granted, no young lady could aspire to Ethel's stature without acquiring a certain weightiness, and this weight, suddenly transposed from one end of the carriage to the other, made the Blondin Car bounce so violently that the pulley slipped off the rope, jammed the cable between the wheel and its framework, and stopped Ethel's progress dead half way across and twenty feet above the railway line. She tried pulling the guide rope to inch the car along without the aid of a pulley, but this needed brute force and Ethel, who was no brute, soon put on her gloves as her fingers were becoming sore from the friction and settled down to await the return of the ghost-hunters.

So she had a grandstand view as the first figure reached the centre of the embankment which bordered the shoreline, glanced back at the pursuing porter's apron and police greatcoat and ran on towards the spindly footbridge spanning the line at West Ferry. From her balcony seat she saw the jostling, shouting masons scale the last few feet of the embankment and pop up in front of the apron and greatcoat but well behind the Inverness cape, which was trying so hard to reach that point on the horizon where the rails converged. She was first to hear and then to see the Aberdeen express approaching from the west under its portable cloud of yellow smoke. She looked on as the train's angular, purposeful, interminably long shape filled more and more of the cutting. She covered her ears as its whistle filled more and more of the damp, autumn air; then the smoke engulfed her. When she peered through the stinking haze, the train and its pall of steam was overtaking the running figures one by one until at last the horizon was all train or the train was all horizon and the imposing lieutenant of police, the panting porter, the belligerent builders and the Craigie Ghost, who was still outdistancing his pursuers, all disappeared from view. But when the express had passed (all trains must come to an end) and the only trace was a winking rear light and a wake of oily steam, when the horizon had re-established itself at the top of the embankment, there were no running figures to break its horizontal monotony. They had all vanished down the far side on to the sea shore.

Ethel's surprise was giving way to apprehension. She wondered when her father would return. In any case, the workmen were sure to come back soon. But minute after minute passed, light continued to fade and she began to shiver. She had decided to shout for help when the carriage began to sway from side to side beneath the cable. A faint cry of panic escaped Ethel as she peered into the gathering dusk first to the north then to the south seeking the source of the shaking. The cause was not to be found in someone pulling the guide ropes from one or other side of the cutting, but in mid air. Inch by inch, foot by foot a man was approaching along the cable from the Stannergate end. Ethel was so taken aback to discover another human being within a few yards that her head swam and she clutched the side of the carriage in dismay. From that angle, all she could see was a pair of heavy boots with smooth soles, devoid of hobnails, and the tail of a coarse pilot jacket hanging below them. The man had wrapped his legs round the cable and hand over hand was pushing himself feet first towards her. She watched mesmerised as the man let his legs swing free and, with a final grunt of exertion, dropped into the carriage beside her. No matter how acute her relief at finding this reassuring presence so unexpectedly by her side, Ethel did not ignore the conventions.

'I am Miss Wilkie,' she said. 'My father is in charge here. He lets me cross from time to time, but the wheel has slipped off the cable.'

'So it seems,' said the acrobat. And in an instant he had handed Ethel his jacket and was pulling on the guide rope with all his might. The little carriage began to move. Gratitude and relief welled up. Ethel wanted to help, but her rescuer seemed so equal to the task she stood aside, pressed his coat to her bosom and watched as he pulled them steadily foot by foot to the far side of the cutting. It was hard to tell the man's age. Perhaps forty, though he was greying at the temples and wore a heavy moustache which concealed his upper lip. His face was fresh and ruddy, a face that had seldom seen the sun but was no stranger to cold and wind and wet. He was powerful, but not tall, scarcely taller than Ethel herself in her high-heeled boots and straw hat. His plain waistcoat and worsted trousers marked him as a working man, but Ethel was sure, wherever he had sprung from, her rescuer had nothing to do with the new bridge. A man as at home hanging upside down from a rope as on solid earth was not a huer of stone or builder of arches.

Etiquette did not require Ethel to remove her glove before shaking hands with the rescuer, who introduced himself as Alexander Yule, late of Newfoundland. Etiquette did not require Alexander Yule, after shaking her hand, to lift it and examine the red marks in the fading light.

'You've burnt yourself on the rope,' he said, delving in the pocket of his pilot coat, 'but this will soothe it.' He uncorked a brown glass bottle with his teeth and quickly spread a few drops of yellowish, oily liquid across Ethel Wilkie's plump palm.

Chapter 3

Absolutely right. What I've just described was indeed the inspiration for one of Forbes Wedderburn's seminal works. I'm impressed by your grasp of the subject. He completed it in his last year at college. Duncan of Jordanstone. An institution of fluctuating reputation, which counts him far and away its most notable exponent of the visual arts. He taught there for a while before moving to greater things. I've no idea where the painting is now. I'm sure you'll know. It's unmistakable with the huge, foreshortened man in mid air and the tiny figures scampering along the bottom edge of the canvas. What did he call it again? *Deliverance*, of course. It was hailed as a late flowering of Scottish neo-surrealism or some such tosh. I'm not surprised there's no record of the story. I've never been credited as Forbes's muse, though I may go down in posterity as his nemesis. No, I'm fine. Perhaps you can switch on the light, then we'll get on if your wee machine has enough tape.

So Jimmy Ritchie, the porter and ghost-hunter, emerged from the sulphurous cloud of locomotive steam and slithered crabwise down the embankment towards a wall above the sodden footpath that followed the northern shore of the Tay above the high-water mark of ordinary spring tides. Was he spurred by the sight of the builders about to claim his prize? Was he intent on impressing Lieutenant Glass, prudently picking his way over slippery sleepers just behind him, or were his boots simply so caked with mud that he could not stop? In any case, he plunged down the embankment and, in one movement, vaulted headlong over the the wall. His muddy boots flew through the air, but instead of finding grass beneath them, found fur. He saw angry brown eyes, felt rancid breath on his face, then a massive paw cuffed him on the shoulder and he fell to the ground in a heap. The panting masons stopped in their tracks. The stumbling, cursing builders gave up and formed a ragged line on the horizon. Even Lieutenant Glass pulled up short, for the sight of a railway porter being tossed by a fully-grown brown bear is enough to divert even the most dedicated ghost-hunter from his purpose.

The porter lay on the footpath with his arms over his head. The bear poked him with its muzzled snout, leaving smudges of saliva on the apron. A wiry little man with steel-rimmed spectacles, who was attached to the bear by a twelve-foot chain, hauled at the animal with all his strength, muttering between his teeth in a strange tongue, while five companions, jumping this way and that, tried to catch hold of the chain and bring the bear under control. Who knows how long it might have taken to rescue Jimmy Ritchie had not one of the strangers on the footpath, a thin, sad-looking man with long grey hair, taken a fiddle from the folds of his coat and despite the rain, which would do the strings no good, struck up a lilting, waltzing sort of tune? Prodding the petrified porter one last time with a powerful but friendly paw, the bear abandoned its playmate, reared on to its hind legs and began to sway and dip and pirouette at the end of its chain as it had been taught.

The leader of the musicians, portly and sly with an enormous moustache, hurried to help Jimmy Ritchie to his feet. The rest of the troupe formed a sheepish cluster round the fiddler and looked up apprehensively at the lieutenant who stood, legs astride, on top of the wall. Breathing as deeply as his exertions would allow, the lieutenant, who had not expected to encounter a German band far less a dancing bear, placed his whistle between his teeth and with a regulation blast, drowned out the fiddler, stopped the bear in mid waltz and sent the itinerant musicians huddling even more closely together on the footpath at the water's edge.

'Who's in charge?' roared Lieutenant Glass, letting his whistle drop on to the chest of his greatcoat. The leader eyed the double row of polished buttons and the whistle still swinging on its silver chain. Removing his broad-brimmed hat, he approached till his eyes were level with the policeman's boots.

'Niemcewicz, your honour,' he said, 'and my wife Bella. We bring amusement to the people.' A sallow, yellow-haired woman left the group and made a deep curtsey. Lieutenant Glass, who had seldom been called 'your honour' and had never been the recipient of a curtsey in his life, folded his arms and glared down from the wall.

'Keep that animal under control,' he said, 'and don't overstay your welcome. You've missed St Mary's Fair. Now, where's the man who jumped over this wall a few moments ago?' Niemcewicz looked perplexed.

'He's here, your honour. He's not hurt one bit.'

'Not him, you fool, the one in the cape.' And the lieutenant held out the skirts of his coat to represent the garment in question and jiggled to and fro in imitation of the Craigie Ghost. Niemcewicz stared back blankly. His wife examined the footpath with downcast eyes. The musicians shuffled about, uncertain whether or not to be amused. Lieutenant Glass leaped from the wall and landed directly in front of their leader. Pushing his face to within an inch of Niemcewicz's washed-out eyes, he bellowed, 'Damn it, you must have seen him. The train only cut us off for two minutes. He can't have vanished into thin air.'

It was all beyond Niemcewicz's grasp. He shrugged his shoulders and spread his hands in mute incomprehension as, one by one, the masons and builders jumped on to the path. They sympathised with the porter, skirted warily round the bear, which watched them through bright little eyes, and rummaged inquisitively among the trunks and instruments which were neatly stowed on a hand cart. The lieutenant made notes in his notebook with a pencil designed to function even in the wet. He scrutinised the musicians in turn with a gaze the keenness of which was intended to forestall any concealment. In turn, they averted their eyes and looked so sad that the lieutenant closed his notebook, dismissed them with a wave of the hand and, mustering his troops, set off eastwards to rendezvous with a constable of the county force who was approaching in the distance with a band of volunteers from Broughty Ferry.

Only the porter did not join the lieutenant to continue the search along the soggy margins of the Firth of Tay. Jimmy Ritchie had had enough. Muddy and indignant, he set off westwards after the German band, who had unpacked their instruments and, to bolster their spirits, played a jaunty, if discordant march as they trudged along dragging their hand-cart behind them. Had the porter possessed a musical ear, had he possessed a knowledge not only of the timetables of the Caledonian and North British Railway Companies but also of four-part harmony, he would have realised that, despite the liveliness of the tune, something was amiss. Despite energetic contortions and elaborate fingering, the clarinet in the hands of the tallest musician, who wore a long loden coat and a pointed hat drawn close round his ears, remained obstinately silent. All through '*Alte Kameraden*' the band played without the benefit of woodwind. For four verses of '*Drei Lilien*', the clarinettist puffed out his cheeks but his instrument gave forth not one note. Jimmy Ritchie did not notice. How could ears attuned to train whistles sort one instrument from another? He followed the band until it reached Stannergate Station, then climbed over the track to the door of his railway cottage, where his wife appeared with the two young ladies who, on account of their recent experience, were still clutching cups of hot, sweet tea.

Twenty minutes later, on a deserted path behind the oil cake works at Stannergate, out of sight of the railway station, the unmusical clarinettist placed his instrument in the hand-cart, slipped out of his borrowed clothes and, from an accordion case that contained no accordion, took a bundle reminiscent of a hastily-folded Inverness cape. Leon Niemcewicz, accordionist and band leader, unstrapped his instrument and approached the lanky figure who was transforming himself into a country gentleman of ample means. Niemcewicz who, like the members of many German bands, originated considerably further east than the territory of the Second Reich, stood four-square before the

Inverness cape and held out his hand. The trumpeter, young and stocky, stood behind the would-be ghost, cutting off his retreat. Caught between two pillars of Slavic belligerence, Peter Pye (why shouldn't I name him now?) fluttered his long, pale fingers beneath the Inverness cape, let them emerge in a fist, and with one upwards movement, released a cascade of sovereigns, half-sovereigns and crumpled banknotes. Peter Pye stepped nimbly past the bandmaster scrambling for money on the wet pathway. The gentleman in the Inverness cape strode swiftly past Frau Niemcewicz and the grey-haired fiddler as they stooped to help their leader. Only when he reached the bear, which went by the name of Kaspar, and its keeper, who, despite the considerable revenue being trodden into the mud, looked on with quiet detachment through steel-framed spectacles, did Peter Pye stop. Words were exchanged; confidences whispered. Ten long fingers lingered in Kaspar's rough, matted hair, then Pye was off towards the gravel pit with great, loping strides. Only the keeper and Kaspar saw him go.

Chapter 4

SO YOU'RE staying at the Queens? Right at the centre of things, or haven't you seen it yet? The old town has been badly mauled over the years, with everybody trying to redevelop the same wee patch. We demolish things, build new ones, then just when people are used to them, knock them down again or even blow them up. But there are a few places where people would still recognise the lie of the street no matter how far back you go. The Nethergate is one. After dinner, you might take a stroll. Just round the corner, you'll find the Overgate, or rather a shopping centre where the old street used to be. That was the ancestral home of the Wedderburns. Oh, yes. Wedderburn was an important name in Dundee. They were running things in these parts long before jute and jam had come and gone. They started as merchants, wrote plays, went into the church. A Wedderburn translated Luther into Scots. They go that far back. And they made sure for a hundred and fifty years that the town clerk was always a Wedderburn. In Scotland the town clerk was just as influential as the provost. Let's say it was as if Dick Whittington had founded a dynasty that ran London for centuries.

Did Forbes claim kinship? Maybe not in as many words, but he let folk know his family went away back. Being called Wedderburn round here does you no harm. I've never checked. Neither did he, as far as I know. But you'll find that in seventy-nine, at the time of the first referendum, when he unveiled that provocative triptych which got up so many unionist noses, he called it *The Complaynt of Scotland* after the work of another Wedderburn who was Vicar of Dundee during the Reformation. 'An inherited talent for mischief,' I think he put it.

If you stroll further east – I'll show you on a map – you'll see the remains of the Dens Mills. Posh flats now, of course. Award-winning designs. But at the time I'm talking about, when Ethel Wilkie taught one class in the forenoon and another in the afternoon to let the children spend half the day in the mill, upwards of three thousand people made a living there. You look surprised. Child labour? I don't suppose they saw it that way. State schooling finished at fourteen then, and families in need could apply for an exemption to let their bairns start work at twelve. It was a form of income support. Baxters, who owned the mills, ran their own school. The children still had some education and the families got the benefit of another wage, however small. And remember, there was always a full-time job for them when they reached fourteen. Money was to be made in the mills by women as much as men, so I doubt there was any pang of conscience when Mr Meiklejohn, the headmaster, introduced Ethel Wilkie to Herr Jochen Dau in the parlour of the school-house later that evening.

In the shaded gaslight, the schoolmaster sniffed Ethel's palm. 'Oleum Hyperoodon Ampullatus,' he said, letting go her hand. 'The oil of the bottlenose whale, said to cure burns, sprains and bruises.'

Quickly Ethel drew a handkerchief from her sleeve and wiped away the last traces of Alexander Yule's unusual remedy. By the mantelpiece, Herr Jochen Dau replaced the bronze statuette he had been examining and turned to Mr Meiklejohn. 'Professor, you astonish me to recognise such a thing,' he said, in an accent which hardly seemed in urgent need of a tutor.

Herr Dau's fame had gone before him. Throughout the century, when the trend had been towards jute, Baxters had stuck to linen. Peter Carmichael, their ingenious engineer, had taught them long ago to keep an eye out for innovation. So when a company agent, sent to the eastern Baltic to buy flax, telegraphed home about a little firm he'd discovered with an interesting line in oilcloth, it was only a matter of time before Herr Dau was offered cabin passage to Dundee and a personal bench in the laboratory high in the tower of Dens Mills. He had taken lodgings in one of the most respectable boarding houses in the city, taught his landlady to cook meatballs with lemon sauce, Koenigsberg style, and become increasingly disillusioned with his grasp of English. When he heard of the company school, he contacted Mr Meiklejohn at once.

The schoolmaster had more than one motive when he suggested Dau should take lessons from his young assistant, who was renowned throughout the district for her pleasant, well-modulated voice and exceptional command of language. Ethel Wilkie was already past the age when most young women were betrothed, if not married. While appreciating her value as a teacher, Meiklejohn had very definite ideas of the propriety of things and had come to view Ethel's continuing spinsterhood with concern. So it was with some satisfaction that he brought Ethel Wilkie and Jochen Dau together in his front parlour and persuaded them to meet twice a week, when Mrs Meiklejohn would serve tea and leave them alone to plumb the finer mysteries of the English tongue.

Don't imagine Ethel was unaware of, or indeed unused to, the attentions of young men. Though there was nothing in her past which could be described as a lasting relationship, she had entertained a variety of widely differing admirers with equally varying enthusiasm since her late teens. She already counted a doctor, a minister and a whole series of local tradesmen among her disappointed suitors, and had soon seen through Mr Meiklejohn's scheme. But she went along with it out of curiosity. Over tea, she noticed Herr Dau observing her in a manner which she recognised as the prelude to attentions of a more particular nature.

Their way home lay in the same direction, and Ethel found herself staying on the tram as far as the Sinderins, though normally she would have got off a few stops before. When they had travelled in silence for some time, Jochen Dau suddenly asked which church she attended. It was an age when religion was seen to be practised, but Ethel was taken aback because she assumed he'd be a Catholic or belong to some strange, northern branch of Protestantism. She said at once that her family had been members of St Mary's for generations and was even more surprised when Herr Dau announced he would attend the service there next day as he was looking for a church that suited him. 'I may meet you afterwards and also your esteemed family,' he said without a hint of embarrassment. And it was Ethel who gathered her things in confusion as the tram rattled to a halt at the crossroads.

Jochen Dau stepped from the platform and was about to offer Ethel his arm when, above the clatter of the departing tram, there came the sound of lively dance music. Beneath a lamppost on the corner where Hawkhill and Perth Road diverged, some travelling musicians were playing. In their midst, a brown bear danced and capered at the end of a chain. Ethel Wilkie and Jochen Dau hurried to join the crowd. Ethel clapped and craned to see as the bear swung to and fro and, despite its muzzle, deftly caught titbits thrown in its direction. Herr Dau proudly cleared the way and beat time to the music, which was more familiar to him than to most of the crowd, with his cane. When a tin cup was rattled by a yellow-haired woman, Jochen Dau was the first to part with a handful of change. When one tune came to an end he requested another, first in German then in Russian to make sure. Only when the bear needed more room, only when Kaspar decided to test the limits of his chain, extend his dance floor and drag his keeper into the yellow pool of lamplight did Herr Dau tire of the performance. When gaslight glinted on steel-rimmed spectacles, Dau yearned to be gone. He hopped from one foot to the other in agitation. He gripped Miss Wilkie's arm so tightly she pulled back in dismay. His Adam's apple jerked alarmingly and before she could resist, he hustled Ethel to the edge of the crowd where he fumbled for his watch, doffed his hat and muttered that he had just remembered a report he must finish. She watched in astonishment as he hurried away along Perth Road and disappeared down Windsor Street towards his lodgings.

Excuse me while I hobble around a bit. As I said, my circulation isn't quite back to normal. The numbness reminds me only too often of those hours in the water, but we'll come to that later. Just be patient, my dear. How can you see the whole picture unless you know what led Forbes and me to do what we did? I hear Louise in the kitchen. She'll bring a fresh pot and maybe a few scones before you check into your hotel. Before you switch off the recorder, I want to tell you what else happened on that momentous day.

Late that evening, when the last Saturday but one of November had only ninety minutes to run, when the wind had turned north-west and the rain, which had never really stopped all day, had changed its angle accordingly; when Miss Ethel Wilkie lay snug between starched sheets and Herr Jochen Dau, alone in his room, was about to stub out yet another cigarette, two muffled figures trudged along the dark quayside of King William IV Dock. They looked neither to left nor right. They ignored the gloomy hulls and masts floating silently above their black reflections. The two travelling musicians had one aim in view. Clutching their instruments beneath their coats, they picked their way over wet manila cables, through rippling rain pools and across railway lines set in glistening cobbles to the Royal Arch, which formed an ornate, deserted, unnecessary gateway to the docks, but welcome shelter.

They shook the rain from their coats and cast wary eyes towards the smudge of light in Green Market which marked the door of the Harbour Head Inn. Save for the Model Lodging House, this somewhat shabby and nautical hostelry offered the cheapest accommodation in Dundee. When they stood blinking and dripping in the overheated taproom, the landlord gave a quizzical, though barely perceptible nod, took down two keys and poured two measures of Holland's gin from a stone bottle. Without a word, the musicians found room at a table between two firemen from the London packet playing cards and some morose Scandinavians from a timber ship.

The landlord, who was called Tommy Allen, propped his arms on the counter and redirected his attention to the three men at the end of the bar. A windfall had let him give up the sea. It was said that when crew were hard to find, Tommy Allen was not above crimping – that is supplying seamen who are in no condition to object to their unexpected re-employment – for a suitable price. Nothing was proved, and sailors were not discouraged from dropping in whenever they were in port. The landlord's thirst for conversation almost surpassed his thirst for whisky, which was very deep indeed.

'The Galloping Cow,' he said, shooting a jet of liquid into the spittoon. 'There was a woman. I kent her in Frisco long afore she bought that saloon on Pacific Street. She took my belt and put it round her thigh for a garter. It wasn't long enough. What a powerful woman. She once broke the back of a lad who tried to kiss her.' He flexed his biceps in imitation of this amazon. Allen had jumped ship in California and found his way home via the diggings. Every conversation with Tommy Allen inevitably ended on the Barbary Coast. But that night he had competition. Wiggy Bennett was back from a trip round the Horn as bosun on a nitrate clipper, and who should have crossed the threshold a moment later but Yule the specktioneer.

I doubt you'll find that one in your spellcheck. On Arctic whaling ships, he was the chief harpooner. It comes from the Dutch *speksnijder* or fat-cutter, a reference to the flensing operations which were also usually under his command.

Alexander Yule might have matched every tale of foul Cape Horn weather with a story of perils in the pack ice. He could have bettered every description of a San Francisco brawl with a first-hand account of lancing a maddened whale from the bow of an open boat; but he preferred to drink his whisky and smoke his pipe in silence.

Who was the third person at the polished bar top listening to Tommy Allen's far-fetched yarns? Between the garrulous bosun and the quiet specktioneer, in overalls that proclaimed his professional interest in coal dust, stood Harry Wilkie, Ethel's younger brother. He was a fireman in the engine house of Lower Dens Mill and had just finished a back shift. Harry had shown scant interest in his father's profession. He had pursued a number of unpromising occupations, but that wet Saturday night, in the smoky warmth, his thoughts were far from coal, steam or linen. He saw himself fresh ashore on the Barbary Coast, strolling down Pacific Street 'Terrific Street' with money in his pocket and a girl on each arm.

'Chicken Devine,' said Allen, getting into his stride, 'was an evil wee man. He tried to knife Bill Maitland, who ran a bar on Battery Street, but Maitland was too quick for him. He grabbed the knife, cut Devine's left hand clean off with one swipe, then threw him into the street. Devine shouted, "Maitland, you bastard, chuck out me fin!" and he snatched his hand out of the mud and took it to a quack doctor who sewed it back on again.' Harry Wilkie supplied the expected question. 'Of course not,' said Allen. 'It dropped off and they had to give him a hook.' Tommy Allen unbuttoned his shirt and thrust a flabby, bare shoulder towards his audience. 'That scar,' he said, 'was made by the self-same hook.'

In the silence that followed this well-rehearsed and, it must be said, familiar revelation, Harry took the opportunity to return to a topic he had raised earlier. He asked about going to sea. Once more the bosun shook his head and laughed and swilled his whisky. Harry was too old. He had left it too late to become an apprentice. And the sailing ship had had its day. Dozens were being scrapped or sold to the Norwegians. In vain, Harry Wilkie emphasised his suitability for employment aboard a steamship. In vain he drew attention to his skill in stoking, trimming and banking fires, in handling coal and ash and regulating the flow of steam. Wiggy Bennett lost interest and Alexander Yule only smiled, puffed his pipe and played with a little whalebone carving that hung from his watch chain. Harry buttoned his jacket to leave, but before he could make his way dejectedly to the door, Lieutenant Glass pushed into the bar followed by a constable with a bull's-eye lantern on his belt.

Glass waved aside the whisky Tommy Allen slid across the counter. The lieutenant was in no mood for conviviality. Numbers did not tally. He was scrutinising faces, consulting his notebook, making comparisons. All evening, suspicion had gnawed and rankled. He crossed the room with three strides and jerked the musicians to their feet. Sheepishly they shook their heads and emptied the contents of their pockets. Coins, matches, pipes and tobacco pouches dropped on to the table among the puddles of beer. The lieutenant signalled that they could pick up their belongings, then suddenly demanded that they remove their boots, which he examined with distaste and dropped on the floor. He cast a glance round the room, nodded to the constable, and without a word, they stepped into the night.

Where were the other musicians? It was not the first time Niemcewicz and his troupe had visited Dundee. They found lodgings in Yeaman Shore with a pork butcher who had started by supplying victuals to foreign ships and now did a brisk trade in all manner of continental produce. Earlier that year, 'O. Gruber – Pork Butcher' had been painted out above his shop window and 'Italian Warehouseman and Pork Butchery – O. Gruber Proprietor' lettered in its place in gold leaf. Gruber was not in the least disturbed by this dichotomy of nationality so long as business was thriving, which was why he had rapidly developed a dislike of the fat musician who ate his food, slept under his roof and regarded money simply as a means of buying a drink if he wanted to stay or a railway ticket if he wanted to move on. Gruber's wife had struck up a friendship with Bella Niemcewicz at St Mary's Fair a few years earlier and persuaded him to offer hospitality to his musical countrymen if they returned. The butcher, a down to earth Bremener, had scant regard for his eccentric eastern guests who originated in the racial melting pot left by the last partition of Poland. He regarded them as no better than gypsies and insisted they stay no longer than a couple of days. Besides, this time there was the bear. What would his customers think if they discovered the lard and oatmeal and castor sugar they bought in neat paper cones had been keeping company with a European brown bear whose greedy snout unfailingly found its way into sweet-smelling sacks and bins?

Only Niemcewicz and his wife were allowed into the house. Kaspar and his gloomy keeper had been lodged with ill grace in an outhouse in the yard. Inch by inch, the raindrop on the storehouse window drew nearer to a dusty cobweb that ran, left to right, across the bottom of the frame. Inch by inch, Kaspar's tongue drew nearer to the end of a trail of grease it had been following across the floor. But the cobweb remained intact; the last smear of pork fat never reached the bear's snout. A crooked forefinger rapped, withdrew, then rapped again at the window pane. Kaspar raised his head and uttered a rumbling growl between sharp, unmuzzled teeth. His keeper watched motionless as the latch was raised and a tall, oilskinned figure stepped cautiously into the storehouse. Peter Pye twisted his wet felt hat between bony fingers and settled himself on a precarious perch of boxes.

'You saved me this afternoon.' Pye smiled ingratiatingly with a wary eye on the bear.

'You paid,' said the keeper gruffly. 'How did you find us?'

Pye's fingers fluttered at the harshness of the tone. 'I always know where everyone is,' he said simply. 'But I owe you a special debt. Your leader didn't want to help me when I landed in your midst beside the railway line. But you took my part. If you hadn't threatened to withdraw the bear from the show he would never have agreed to the temporary addition of a new, totally unmusical member to his troupe. I would not be standing here.' Pye drew a green glass bottle from his pocket and held it out. The keeper looked carefully at the label through wire-rimmed spectacles and put it to his lips.

'Why were they after you?' asked Kaspar's keeper with surprising fluency. 'Are you a thief? Did you escape? I know what it is to be pursued by the gendarmerie, whether or not accusations can be proved.'

'Don't take me for a common criminal,' said Pye. 'I have ample means and not gained one penny dishonestly unless, of course, you think an annual dividend from the family jute mill is itself a crime. The interest shown by the lieutenant and his inept followers stems from my deep-seated preoccupation with observing the phenomenon of fright in the female. As a child, I chased cows. Complaints were made; lawsuits threatened. Later, I persuaded one of our housemaids, on the promise of my entire weekly allowance which probably exceeded her wage, to come to my room one night clad in her shift. She entered, as agreed, on all fours; in the posture, if not with the grace, of your delightful companion. When I lifted my razor strop (I had only just started shaving) I noticed she had inserted a folded handkerchief between her teeth, the better to honour her vow of silence. Surprise is the most powerful instrument of any researcher. As she tensed every muscle, expecting at any moment to feel the sting of leather on her buttocks, I took my chamber pot from where it had been placed out of her field of vision and poured its carefully fermented contents over her head. The treachery of woman. All honour deserted her. Leaping up, she hurled the pot, which was an attractive piece of Wemyss ware, against the fender. Spitting out the handkerchief, she screeched like a banshee. When my panic-stricken parents burst into the room, they found me under the bed and the maid lashing out insanely with the strop whenever I tried to leave my sanctuary. Next morning she was gone. She bought a millinery shop in Aberdeen: a very sudden rise to the property-owning class. And I was sent to school in Edinburgh. From then on, I confined myself to experimenting on strangers in the open air.'

Peter Pye stepped into the pool of lamplight, crouched down and released a little catch set into the heel of each boot. A twang of steel and he was catapulted to the rafters. The keeper gasped. Kaspar lashed out viciously, but his angry claws found only a shadow on an empty corn sack. The Craigie Ghost hung from his elbows, looked impishly down on the man and the bear and laughed till tears ran down his cheeks while the lamp swung from its hook in the roof beam.

'Are there boarding schools where you come from?' asked the Craigie Ghost from the rafters. 'They are probably very different from the one I attended, but I suspect they share an equally strict attitude to dress. Everything has to be in proper repair, and as footwear in general and young men's footwear in particular is subject to all manner of ill-treatment during the course of private education, it was not long before I made the acquaintance of a cobbler who lived in the seaport adjacent to the city in which my school was situated. Do you believe in the power of coincidence? I do, or I'd not be here sharing your delightful company. The cobbler, whose name need not concern us, was of interest to my schoolmates only because of his extremely reasonable prices. He was of interest to me, however, because of the two pastimes to which he devoted his off-duty hours: namely clocks and bottles. His interest in bottles was simply to get to the bottom of every one that came to hand. Whether the contents were whisky or gin, beer, wine or porter mattered not, so long as the bottle was capable of being emptied. His interest in clocks, however, went deeper, if it is possible to go deeper than the bottom of a bottle.

In a corner of his back shop, beside off-cuts of leather, tins of nails and dusty, disused lasts he kept a stock of cog wheels and ratchets, mild steel and spring steel, pinions, punches and balance wheels necessary for repairing and reconstructing the ancient clocks with which, I believe, his home was festooned. I stumbled upon this trove by accident, indeed by coincidence, when searching for a pair of boots he had been repairing for me. The juxtaposition of steel and shoe leather fired my imagination, put flesh on the bones of an idea that had been with me ever since I had so abruptly abandoned my experiments. Broaching the subject was not easy, but the gift of several interesting bottles and, as always, the promise of ample reward smoothed my path. I sketched a rough outline of my proposal in French chalk on his worn workbench. He was sceptical. Sovereigns changed hands and he agreed to have finished drawings ready for the following week. His design met with my complete approval. I advanced more money, and within a month was the possessor of the finest spring-heeled boots in the land.'

'Surely the story of your boots has become famous and spread even as far as Edinburgh. Maybe they have even been mentioned in the newspaper. And yet the shoemaker says nothing. He has not told of his part in this. Does your money or fear of the law keep him quiet?' said the bear keep.

'Sea water,' said Peter Pye. 'The answer is to be found in the brackish saline solution where the Water of Leith meets the Firth of Forth. Anticipating what you have described, I visited him shortly after delivery of the boots. A seaport is the most unfortunate place to live when your interest in bottles is as great as our cobbler's. There was a thin skin of ice. Snow deadened our footfall. He dropped from the quay like a stone and the ice closed over him. Do you believe in predestination?' Pye asked from between the rafters. 'I believe it was fate that brought us three together.' He crooked his leg across the beams and one by one dropped sovereigns to the floor as he spoke. 'In one last experiment, I want to use your services and those of your companion who shows such bestial antagonism to spring-heeled boots. The Craigie Ghost is becoming too well known. My boots are talked about all over with wild exaggeration. More than once I have been close to capture, and today's debacle was the last straw. When I sprang a full six feet and landed before those two hussies on the road, their reaction was to giggle rather than scream. Only when I pinched them so hard that they squealed did excitement give way to tears and amusement turn to fright. The supreme element of panic was lacking. I need something new, something quite unique to finally lay the Craigie Ghost to rest, and in our meeting I know I've found the answer. As I said, I believe in predestination.'

Slowly, the keeper got to his feet. The bear raised his head, rattling the chain on the flagstone floor. 'I too have discovered something today,' the keeper said very quietly. 'Do you not have a saying that one good turn deserves another?' And from behind a barrel of butter, he took a bottle of schnapps which he uncorked and passed to the Craigie Ghost.

What did you say? Beyond belief? Don't you recall the charcoal sketch of a spring-heeled figure hanging like a crucifix from a network of rafters? The shower of coins was picked out in yellow chalk. It metamorphosed into a shipyard worker in the central panel of *The Complaynt*; the rafters became a scaffold, the coins a cascade of sparks. Forbes Wedderburn knew all about what happened between sacks of flour and tubs of pickled pork in a back court in Yeaman Shore. And now I'll let you get away. You've had a tiring drive and I see from your expression that our first wee chat has not been quite what you expected. Don't come before ten-thirty tomorrow. My physiotherapist is due first thing, which always drains me a little. The road into town is quite simple, second right and straight ahead. And give a wave to the chap in the Montego as you pass. He'll still be there.

Chapter 5

SORRY TO make you come all the way up here, and with such a heavy bag too. I won't get up. The muscle-cruncher has left me feeling as if I've run a marathon. You can see why I made my study at the top of the house. The panelling is original, but I confess we replaced the window. Its panes were quaint, but broke up the view like the grid on a map. So out it came. Have I shocked you? My instinct for conservation runs along quite restricted lines. To lose an original window when the house has thirty more doesn't concern me, but the loss of even one item from my collection would fill me with distress. Take a look through the telescope. Despite the haze, you should see most of the Fife coast. No. At this state of the tide, the sand bar is invisible save for a slight lightening near the horizon. You've made good use of our late start. I recognise some of the books, but those must be quite new. Our bookshop does Forbes Wedderburn proud, supports the local hero. No doubt you'll put them on expenses. But before we open the pages and make comparisons, there's much more I should tell you. The tape recorder will be fine on the desk.

'Far away from here,' said the keeper of Kaspar the bear when their visitor had dropped from the rafters and resumed his previous perch, 'on a cold river emptying into a sea not too unlike your own, there is a city with wharves, quays, factories and timberyards in which I'm sure you'd feel at home. Apart from its impressive fortifications and the preoccupation of many of its inhabitants with amber, Koenigsberg is like any other seaport. It exists through trade.

'Among the factory workers and stevedores there lived a sailmaker who went to work by tram and repaired main courses and mizzen courses, topsails, staysails and jibsails in his loft above the river. Maybe he grew tired of patching so many old sails and making so few new ones. Maybe the sight of more and more steamboats ploughing up and down the river regardless of prevailing winds offended him. Whatever the reason, he put his business up for sale, withdrew his savings from the Credit Bank of East Prussia and prepared to start a new life on the shores of the Hudson. Don't imagine he took this decision lightly. Before he set sail, he already had a letter confirming his appointment with the Universal Canvas Company, which was desperate for skilled men to make mess tents and marquees for the American railroads. His only reckless act, Mr Pye, was to book three tickets; for though he and his wife were quite at liberty to set up house in the Land of the Free, his eighteen-year-old son, an only child who was already proficient in the family trade, had yet to honour an obligation to the regional conscription office. You must find it hard to imagine conscription, but where I come from such matters are taken very seriously indeed. There seemed to be no possibility of the young man sailing to a new life when, by chance, a distant relation on his mother's side died, leaving him heir to a small-holding some distance inland. He was beside himself with delight.

'At that time I led a precarious existence as a professional musician. I had left university when my father died. My incomplete studies had given me an understanding of English, a loathing of Latin and the ability to play the violin from music and by ear. My ambitions were modest. I played at working-class weddings and in the Café Métropole, while shopkeepers and corn chandlers and railway workers drank beer and played skat under the dark-green lampshades. My father kept a lock on the canal. He disappeared into its icy waters in the winter of seventy-nine. Mother survived only another year and, as expected, my younger brother Jochen and I were obliged to move from the company cottage. I rented a shabby room in the old town. Jochen found work as a representative for a firm which produced canvas and sacking. He travelled all over the region, selling his wares to millers and potato farmers. We scarcely met from one month to the next, and it was with some surprise that I saw him making his way between the café tables one evening when, according to his schedule, he should have been in a town many miles to the south. I finished playing and went over. He swallowed several gulps of beer before he could tell me his news. He had received the freehold of a small-holding near the Russian border. His time spending night after night in comfortless inns was over. He was a landowner, which, in our country, meant his future was assured.'

To Peter Pye, the hopes and aspirations of an East Prussian peasant were as unfathomable as those of a Hottentot. He peered at the keeper of the bear through narrow, bewildered eyes. 'What had your brother done to deserve such a reward?'

The keeper ran his fingers through the hair on the back of the bear's neck. 'He had sold his identity. He had agreed to exchange his mundane life as a travelling salesman, rejected by the conscription board on account of a chronically weak chest, for that of a young sailmaker about to be unwillingly called to the colours.

'The deception was not too difficult to achieve. Both young men were of much the same height and colouring. My brother was barely two years older than the other man, and could easily pass for the same age. Sailmaking is not a common profession, but Jochen worked in the canvas business. He could convince any layman that he had just finished his time as a sailmaker's apprentice. His unsatisfactory medical examination had taken place two years before. As a precaution he grew a moustache, but no one suspected a thing when he presented himself at the inspection centre, this time with papers in the name of Egon Lorenz. He joined the gloomy, naked queue and waited for the inevitable verdict on the sorry state of his lungs. Then things went wrong. He had expected to face a bored major of the 6th East Prussian Infantry, but found behind the baise-covered table a Korvetten-Kapitaen of the Imperial Navy who studied his papers with alarming interest while a surgeon-lieutenant in blue serge and brass buttons performed the customary proddings and soundings. There was a whispered consultation. He was ordered to take a few more deep breaths. The surgeon nodded. The Korvetten-Kapitaen lifted his rubber stamp from the inkpad and Jochen was in the navy. Heaven knows how he broke the news to the young man waiting in a nearby café for an exemption certificate in the name of Egon Lorenz. I imagine mutual recriminations. Lorenz would blame Jochen for exaggerating his disability. Jochen would blame Lorenz for not warning him that the interview fell in that one week of the year when conscription passed from the army to the navy, in whose eyes a sailmaker's training weighed much more heavily than a whistle in the lung.

'I am amazed how you exist without the slightest concept of identity papers. Had this afternoon's little event happened in any other country, the policeman would have demanded to see our papers and you would have been exposed. But it simply did not occur to him. In Prussia, papers are more important than their owners. There was no alternative for the two men but to continue their deception. Jochen awaited his call-up papers in the name of Egon Lorenz, and Lorenz bade farewell to his parents and set about finding work in the name of Jochen Dau until a discharge certificate would release him to join them in New York and Jochen to settle on the rim of the Lithuanian forest.

'When next I saw Jochen, he was desolate. In four days he was due to present himself for basic training at a torpedo boat base in Elbing, many miles further west. Though the deeds were in his pocketbook beside a travel warrant, he had not yet visited his holding. I agreed to go with him to see what arrangements could be made to look after the land until he found a way of extricating himself or finished his two years beneath the imperial flag. The plot lay in a fold of low, scrubby hummocks between the railway line and Eydtkuhnen, which marks the border with Russia and where a surly Pole hired us a gig. It was dusk when we saw what Egon Lorenz had exchanged for a passage to the New World.'

Yes. Over there. Bottom shelf. But you won't find East Prussia in the atlas these days, my dear. To find the scrap of ground being discussed in Mr Gruber's storeroom, you must look for Kaliningradskaja Oblast: a geographical thorn left in the side of the emergent Baltic republics. Russia grabbed East Prussia after the war. Koenigsberg became Kaliningrad. They based the Baltic fleet there. It was a closed city. Now it's hemmed in by Poland and Lithuania, completely cut off, but the Russians won't budge. And who can blame them? The German settlers were all thrown out and I doubt if their neighbours would welcome them back.

You know, film people used Dundee to represent Moscow not so long ago. It seems our council estates capture the spirit of domestic Stalinism. Drive round and have a look before they blow them all up. And while I'm on the subject I noticed a picture postcard pinned behind the bar at the golf club recently. Why would anybody produce let alone send a card of the municipal flats at Dudhope Court? It was actually Kaliningrad, which one of our more eccentric members had just driven through on his way round the Baltic. Now there's a thing. And here's the coffee. Just put it down there, thank you, Louise.

'The place was pitifully small,' said Kaspar's keeper, whom we must now also call Dau. 'Scarcely larger than one of those allotment gardens city dwellers cultivate at weekends. At first it seemed we were alone on the untidy patch of dried mud that served as a farmyard. Our gig had set dogs barking at every farm we passed, but here, where we expected a welcome, we found only stillness and shadows. Every window of the little wooden house was shuttered, every door barred. We were about to head back to the village when a light appeared at the end of the yard. An old man approached and held a storm lantern suspiciously in our faces. He asked our business in Lithuanian, then in German. Jochen introduced himself as the heir to the property, and me as a friend from Koenigsberg. The old man fumbled with the lock and in a moment we were in the kitchen of my brother's new house. It turned out that the old Lithuanian, who readily accepted Jochen's story, was a farm labourer employed by the notary to act as caretaker until the new owner appeared. The house was bare, but Jochen produced a bottle of kümmel and began a conversation that ranged over potatoes and broad beans, oats and seed corn. His weary days selling sacks to farmers had borne fruit. Before the bottle was a third empty, plans had been made and a bargain struck. In exchange for use of the outbuildings and a generous share of the produce, the old peasant would look after things until my brother completed his military service. Still the old man seemed uneasy. At last he revealed that, apart from some geese and chickens (the cow and goat had been sold), there was on the small-holding one piece of livestock to which he took exception.' The keeper made a hissing noise between his teeth. The bear moved closer, nuzzling his leg with its snout. But its little eyes never left Peter Pye.

'I met Kaspar the next day when the old man took us to a broken-down pig sty. The bear was in pitiful condition, surrounded by excrement and pieces of discarded food and chained so tightly he could scarcely move his head. The old man was terrified of the animal and had only given it water and an occasional bucket of swill more suitable for the long-departed pigs than a fully-grown brown bear. When we asked him how he came to be in charge of such an unusual item of livestock, he tapped his forehead and told us it came with the farm. Didn't we know the previous owner was strange?

'A year or so ago, the bear had been discovered chained to a stake in a little grove beside the St Petersburg railway line. A search had revealed the body of its presumptive owner, struck, it seemed, by a train while collecting wood for his campfire. The gendarmerie could only discover that the man, who appeared to be Russian, had been seen in the Vilnius district and seemed to be heading westwards to entertain villagers in East Prussia. No identity was established; no relatives traced. The man was buried at the expense of the state, but the state could not be expected to meet the requirements of a European brown bear which had become particularly aggressive since its master's demise. It was about to be shot when the previous owner of the small-holding, near whose land it had been found, offered to keep the animal. On the understanding that it was at all times kept fully under control, the bear was handed over and lived happily with the eccentric old bachelor until he too passed away.

'Four days is a short time to cement a friendship, Mr Pye, but my nature combines patience with determination. Though the farmer had no doubt offered the bear every kindness, a vital element was missing. He had been totally unmusical. When I cautiously played a few bars of a waltz, the bear's reaction was most interesting. It swung its head, then its shoulders. Had it not been so closely tethered, it would have danced there and then. I rewarded it with a few titbits, loosened the chains and again took up my fiddle; and while my brother measured boundaries, inspected poultry, discussed livestock and ploughing and sowing, I drew forth from the memory of Ursus Arctos all the dances and tricks it had learned from the teacher whose career had been cut short by the Prussian State Railway. By the time Jochen was ready to leave, my mind was made up. I would continue the tour embarked on by the unknown entertainer from the east. With the bear, whom I christened Kaspar after another famous foundling, I would spend the duration of Jochen's military service travelling westwards from village to village. I knew how readily country people would pay for anything that enlivened their existences. Surely a performing bear would be a success. Jochen gladly parted with his unexpected acquisition, wished us good luck and set off for the depot at Elbing to keep his nautical appointment.'

Pass me that book, please. The big one. That's it. While you're changing the tape, I'll see if I can find something to help you understand why I want to start at the beginning, no matter how obscure it may seem. *Wedderburn. The Plastic Years.* A time when Forbes fell under the influence of Pop Art, as it was called. Out of fashion now, of course, but Forbes could anticipate a trend. He was never a leader. His knack was to spot what would sell. Warhol and Lichtenstein made the running, but long before anyone here had cottoned on, Forbes was turning out what he called 'plastics'. Here's what I was looking for. Pity the reproduction's so small. A minor work, but you can see quite clearly what it is. A graded background of vivid blue on which has been superimposed or glued, if you like, a brown teddy bear surrounded by six small plastic pigs. What does the caption say? *In the Sty. 1962 – Private Collection.* You seem a little fazed, my dear. Have some more coffee and I'll carry on.

'Almost six months had passed,' said the keeper of Kaspar the bear, 'before I heard there was a letter awaiting me at the post office in Bromberg. It was from Jochen. His induction into the navy had passed off relatively smoothly. He had endured the rigours and indignities of basic training with good grace, in the hope that he would be returned to civilian life immediately after his next medical inspection. When three weeks had passed, he reported sick in the prescribed manner, presenting himself before the medical officer with a description of chest pains and a tightness about the ribcage that made breathing difficult. Instead of a medical discharge, he was handed a bottle of expectorant and told to resume duties forthwith. He tried again the following day and the day after that; and by this time, the combination of draughty barrack rooms, vile expectorant and the motion of the torpedo boat on which he was obliged to train each day had set off a genuine irritation in his bronchial tissue. Genuine or not, his application for an examination by the surgeon lieutenant was flatly refused. He ended his letter in the lowest spirits, with the news that he had lasted barely a week as a sailmaker's assistant. The petty officer in charge had called him the most incompetent tradesman he'd seen, and had him regraded to assistant cook. In this capacity he was about to set sail for manoeuvres in the Gulf of Danzig.

By the time the Baltic fleet had completed its exercise, I had made my way to Elbing. I cheered and waved like the others as the torpedo-boat squadron approached harbour, though it was impossible to distinguish individuals in the sea of blue jerseys on deck. Jochen was not among them. When I called the next day at the Kommandanteur and introduced myself as a close friend of conscript Lorenz, I was shown into the presence of an elderly petty officer who told me that Lorenz had died in an accident off the coast of Gotland. There would be an inquiry, but from what he could gather Lorenz, who had been complaining of sickness, had deserted his post and crept into a larder to sleep. A sudden manoeuvre in heavy seas had dislodged a side of bacon from its hook. It broke his neck. Death had been immediate. The petty officer, who offered me a sympathetic cigarette, was glad I'd called. His records showed Lorenz's only relatives lived in America. They had been informed, of course, and might even be due some compensation, but shouldn't bank on it because Lorenz should never have been there in the first place. Maybe I'd like to take his personal effects in the meantime. The body had been buried at sea, as any sailor would have wished. I signed the form and left with a cheap, fibre suitcase that contained, as well as a shirt and a threadbare suit, a pair of much-mended lacing boots which would never tread the soil of my brother's holding.

'Let's not dwell on fate, Mr Pye. I could do nothing to alter the course of events without incriminating myself. I remained silent while the same notary who had made over the small-holding to my brother, arranged for it to be disposed of by public auction and the proceeds sent to the unfortunate young man's parents whose address was given as Horatio Street, Manhattan, New York. Imagine how often I thought of poor Jochen, racked with pain, sleeping fitfully on naval flour sacks and dying beneath the weight of salt pork in a stormy sea. I travelled the country, sometimes with Kaspar as my only companion, sometimes in the company of other musicians I met at fairs and festivals. Don't suppose I could have returned to my precarious but stationary existence as a café musician. What would have become of Kaspar? How could I abandon the creature which was a constant reminder of the folly that had taken Jochen's life and disrupted my own?

'Dau is a common name on the Baltic coast. In my wanderings, whenever I came upon it painted above the door of a business or in the post office directory of a larger town, I made inquiries, asked if a young man named Jochen lived there. In towns and villages, I asked if a Jochen Dau had appeared out of the blue looking for work, or if someone of that name had recently taken passage to America. And I tried the network of contacts used by fairground people and gypsies, into whose company Kaspar and I were becoming increasingly accepted. It was eight years before a showman at the *Volksfest* in Posen pointed out an article in a

Berlin newspaper. It concerned a prize which had been won by a small linen mill in Memel. While experimenting with protective coatings for the production of oilskins, they had discovered a type of oilcloth which not only was easily washable but stood up to heat. More work had to be done, but the Federation of German Linen Manufacturers had no hesitation in awarding its annual medal to Messrs Simon & Kaiser. Herr Kaiser had been accompanied to the ceremony by Herr Jochen Dau, the employee whose chance discovery might well prove a most useful and profitable addition to their range of products.

'Herr Kaiser's preoccupation with oilskin is quite understandable. Memel is Germany's most northerly and easterly port. It exists by fishing and by exporting Lithuanian timber and flax from the vast Russian hinterland to which it clings. Herr Kaiser would not see us when, some ten days later, Kaspar and I stood in the yard of his factory and watched gulls circling in the drizzle. Herr Kaiser had been betrayed. He sent a bald underling to tell us, from beneath an umbrella, which he refused to share, that Herr Jochen Dau was no longer an employee. He had been lured to England to reveal his secrets. Indeed, Dau had arrived from nowhere. Herr Kaiser had noticed his talent and taken him under his wing. When Dau had spoken of trying to join his parents in New York, Kaiser had even increased his salary. Now he was gone. There was no forwarding address. The clerk looked as if he'd like to hit me. Had it not been for Kaspar, who terrified him, and the increasing number of faces drawn to the mill windows by the rumour of a bear in the yard, I think he would have done. A local innkeeper soon remembered who had tempted Jochen Dau to cross the sea, if not to America at least as far as your surprising country. He wrote down the name of a company and a town, though I fear he too said it was in England.

'I met Niemcewicz in Hamburg. He is a man of crude sensibilities and a mean nature, but he was proposing to tour Britain and I asked to join him. He described previous visits; how he had played for fisher women who travel round the coast by the hundred to pack herring; how he had played at horse races attended by the richest men in the land. Not even in Berlin had he known such rewards. It was his habit to take a ship to Aberdeen and work down to the Channel coast. I asked for names. He mentioned places at random, often repeating himself as he tried to remember the unfamiliar towns. Stonehaven . . . Montrose . . . Arbroath . . . You know the name I wanted to hear. When he pronounced the six letters, I struck a bargain at once. Our little band has been in the country for several weeks now, but only today, when we entered your city by way of Broughty Ferry, only when I smelled the distinctive odours of jute and boiling whale oil was I sure I'd reached my goal. You say you know where everyone is in this town. Don't you have an expression, Mr Pye, "one good turn deserves another"?'

Chapter 6

Two tornadoes. Just dropping below the horizon. As well as the home of golf and a cradle of learning, Fife is host to these noisy blighters. Another good reason for reglazing the window, you see. Not so long ago there were helicopters too. They fished the occasional pilot out of the drink, but spent most of their time rescuing climbers and yachtsmen. If they'd still been here, maybe I'd have more feeling in my toes. Still, the physiotherapist tells me I'll see the last of her in a fortnight. Then I can take up ballroom dancing. Please. Look around as much as you like. No Wedderburns, I'm afraid. Forbes's efforts have never suited my taste, nor my pocket. But those prints and paintings have a value of their own. The whale fishery has attracted few artists. Examples are rare and pictures showing the actual hunt, not just individual ships, are rarer still. For years I've corresponded with a professor in New England. Our passions match nicely. I have put several items like ancient log books his way, and he is the source of much of the scrimshaw in the glass case behind you. I suppose my collection must rival in quality, if not in size, the one in Broughty Castle. You can see the castle from the window, guarding the estuary out there on the point. A suitably remote and watery spot in which to display evidence of the city's less than politically correct past. You must visit it for background, don't you think?

But before you do, stroll across from your hotel and look at the City Churches. They're quite unique. Three separate kirks built round one fortified steeple; the result, I believe, of the English burning the original church, but a typically Dundonian way of turning a setback to advantage. St Mary's can't have changed much since that damp, inclement Sunday, the last one in November 1899, when Miss Ethel Wilkie took her seat between her mother and her elder brother three rows from the front of the nave on the right side of the aisle. They arrived early. Ethel had little opportunity to examine the congregation and perhaps pick out the refined features of Herr Dau among the black-clad worshippers awaiting the minister in a silence punctuated by seasonal coughing. The congregation rose and, as the minister ascended the steps and turned to face them, arms outstretched, their voices, thin at first but gathering assurance at every word, broke into the hundredth psalm, the Auld Hundred. In the back row, wedged between a stout matron and a stouter fishmonger, Herr Dau gave up trying to find the words in an unfamiliar hymnbook and inserted two well-manicured fingers between his starched collar and his neck which was already moist with sweat. Three rows from the front, Miss Ethel Wilkie became aware of a voice directly behind her. It was neither unpleasant nor unmelodious, but so loud it seemed more suited to shouting against the wind than the discordant tones of Dundonians at worship. Besides, the more they sang, the more she was convinced that she'd heard the voice before and that it was aimed specifically at her. When she took her seat as the last chord of the long amen died among the rafters, the flush on Ethel's cheeks could not be attributed entirely to her vocal exertions.

High in the dark pulpit, the minister clutched the gilded lectern in both hands and embarked on the text, which he took from Acts 27 verse 29. 'Then fearing lest we should have fallen upon rocks, they cast four anchors out of the stern and wished for the day.' Four rows from the front, unseen by the minister, unobserved by the worshippers who flanked him, heads bowed in private thought, Alexander Yule lifted a hand and let it rest on the back of the pew in front of him. The hand was callused and rough but seldom had the wood, polished by the backs of generations of worshippers, been touched more lightly. Slower even than the rumbling voice of the preacher, Alexander Yule slid his hand first one then two inches along the back of the pew till at last it rested directly behind Miss Ethel Wilkie's head. With the tips of two fingers he gently caressed the soft hair and even softer skin at the back of her plump neck.

'And now be of good cheer,' said the minister. 'For there shall be no loss of any man's life among you, but of the ship.' And he spread his arms in his gown like a great black crow and peered down on the congregation. He saw baillies and councillors; he saw tradesmen and journeymen and labourers; he saw housewives and servants; he saw weavers and winders and sack machinists from the mills, and their children who worked part time and their husbands who often had no work at all and stayed at home to boil the kettle; he saw bent grey heads. He saw the unexpected face of Alexander Yule and the unknown face of Jochen Dau. 'For there stood by me this night the angel of the God, whose I am and whom I serve.' Yule, who had stopped moving his hand when the preacher's gaze descended on his flock, felt a far from unpleasant pressure against his fingertips. 'Wherefore, sirs, be of good cheer: for I believe God it shall be even as it was told me,' proclaimed the minister. Three rows in front of him, he might have seen Ethel Wilkie's eyelids grow heavy and the hint of a smile form at the corners of her mouth, but the minister was adrift with Paul in the Sea of Adria and saw nothing.

Wedged in the last pew, Herr Dau also let his thoughts wander to foreign seas, but his imaginings were of chill Baltic winds and the treacherously steep waves found only in shallow waters. He thought of sail lofts and linen mills and the conscription office of the Koenigsberg region. He thought of the face he'd seen the day before; so familiar yet so strange, as if a faded, forgotten photograph had come to life. 'And so it came to pass that they escaped all safe to land.' The minister lowered his arms and scanned the rows of faces before him. 'Would you have had Paul's faith in the face of such a tempest? When you are assailed by the troubles and perils of life, can you say, "I will cast out my anchor into the deep and trust in Him?" ' Whether or not the congregation was equal to the question, they lowered their heads as the preacher rumbled on. 'Think of Ralph the Rover, who cut the abbott's bell from the Inchcape Rock only to perish there himself in stormy seas.' Herr Jochen Dau was beginning to feel unwell. The humid warmth in contrast to the cold outside made him shiver. His total consumption that day had been two cups of coffee and six cigarettes, the last of which he'd smoked in a shop doorway waiting for Ethel to enter the church. Herr Dau's empty stomach gave a heave. 'Think of Winstanley,' said the voice from the pulpit. Dau could not understand the word. 'He built a lighthouse on the Eddystone Rock and swore his tower would endure despite the wrath of any storm. He even hoped he might be there during the greatest tempest ever known. And it came to pass he was in the lighthouse when the worst storm ever known in these isles dashed against the coast. That was in the year of our Lord 1703. The keeper begged him to try to reach land, but Winstanley only laughed. He laughed in the face of God. The seas rose to the height of mountains, the tempest roared with the wrath of the Almighty and hurled itself against the frail structure on the rock.' Dau felt seasick. He rose and squeezed his way to the end of the row, handkerchief pressed to his lips. As he stepped into the aisle, his coat-tail dislodged the fishmonger's knob-headed walking stick from a rack at the end of the pew. It clattered to the ground and, as the ancient flagstones were on a slope, rolled down the aisle with increasing momentum. 'When the people looked out from the shore,' said the preacher, 'what did they see?' The people looked and saw Herr Jochen Dau try to stop the stick with his foot. In the process he kicked it even further down the aisle till it came to rest against the pulpit steps. 'When morning dawned,' said the minister, 'they saw that the lighthouse had disappeared from the rock. No trace of it or its occupants was ever found.' With a hand to his mouth, Dau stooped to retrieve the stick. Children began to squirm and snigger. 'Be humble in the face of the Lord,' roared the minister from above Dau's head.

'*Verzeihen Sie*,' said Jochen Dau.

The minister opened his mouth but no sound came. Even the children were silent, as if by uttering those two outlandish words,

Dau had cast a spell upon them. Slowly, Herr Jochen Dau picked up the stick and walked back up the aisle. He replaced the stick in its rack and turned towards the door.

'Be not proud,' the voice from the pulpit shouted at Herr Dau's departing back. 'Think on Winstanley. Think on that bare rock.'

'What did he say to the minister?' the children asked one another, twisting in their seats to see the door close behind Herr Dau. 'Kronje! He said, "Good for Kronje!" He must be a Boer. A dirty Boer!'

'Poor Jochen,' said Ethel Wilkie as she turned like the rest of the congregation to watch Dau's departure.

'Wait for me outside,' said Alexander Yule, who had not turned round. He looked full in Ethel's face which coloured even more before his eyes.

No. You won't find a picture in any of the books. To the best of my knowledge, no Wedderburn drawings exist of bible-black ministers. Locks of maidenly hair or ebony-headed walking sticks don't feature in any of Forbes's plastics. He was not inspired by events that day in the church, though to my mind they are a crucial part of the story. But Forbes made up for it. What happened next day was the source of no less than five graphic and plastic works over the years. You'll recognise them as I go on.

Gas jets were still burning that morning in the shop in Yeaman Shore. Mr Otto Gruber was in the process of adjusting one of the mantels when the little glass strips above the door tinkled and Mrs Jemima Ritchie entered the premises. The Italian warehouseman and pork butcher stepped down from the chair and greeted his first customer of the day with a curt nod. The greeting was uncharacteristically abrupt for a businessman who knew the value of maintaining amicable relations with the ladies of the town, but Gruber had much on his mind. That morning, long before even the earliest shoppers were about, Niemcewicz had announced that he intended to cross on the ferry with his troupe and try his luck along the north Fife coast. He would return on the last boat. Gruber's joy at being rid of his shifty guests, if only for a day, evaporated when he was told that the bear would not be accompanying them on the excursion. According to his keeper, Niemcewicz had explained, Kaspar was inclined to feel out of sorts from time to time during the winter months when, in the natural course of things, he should have been in semi-hibernation. On such occasions, the only remedy was to let the animal rest for a day and sleep off its indisposition. Hence the continued presence of the bear and his keeper in Gruber's storehouse across the yard, and Gruber's growing consternation in case they emerge from their lair without warning. Already he had been obliged to invent ridiculous pretexts to prevent his shopman and delivery boy from going into the storehouse, and he kept a wary eye on its green door as he served the railway porter's wife.

'Did you hear about my man?' asked Mrs Ritchie, settling herself on a chair beneath the gas mantle. 'He nearly caught thon ghost on Saturday. Thon ghost that chases women and the like.'

'I think we'll find that the culprit is not a ghost but an impudent young fellow,' said Gruber. He scooped a lump of lard from an earthenware tub and carried it towards the scales on a sheet of greaseproof paper.

'Twa lassies came running intae the station and said the ghost had jumped oot on them up the back road. Jimmy went tae have a look and there was the ghost as bold as brass on the railway line. Jimmy chased him till a train came in between them, and after that they couldna find the ghost at all. Not even the polis could find him, and all Jimmy got for his trouble was a sair back and scarted arms.'

'The ghost fought with your husband?' Gruber said with surprise.

'Dinna be daft. It was a bear that did it. Thon foreigners with a bear. It louped on Jimmy when he was chasing the ghost.'

The lard shot from Gruber's hand and landed on the scrubbed floorboards. 'Surely it must have been an accident,' said Gruber as he stooped to retrieve the white lump which had fallen sticky side down. Mrs Ritchie pursed her lips and said nothing. While Gruber was grubbing about on the floor, Mrs Agnes Pitkethlie came in. She and the porter's wife exchanged nods.

'Did you hear about my man and the Craigie Ghost?' said Mrs Ritchie.

'Did you hear about thon Boer throwing his stick at the minister in St Mary's Kirk,' said Mrs Pitkethlie. Gruber got to his feet and wiped his hands on his apron.

'Throwing a stick,' he said. 'In a place of worship.'

Mrs Pitkethlie stepped across to where a second high-backed chair was placed beside the counter and settled herself down. 'I wasn't there myself, mind.' she said. 'We've gone to the Free Kirk since the disruption, but I heard it frae Mrs Wilkie that in the middle of the service, this Boer jumped up and threw his stick at the minister and started shouting, "Good for Kronje" and "Hurrah for the Boers" and all sorts of terrible things in Dutch till the beadle and the elders chased him oot o'the kirk.'

'Would you believe it?' said Mrs Ritchie. 'I was just going tae say tae Mr Gruber that there are far too many foreigners aboot. What richt has a Boer tae gang tae St Mary's Kirk onieway? We're supposed tae be fechtin them. And thon Germans with the bear. Did you know it louped on my man when he was chasing the Craigie Ghost?'

Mrs Pitkethlie, more sensitive, perhaps, than the porter's wife, coloured and said, 'Of course she doesn't mean you, Mr Gruber. You're just like one of us.'

In contrast, Gruber's complexion became noticeably less ruddy. As he busied himself with a fresh lump of lard, troublesome memories returned of the curious stares and suspicious glances when he had first settled in the city. And only three years before, several valuable accounts had been discontinued when news broke that the Kaiser had congratulated Kruger on his defeat of the Jameson Raid. 'We call them "German Bands", said Gruber. 'But most of them come from Bohemia, you know. It's in Austria Hungary.' He turned towards the scales beneath the side window. As he did so, the storehouse door opened and Kaspar's keeper wandered into the yard, unbuttoning his trousers as he went. The ladies, neither of whom could see the cause of Gruber's dismay, looked up in surprise as he let out a gasp and dropped the lard into a butt of pickled pork.

'Oops-a-daisy,' said Mrs Jemima Ritchie.

'Poor Mr Gruber,' said Mrs Agnes Pitkethlie. 'Some days just nothing goes right.'

The keeper relieved himself in the corner of the yard then strolled down the close leading to the lane which ran at right angles to Yeaman Shore. He peered up and down through wire-rimmed spectacles. A large, two-horse van stood at the end of the lane. One horse raised and lowered its head in a repetitive, nodding motion that rattled the harness and agitated the plume of steam round the animal's nostrils. The driver waved his whip towards the keeper who spat in the gutter and walked back up the close towards Gruber's storehouse.

Mr Gruber did not see his unwelcome guest return to the storehouse. He did not catch a glimpse of the keeper as he emerged with Kaspar the bear, who, far from being in a state of torpor, strained eagerly on his chain and looked about with quick little eyes. For as soon as he realised the keeper was awake, Gruber had distracted the ladies by drawing their attention to a particularly desirable cut of pork which, only for the day he announced, was on sale at half price. At the end of the lane, the keeper pulled hard on Kaspar's chain and looked towards the driver who was now holding wide the doors at the rear of the van. The keeper climbed into the dark interior, and slowly, with some coaxing and the temptation of sugar broken from a stick in Gruber's storeroom, the bear lumbered after its master. Whose heart was in his mouth lest someone turn the corner? Who closed the double doors and slid the bolt in place? Beneath a carter's oilskin cap, behind the best grey muffler money could buy, Peter Pye licked his lips and flicked his whip over the patient horses.

Chapter 7

THE WINDS that prevailed over Dundee were west-southwest. In November they veered northwest; but whether fresh from the fruit fields of Gowrie or sharpened by salty ozone, the wind that blew along the northern coast of the Firth of Tay on a Monday was welcome only if it was a drying wind. Long before daylight, practised fingers were held up to the wind. In cottage kitchens, in washing houses adjoining the villas of West Ferry, in lean-to sheds propped against tenement walls, in Hilltown and Craigie, in Blackness and Lochee and in the public wash house standing in its bleaching green in Constitution Road, where full advantage could be taken of drying winds, water was drawn, fires kindled under coppers, wash-boards, scrubbing brushes and blocks of soap were assembled. Clothes ropes were uncoiled. In short, on every Monday with a drying wind, and what day can call itself Monday without one, operations got under way to cleanse the garments, bed and table linen of the city and in the process add to the ice-cold, restless water of the Tay a warm, steaming stream grey with hard-earned dirt and soapy through honest toil.

Solid stone, the public wash house stood in the shadow of the Royal Infirmary with a door at either end and twelve narrow windows, all steamed up. One door opened on to the path which led from Constitution Street to Dudhope Street, and at this portal the many housewives and maids-of-all-work and the few professional washerwomen who used the municipal facility carried baskets and bundles heavy with fetid linen. The other door opened on to the drying green, where, suspended between wrought-iron poles, propped above the damp grass by wooden stretchers, the results of earlier labours billowed freely in the drying wind. Sheets intended for single and double beds, pillowcases and bolster-covers, table cloths and tea towels stood stiff in the wind, pointed south-east and followed the trail of smoke from the wash-house chimney. Shirts and overalls, vests, drawers and chemises that the previous day had luxuriated in the Sabbath warmth of their owners' bodies now displayed themselves shamelessly. And on the drying-green wall, hands deep in November pockets, gazing mindlessly at the sea of fluttering linen sat Toddie Law. Toddie Law, fourteen years old, but neither man nor woman. Toddie Law, round as a barrel with pudgy knees and blank eyes encased in rolls of flesh. Toddie Law, figure of fun and pity who wisna wise because widow Law was always a bitty queer hersel . . . an whose bairn was Toddie onieway? Old Law was died twa year afore . . . an was that no scandalous how she widna wean the bairn an let it sook till it was nigh five year old? Toddie Law sat on the low wall and watched the north-west wind flap the moisture from fresh-mangled linen.

In the washing house, twelve women scrubbed at twelve stone sinks, two by two. Six women stood by six copper boilers, one by one, prodding the steaming sludge with wooden batons. Four women toiled at four patent mangles, wringing out the last vestiges of the week's dirt. And everywhere in this supremely feminine scene, where every voice was high and every elbow plump, where kerchiefs held back hair from pink, polished faces, where skirts, unfashionably short to avoid the sodden floor, were in a constant state of agitation above stockinged and unstockinged legs, everywhere in the public wash house there rose an endless, all-embracing cloud of steam. It veiled red arms, elbow-deep in water, deadened shrill bursts of laughter and filled the end of the wash house nearest the path with an impenetrable mist. Who was about to join the ladies in the warm, succulent steam? On the gravel path, the keeper waited till the last laundress entered the building before coaxing the uninvited guest from the van. On the deserted path, the Craigie Ghost tarried only long enough to see him tie a loop of rope round the handles of the double door before releasing the catches on his spring-heeled boots. The ladies in the wash house did not immediately notice their unexpected visitor, but gradually it occurred to them that the figure at the far end of the room, though wearing a kerchief and voluminous gown, held herself in a curiously four-legged posture. Not until Annie Macfarlane, groping for a bar of soap, met a decidedly unladylike though not unfriendly swipe from a hairy paw did concern begin to spread. Not until first one then another found the front doors tied did bewilderment give way to flight. One by one, the twelve flushed women left their sinks, the six stout women neglected their coppers, the four sweating women abandoned their mangles and altogether rushed towards the far door that blinked pale sunlight through the steam at the end of the building. But there were obstacles. Hurrying feet slid on soapy flagstones. Oh my god! Oot the road! Help, Maggie! In their haste, the ladies tripped on buckets and baskets and bundles of washing. The laggards fell over those already on the floor and soon the space between the mangles and the doorway was wedged with squirming women who, regardless of modesty, waved their arms and legs and pulled each other's clothing to regain their feet.

You know who watched as the ladies rolled around on the floor which grew wetter and slippier as water spilled from unattended faucets. You know whose eyes rolled as, one by one, the ladies revealed plump thighs and plumper buttocks, for many had their drawers in the wash. You know whose spittle drooled on dishevelled linen kerchiefs and matted locks. The Craigie Ghost lay spread-eagled on the slates of the wash-house roof and gaped at the chaos through an open skylight.

The poor eyesight of the European brown bear is more than compensated for by its hearing. When Kaspar was coaxed into the steamy wash house, draped in a long sheet and with his head wrapped in rags to look like a bonnet, he was not in a bad mood. When the ladies fled before him, he was unsettled by their sudden movements, but not unduly annoyed. He had been about to perform a trick. But when they fell to the floor, when their screams reached a pitch that pierced the wrappings round his head, Kaspar lost his temper. He reared eight feet high. Eight feet of diabolical washerwoman in bonnet and gown. Satan's beast breathing sulphur and brimstone. And his feet were as the feet of a bear and his mouth as the mouth of a lion. Kaspar snapped his jaws behind the muzzle which his keeper would not remove at any price and advanced on the hapless ladies on hind legs. The Ghost drooled, the keeper waited, the drying wind blew, the washing billowed, the idiot sat on the wall and on the wet flagstones, the washerwomen, one by one, found their feet. Pulling and pushing, they burst into the watery daylight. Annie Macfarlane, Muriel Brown, genteel Sarah Lindsay, who wore shoes and stockings and was married to a printer, Chrissie Spence, who was Baillie Williamson's housemaid and clutched her mob-cap in her hand, all rushed headlong through the back door into the billowing mass of washing. Sheets swatted polished faces. Stretchers slid. Fingers clutched. One by one, gypsy clothespegs surrendered their grip on sagging ropes, and laundry which two seconds before had been ready for ironing, collapsed to deck the struggling, screaming ladies in festive disguises. Last of all came Nan Galloway, a washerwoman for forty years, as broad as she was long, with arms like hams. In the doorway, Nan looked round, and took a last look at the devil whom she was convinced had possessed the wash house. Avoiding the mêlée on the grass, she waddled across the drying green and scrambled over the wall. So no one saw the keeper slip into the wash house. No one noticed him coax the remaining occupant, who was lapping water from an overflowing sink, back down the row of coppers to the far door, the restraining rope of which had been cut by a vanman who, despite his oilskin cap and stylish muffler, could not conceal his twitching mouth and wildly excited eyes.

This might have been the end of the mildly apocalyptic events at the public wash house had not Harry Wilkie been working overtime. Maintenance was under way at the Dens Works, and Harry had spent the whole night shift plus three extra hours crawling in the belly of a cold boiler to clean its tubes and smoke box. He was making his way home when he heard the women screaming. How it came about that, except for the occupants of the van which was already turning into Dudhope Street, Harry was the only male to hear the women's screams we shall never know. Old Waldie, deaf as a post, had shovelled coke into the wash-house furnace throughout the drama. Harry ran down Constitution Street, saw the whirl of arms, sheets, fists, linen and washerwomen, vaulted the wall and rushed to their defence. If only caution had prevailed. If only his face had not been barkit with soot. If only a sheet had not wound itself round his head. If only he had not knocked down widow Brown in the muddiest part of the drying green, he might have forestalled the sudden burst of passion that rose in the breast of the idiot sitting on the wall. Moving more quickly than had ever been known, Toddie Law seized a wooden stretcher from the mud and with unrelenting fury belaboured Harry Wilkie's back and arms and legs. If only Gray, the slater, had not left a stache of slates behind the drying-green wall, Nan Galloway might not have begun an indiscriminate aerial bombardment. Behind a barrier of curses, she hurled slate after slate into the struggling crowd until, as if by magic, the remaining washerwomen squealed and tripped and stumbled off down the path, leaving Harry Wilkie and Toddie Law prostrate beneath the soiled banners of the washday battle.

No one was blamed. Lieutenant Glass made notes in his notebook, once Harry's head had been properly dressed, and announced that the whole affair was the result of hysteria created by an optical illusion caused by the steam. Maybe he scarcely believed his own conclusions, but everyone had forgotten the van at the end of the lane and he could find no other explanation. There was no case to put before the Fiscal. The next edition of the *Courier* carried a poem by a local academic who hid behind the pseudonym 'Cavillator' and satirised that Monday's events in the style of Tennyson's 'Charge of the Light Brigade'. In the days that followed, Harry Wilkie became something of a celebrity in the city, and in the end, benefited from his brush with the supernatural in an unexpected way.

Even the idiot gained from the washday battle. Toddie Law lay in a stupor for six hours after being struck on the head by one of Nan Galloway's missiles. At the seventh hour, she sat up, opened piggy little eyes that seemed to notice much more than before, and demanded something to eat. From that day, Toddie Law began to change. The pudginess of thigh and waist and neck that had defied all uninformed guesses at gender began to recede. An unmistakably feminine outline appeared beneath Toddie's shabby clothes. The voice, previously known for infrequent, strident and unintelligible ejaculations, began to insist in no less strident terms on the identity of Miss Thomasina Law. Within a year, she took up the post of second scullery maid in the household of Baillie Williamson. Thomasina approached her duties with a ponderous dedication, though often she would gaze fixedly at billowing lines of washing.

And seventy-five years later, Forbes Wedderburn, deputy head of drawing and painting at Duncan of Jordanstone, torn between the security of college and the ever more tempting prospect of international fame, took the little tale which I told him much as I have told you, and transformed it into *Bestiary I.* Look closely, my dear. Amidst the whirling shapes, which have been interpreted as representing female subjugation or woman's struggle against domination (Forbes never would tell which), you can see the distinct outline of a muzzle on the stoutest figure. The fact that, to my eye, the figure resembles Nan Galloway much more closely than Kaspar the bear must have been Forbes's little joke. It paid off. The feminists, who were just beginning to flex their muscles, claimed the painting perfectly summed up how men exploited women, forcing them into an endless whirl of work and eroticism but gagging them from expressing their true feelings. Forbes appeared late one night on television. He sat like a pasha between a raw-boned Australian in muslin and a bleach-blonde American who had written a book. For twenty minutes the women turned the air blue, but they saw Forbes through motherly eyes and soon were performing all the girlie little tricks they both claimed to despise.

Forbes was bitten by the bug. From then on there was no doubt which direction his career would take. Media commitments ate more and more into his teaching time. For a while he tried to keep all the balls in the air, and I dare say the college indulged him for the sake of publicity. Commercial forces were already stalking the halls of academe. In his last year before standing down and accepting the honorary post of guest lecturer, he produced a remarkable amount of work, including numbers *II* and *III* in the *Bestiary* series. There was a fourth piece produced that year, though it won't be found in any catalogue. I suppose I'm one of the few to have seen it.

As I remember, something arose concerning the estate of a mutual relation. My office is within walking distance of the college so I suggested he drop in, do the business then have lunch. But Forbes's schedule was too tight. In the end, I agreed to visit his studio that evening. As I walked towards the college through the drizzle, I remember feeling that I too had fallen for the manipulative Wedderburn charm. I had visited a few exhibitions but did not know the college well, and it took a while to find the studio in which Forbes was working. He always walked a thin line between the graphic and the plastic arts. For this project, with some ill will I discovered, he had borrowed a studio from the sculpture department. He needed its pulleys and tackles and power lines. I found Forbes in a state of agitation. Charm had been replaced by edginess, and it was clear I had no chance of talking business until he had solved the problem with which, it turned out, he had been wrestling all day. There was a screen to shield Forbes's work from prying eyes when the door opened into the corridor. Behind this, on a portable plinth some two feet from the ground, I found an extraordinary creation in shiny material which I later found to be fibre glass. At first glance, it seemed to be a fat woman standing legs apart, arms folded, and dressed in a voluminous skirt of silver foil. The head was thrown back, but where the face should have been was filled by a long, cylindrical, animal snout held on by leather straps. It was, of course, a gas mask. But painted to match the figure and tilted in that particular way, it seemed to me that Forbes had succeeded in reproducing with startling impact, the very image of Kaspar dressed for the wash-house battle.

Forbes was not content with the unsettling figure on the podium. A vital element was missing. What had transformed Kaspar from a mild-mannered European brown bear to a devilish washerwoman was not the inept and comical attempt at disguise but the swirling wreaths of steam through which he had emerged. Forbes had pondered. He contacted the production manager at the local repertory theatre, who suggested dry ice. Equipment had been hired from people who supplied pop groups that had taken to appearing knee-deep in mist. But what might have worked on stage was a failure in the studio. The white fog refused to rise more than a few feet. When Forbes increased the concentration, it simply billowed relentlessly from beneath the aluminium foil skirt and filled the entire studio with knee-deep haze, which soon found its way into the corridor and the rooms in which Forbes's long-suffering colleagues were working. Tempers had frayed. A solution had to be found. Forbes had spent the afternoon tracking down two powerful fans which he had hidden below the podium in the hope of blowing the white cloud up round the figure in a suitably impressive impersonation of steam. He stood before me in sweat-stained overalls and ran his hands through his hair. It was time to test the system. I would not get his attention till he had sorted things out, so I agreed to help. Forbes disappeared behind the figure of the washerwoman with the upturned snout. White mist began to roll from beneath the hem of the foil skirt. Forbes shouted. I threw a switch which not only turned on the fans, but also lit a couple of spotlights arranged to cast an eerie bottom light on the sculpture. Forbes struggled through the mist. He rushed to switch off the strip lights at the wall, then turned to view his creation. We stood in utter silence save for the whirring of the fans which dissipated the fog to the farthest corners of the studio and blew the washerwoman's skirt up round her hips in a grotesque parody of Marilyn Monroe in *The Seven Year Itch*. I'll never forget the shock on Forbes's face. He elbowed me aside, cut the power and restored the devilish washerwoman to decency. But he had caught my eye. The damage was done. Forbes abandoned this capricious item of *Bestiary*. The fat woman in gas mask and foil skirt was not seen again and in all our future dealings he never once mentioned her existence.

I beg your pardon? Yes, I suppose sketches and working drawings may exist somewhere. Quite a find for whoever brings them to light; but you must be patient. If the time comes to pick over old bones, you'll have to join the queue. Believe me, my dear, what you're collecting on BASF Ferro Extra 1 will open more eyes than a dozen faded sketchpads.

Chapter 8

ETHEL WILKIE'S first lesson with Herr Jochen Dau was embarrassing. Dau smarted from the incident in St Mary's Church, and Ethel blamed herself for having ignored him. He had waited bravely in the same doorway from which he had watched her enter the church, but Ethel had taken the arm of Alexander Yule and passed by on the other side. When Mrs Meiklejohn had placed the tea things on the sideboard and withdrawn, Ethel Wilkie and Jochen Dau sat down and avoided one another's eyes. Ethel began to recite words and phrases she had prepared beforehand.

'Fat, far, fate. Mould, soul, sold. Gold, galled, goal.'

Carefully, Dau repeated the words, pausing only when the meaning was unclear or the pronunciation eluded his tongue.

'Round and round the ragged rock the ragged rascal ran.'

Maybe repeating meaningless words helped to dispel their embarrassment. At all events, teacher and pupil found their selfconsciousness ebbing away as the lesson progressed. Herr Dau pulled his chair closer to that of Miss Wilkie. He noticed that she did not brush away the hand which he had rested on the arm of her chair so that his fingers touched the black passementerie of her sleeve.

'Peter Piper picked a peck of pickled pepper.'

Beyond the half-drawn curtains, the playground lay in darkness punctuated only by two blurred street lamps. They cast pools of gaslight over the railings and picked out black switches fanning from the crown of a pollarded poplar. Ethel Wilkie opened a grammar book flat on her lap.

'It is most important when learning the English language to master the pronunciation of the digraph "th",' she read. 'This is achieved by placing the tip of the tongue lightly between the teeth and breathing out over its surface. Th . . . th . . . th. The sound, which occurs with great frequency in English, has been found to cause considerable difficulty to foreign students. Those whose native tongues fall within the Romance group of languages tend to corrupt it to "d", while those of the Germanic tongues render it as "ss". Th . . . th . . . th,' said Ethel Wilkie.

'Ss . . . ss . . . ss,' said Jochen Dau, leaning over to look at the book and savour the scent of soap from Ethel Wilkie's neck. Ethel shook her head.

'Watch carefully,' said Ethel, and Jochen Dau watched as she parted her small, teeth to reveal the wet, pink tip of her tongue. 'Th . . . th . . . th,' said Ethel.

Very carefully her pupil opened his lips, let his tongue play on the edge of his upper lip, then pressed his mouth against her cheek while his arm enfolded her shoulders in a firm embrace. Ethel felt the grammar book slide to the floor. She felt the smooth, hard texture of Dau's jacket beneath her fingers as she twisted her face aside to gasp for breath. She said, 'Please get on with the lesson. There is very little time left. Now try again. Th . . . th . . . th.'

'Th,' said Herr Jochen Dau with a sly grin.

From beyond the school railings came the distant bumping of a drum, and the increasingly distinctive sound of a little band. Guitar, fiddle, accordion, clarinet, the notes wafted through the chilly air and formed themselves into a jaunty march. Above the music, frail as a reed, came the sound of a woman's voice singing with the band.

'Denkste denn, denkste denn, du Berliner Pflanze.'

Jochen Dau went to the window. 'They are playing a march of the Prussian army,' he said. 'The man who composed it was given a clock by the Tsar.'

Ethel said, 'You don't like those people, do you?'

'They are good for nothing. We call them *Schnorrer*. They are not Germans; more like gypsies.'

'They frighten you. Why are you afraid of the man with the bear?'

Dau stooped to pick up the book. 'He reminded me of someone I knew.'

'A friend?'

'Someone who is dead. Not a friend. The musician looked like this man, only smaller and older; as if the dead man was in disguise.'

'You looked like you'd seen a ghost.'

'I was shocked. But now I must laugh. I am sorry if I startled you.' Dau handed Ethel the book. 'I am never going back to Germany,' he said. 'Dundee is my home. I belong here, where my ability is respected. I can give much to this city. I can give much to you.'

Ethel crossed to the window. Mist was forming moist banks, over the blotches of gaslight. Ethel said, 'Not so fast, Herr Dau. First we must transform you into a Scottish gentleman. Now repeat after me: these, those, there, then, them, that, this.' But her student stared silently at his reflection. Fading in the mist, the woman's voice came between them like the cry of a distant bird.

'Denkste denn, denkste denn, du Berliner Pflanze . . .'

You seem restless. Has my tale of late Victorian passion left you unmoved? Granted, it lacks the vigour of the wash-house battle. Forbes was never inspired to re-create Ethel Wilkie's black-beaded sleeve in two or three dimensions. But I assure you, the dilemma faced during the last weeks of the nineteenth century by the assistant teacher at Baxter's Half-time School is why you are standing in a study in West Ferry instead of a gallery in Mayfair. You'll get your scoop, don't worry. A little patience is all that's needed. Listen to what happened later that night in the Harbour Head Inn.

'Ca' that a sair heid? When I was in Frisco I saw a man who had been scalped and lived tae tell the tale. An it wisna a redskin that had done it but a Swede.' Tommy Allen cast a meaningful glance towards a half-drunk Scandinavian sitting in the corner.

'What did it look like?'

Allen slowly wiped a glass. 'Oh, just like the bare bone, but kind of greasy, like the skin on a white puddin. He used to hide it under a wig, but he'd gie ye a look for a couple of dimes or a glass of gin.'

Conversation had centred on cranial injury since Harry Wilkie had appeared with his head freshly bandaged from the battle on the drying green. Harry stood at the bar, accepted the commiserations and refreshments thrust upon him and speculated with the others on what had caused the remarkable incident.

'When it comes tae viciousness, women are worse than men,' said Tommy Allen, who believed there must have been a secret feud between the washerwomen. And he cited numerous incidents from the Barbary Coast to prove his point. Others blamed panic and hysteria. Wiggy Bennett, on a run ashore at the Cape, had seen two hundred Kaffirs dash headlong into the sea when clouds passing over a flag pole had convinced them it was going to fall on them at an open-air prayer meeting. As for Harry, he pointed out that his sister Ethel, who knew several of the ladies concerned, thought a less hysterical bunch would be hard to find in Dundee.

Alexander Yule, who had been smoking quietly and paying scarcely any attention to the conversation, looked up at the mention of Ethel's name. He had been unaware of the relationship between the attractive school mistress and the hero of the drying green battle. Yule stroked his chin, then signalled that their glasses be recharged and beckoned Harry to join him at a table some distance from the crowd at the bar.

So it came about that, when Harry Wilkie took his place at the family supper table that evening, he announced his intention of applying for the position of fireman aboard the whaling ship *Ultima Thule*. He bore the ensuing protests stoically. He had never been to sea, but a boiler was a boiler anywhere and there was nothing he didn't know about stoking a furnace. When his tearful mother conjured up visions of perishing in Arctic wastes or drowning in icy seas, Harry pointed out that such accidents, though not unheard of, were more likely to befall those who hunted whales and seals from open boats or on the ice. Firemen who never strayed far from the warmth of the engine room were seldom subjected to such perils. His father was more persistent. Whaling was in recession. Hadn't he heard that ships which regularly caught twelve or fifteen whales each season were now lucky to catch two or three? The old stonemason, who considered himself nobody's fool but doubted that this quality had been passed on to his younger son, hooked his thumbs into the armholes of his waistcoat, rocked back on his chair and fixed Harry with one of his most penetrating glares.

'Who put you up to this nonsense anyway?' he asked. 'Don't you know that fisher folk are as thick as thieves? You've as much chance of getting a job as fly in the air. You've got a perfectly good job. Do you think Baxters will take you back when you get fed up with chasing whales?'

But Harry mildly pointed out that the whaling community was by no means as clannish as the folks along the coasts of Fife and Angus who made their living from herring. There was no comparison; and besides, someone with influence in the business was prepared to speak up for him. This served in some measure to placate his father, who fell to eating his meal in silence. Though his mother bustled about, determined not to look him in the eye, Harry knew that the worst had blown over. His elder brother, Tam, visited only at weekends. He would have to wait a week for his scorn. And while her father and brother supped their broth in silence, the portion set aside for Ethel simmered in the pot until her mother, shaking her head in despair, lifted it from the fire.

Ethel's thoughts were far from soup. Ethel was crossing the dark schoolyard on the arm of her pupil Jochen Dau, and though the night was far from pleasant, they walked home rather than take the tram. It was therefore very late indeed when Ethel learned the news from her mother who was the only one not yet in bed. Separated by lath and plaster, the Wilkie family lay with their thoughts. In the proprietorial bedroom, the thoughts formed themselves into a conversation that began, 'You should have kept him at the stone dressing. He's never really been happy in that mill. What if we never see him again?'

And continued, 'Some hope. Thon dunt on the head must have knocked him daft. Fishing for whales, if you please. Give it a week and he'll be fishing for his job back, if he's ever fool enough to leave it.'

If his parents debated the matter further, and there is no reason to believe they did, their voices must have been muffled by the darkness and the bolster, for in his tiny bedroom, Harry could hear nothing but the wind howling in the flue and the sporadic rattle of rain against the window. In his imagination, he was already aboard the *Ultima Thule*, beating through silver Arctic waters in search of what? Harry's knowledge of whales and those who hunt them consisted of vague and distant memories from the pages of Herman Melville. Indeed, during their conversation, Yule had been more concerned with establishing Harry's familiarity with tubular boilers than unfolding tales of the deep. So in Harry's tired, excited and still mildly concussed mind, a whaleman, an engineer and a sub-sub librarian interrogated him all at cross purposes until sweat broke on his brow and the bedstead creaked in sympathy with his restlessness.

'This whale's liver was two cart loads' . . . 'After firing, the ventilating grid in the door must be kept open for a minute or so' . . . 'Ten or fifteen gallons of blood are thrown out of the heart at a stroke with immense velocity' . . . 'Do not get up steam from cold water in less than six hours' . . . 'The bone-bearing whales winter in Hudson's Bay. In early spring they come out into the Davis Straits and go north' . . . 'Each safety valve must be lifted by hand to see that it is free' . . . 'You know, the Italians are paying twenty-three pounds a ton for oil these days.'

Across the landing, a slit of yellow light marked the base of Ethel's door. Her lamp stood near the edge of the marble-topped washstand, its calico shade cast the full benefit of its mellow light in a pool before the mirror. Ethel peered at her reflection. A brush rested on her lap, but she made no attempt to pass it through the thick, auburn hair which fell past the bosom of her night gown. Framed by the enamelled rectangle, her face peered back, an oval face, tending to heaviness round the jawline, but none the worse for that. In 1899 fashion demanded weightiness in a woman, which has never quite been in vogue since. A face with dark eyes, perhaps slightly small, arched brows, perhaps slightly thick, and a brow the normal smoothness of which bore the temporary imprint of a frown. A reversed face, but one with which Ethel was tolerably pleased. She pursed her lips, breathed a silent whistle and frowned at her reflection, deepening the furrow on both brows. Not for the first time these days she was left with a vague sense of defeat. Despite Dau's forwardness, she found a pleasing sensitivity in his attitude. Perhaps he had put his feelings on a physical basis to overcome the debacle in church. On the way home, she had listened with satisfaction akin to smugness as Jochen Dau haltingly laid bare his plans for the future. At the garden gate, she had allowed her admirer the reward of two kisses, which, had the nearest lamp not been yards away and every window in the street dark, might have caused tongues to wag. But circumstances justified the risk. Ethel knew exactly what she thought about Mr Jochen Dau. In contrast to his exotic name, Dau was a very down to earth person indeed. His talents would take him far in the field of linen oilcloth, and as it seemed that tables would not go out of fashion and all tables had to be covered, Dau's increasing prosperity went without saying. She had been impressed to hear that his parents lived in New York, though had she met his father, content with his pipe and porter, or his mother, who in all the years had never mastered English, she might have placed Dau slightly lower on the social scale than she did. Only his standing in the community, the problem that had brought them together, might have given cause for concern; but Ethel Wilkie had complete confidence in her educational ability. If Jochen Dau wanted to become accepted in Dundee society, rest assured she would see to it that he was. His foreignness intrigued rather than irritated her. Walking up the short path, she found herself repeating 'Frau Dau . . . Frau Dau,' and was disappointed when she realised that, to German ears, the title must have sounded mildly amusing.

To Ethel's mind, Dau was firmly in his place. A category had been found. He was not the cause of the bipartite furrow above the brows in the mirror. It was Alexander Yule who refused to fit a pigeon hole. How could she even consider being seen with him? A whaler who reeked of oil and blubber and who carried a little bottle of the ghastly stuff in the pocket of his pilot jacket. Ethel rubbed her right palm against her nightdress. She remembered Yule shinning along the rope and perilously plucking her from mid air. Her spine tingled and she touched the back of her neck. How could he have dared to touch her in church? If only poor Jochen had not made an idiot of himself with that walking stick, Yule would have had no opportunity to take her arm outside the church. When she had laughed and hurriedly thanked him once more for helping her, he had squeezed her arm and said, 'I know what you're trying to say. A whaling man should not be keeping company with a schoolteacher. Remember,' he had called before disappearing into the Nethergate, 'oil's making twenty-three pounds a ton these days.'

With that, Alexander Yule might have passed out of her life, leaving the field to the eminently more suitable Mr Dau. Instead, he had gone behind her back. Out of the blue, he had subverted Harry, lured him away to sea with heaven knows what promises of riches and adventure. Not for a moment did it occur to Ethel that Harry might have been offered the position on merit. The skills needed to tend a boiler were unknown to her, and she imagined that her younger brother spent his day simply shovelling coal, which shamed her. When speaking of her family in polite society, she tended not to mention him at all. So it was clearly not because of Harry that Yule had made such a ridiculous offer but because of her. Did he expect her to beg him to change his mind? Ethel drew the brush through her hair with such vigour that the lamp rattled on the marble surface of the washstand.

What's that, my dear? I can't help feeling your attention is drawn more to your books than to my little tale of Ethel Wilkie's thoughts behind lath and plaster. But maybe in your room at the Queen's, when you replay the tape, the significance of Ethel's dilemma will sink in. Ah, yes. Forbes did that drawing some years after the *Bestiary* series, though I see why you think there might be a connection. It's tempting to see the naked man being led by a bear as an ironic reversal of what had gone before. In fact, though the caption does not say, it was a sketch for a proposed poster. Forbes had become interested in animal rights. No doubt he was courted by numerous worthy causes, but he chose to lend his influence to those who campaigned against the exploitation of various species across the world. Don't for a moment imagine him liberating beagles or torching factory farms. Forbes enjoyed a smoke and was one of the most enthusiastic and knowledgeable carnivores I have met. But it was a fashionable cause, and while several stars simply lent their names and fading looks, Forbes contributed ideas for publicity. I can't remember why nothing came of it, probably cost, but that little drawing represents his first attempt to sting the national conscience. I suppose it was the first step on the path which led to disaster. But that must keep till later, when all the facts are in place. Of course you may leave the books here. I'll enjoy leafing through old memories, though I really should get on with my defence. Shall we say the same time tomorrow?

Chapter 9

YOU WAITED my dear! I tried to postpone our meeting, but you'd left the hotel and I didn't think to ring your editor for the number of your mobile. I'm sure you keep one in that enormous bag. I've never held with them myself, call it the innate conservatism of the law, but I'd be the first to admit they're useful in extremis. You'll gather the day has not gone quite to plan. I had been expecting a call, but when Inspector McCreath rang the doorbell at eight this morning it was still a shock. My faith in my own judgement has also been somewhat dented, for who should be with him but the gloomy soul with the Montego and thermos flask. One DC Bell, it appears, not a hack from the tabloids after all. And I thought I knew every detective in Dundee. Why they should waste time and money getting him to sit for days outside my front door defeats me. I'll ask the Chief Constable when I see him. Anyway, they found the body last night, not at Buddon or Tents Moor Point as you might expect, but slap on the shore at Tayport. You can see the place from here. We'll have a closer look through the telescope when we go up to the study. Right now coffee is in order. In fact, we need a dram. It's not every day you see a renaissance man stretched out on a slab. Yes, Louise, I'm sorry. Bad taste. Times like these breed sick jokes. A defence against the unthinkable.

What's that, my dear? No doubt. No doubt whatever. His survival suit was quite recognisable. If only he'd done it up properly. And he hadn't even lost his boots, as I did. I fear there wasn't much left of his face or fingers. Crabs and lobsters, apparently. I doubt we'll be visiting any restaurants in Fife for a while. Sorry, Louise. A little water, my dear? Not at all. He would have approved of a woman who takes her malt neat. So here's to Forbes Wedderburn. He went out with a splash.

Good point. We can expect renewed interest from your colleagues any moment. McCreath put out the ususal bumph first thing this morning: 'The body of a man was found on the shore at Tayport late last night by a local resident walking a dog. No name will be issued until the man has been identified and relatives informed.' But the penny's sure to drop soon. We'll let the ansaphone take care of the gentlemen of the press. I don't have much appetite, Louise. They're doing the post mortem as we speak. But if you insist, let's have something light on a tray in the study.

I understand your agitation, my dear. When front pages are about to fill with confirmation of Forbes's death, I'm filling your tapes with stories of schoolteachers and whalers and shifty Europeans whose lives converged almost a hundred years ago. But as I said at the start, I have an overwhelming desire to get to the bottom of things. While others are producing columns of noble, bland sentiment and reassessing the value of his work, which I dare say will rocket, you are being led, however slowly and with many diversions, to what motivated Forbes's last creation; indeed to what led to his death. You look sceptical. Let me for the moment abandon Ethel Wilkie's hypothetical imaginings behind lath and plaster and show you this letter. It came last year towards the end of August. It must have been delivered on a Saturday, because I was working here on my collection. Louise brought it up before my coffee had grown cold, before I had so much as uncovered the tray of scrimshaw I had hoped to classify. She stood there, bare toes deep in the carpet, and though her left hand held at least a dozen envelopes of significance to our mutual existence, the single slim sheath in her right hand demanded all the attention. She was annoyed when I simply laid it with the other mail on the edge of the desk.

'At least he's taken the trouble to write,' she said, 'instead of descending on us as you thought he would.' Louise was already flushed and excited. I was not surprised. She normally exudes stability and common sense. A supper table including a sheriff or even a High Court judge doesn't daunt her in the least. But the mere suggestion that she act as hostess for a few days to an overexposed media personality turns her into a teenager. Granted, Forbes moved to Hampstead shortly after we married, but we often met on his frequent visits to Dundee and our rather less frequent ones to London. Though we had never stayed under one another's roofs, this had happened more by chance than design and I knew even then that Louise had fallen under Forbes's spell. Surely you remember *Fitting Images*, when Forbes invited us, for three months, to trace with him the major influences of contemporary design. Louise, who had shown little interest in things aesthetic, watched every episode.

'Why don't you show more interest?' she said. 'After all he is your second cousin.'

I can't deny it. When Forbes beamed from the TV screen behind his fashionably tinted spectacles; when he appeared in the Sunday supplements beside his latest creation, I was always reminded that, however unlikely it may seem, we had a pair of great grandparents in common. It started with a call to my office. I was in court. When I returned, my secretary told me a Mr Wedderburn had phoned. He wanted me to assist him with a new project, and would explain the details later. She hadn't caught the name, but he was calling long distance from the Far East she thought. And that was that until the letter. With this knife (the handle is carved from the tooth of a sperm whale) I slit the tasteful, dove-grey envelope and withdrew two sheets of hand-made paper embossed with a logotype of Forbes's own devising applied to all graphic works purporting to come from his hand. Let me read it into your recorder. I can have a copy made for you later at the office if you wish.

Hotel Ambassador, Teipei, Taiwan. 21 August

Dear Gilbert,

How are you, you old whaleback? You may have heard what I'm up to out here. I've been trying for months to erect a small bronze on one of the tiny islands, little more than rocks, that trail like a streamer across the East China Sea from Japan. At first all went well. The British Council played ball and the Japs were all smiles until they discovered my motive. I wanted to draw attention to the ludicrous situation which allows Japan to kill whales, ostensibly for research, then sell the meat on the open market. Admittedly I cheated a little. My drawings and the first maquette showed a jolly, almost heraldic whale flanked by a stylised scientist complete with microscope. I think the Japanese interpreted it as some sort of tribute to cetacean research. However when the finished work was unpacked (it was cast in the States) I had added a second heraldic supporter: a greedy little Tokyo gourmet with drooling chops and chopsticks at the ready. Attitudes changed. My hosts, who had offered a whole range of sites for the work, suddenly became keen to preserve the natural beauty of their coast. My bronze would encroach on this worthy aim. In fact, I doubt if they minded the sculpture much. Stylised animals and fat gentlemen abound in Japanese art; you may even have one or two miniatures carved in your beloved bone. No, they sensed a set-up. Regrets were voiced. The British Council retreated into their gins and tonics and hoped I would go home. And I might have done, had I not been accompanied by a ton of bronze, specially treated to withstand the electrolytic action of the sea. It struck me there was more mileage to be had in their refusal of the sculpture than their acceptance, and I set about persuading the Taiwanese, who have a healthy suspicion of their northern neighbours, to give me a site on a rock in their national waters where the work could face accusingly towards Japan. So here I am, in air-conditioned splendour, being buried beneath a mountain of red tape. To escape the boredom of official procrastination, I have been wondering how to make a similar statement nearer to home. Thoughts have not yet gelled, but I am sure in writing to you, I have found the right man to advise me, for I can never think of you without calling to mind the pictures and carvings and photographs with which, even as a youngster, you used to surround yourself. How often must I have called on you as a child, eager to show you some trivial acquisition? How often must my enthusiasm have given way to awe when shown into your little room? Despite the clouds scudding behind grey panes, despite the brass bed and the wardrobe mirrors, I am convinced to this day that your bedroom was at the bottom of the sea. For beneath a greenish glass lampshade, behind sea-green curtains, on a green-baise table top, you laid out your embryonic collection. Crudely carved whales, rescued from junk shops or the flea market. A rubber toy whale that spouted water. Two whales' teeth. A primitive drawing of whales incised on bone. While round the walls, some in home-made frames, others simply pinned to the pale-green wallpaper, there swam a whole procession of two dimensional whales. Some coloured, some in black and white, blue whales, sei whales, sperm whales, right whales and finner whales followed one another nose to tail round your room. How could a Dinky Toy or a football compete? Although you are barely five years older than I am, the whales made you seem so much more. When you announced you wanted to become a lawyer I was astonished. I had always imagined you adopting a watery profession: a sailor, or fisherman, or even better, a deep-sea diver, right down beside your beloved whales. Who better to advise me on my next aquatic project?

I hope to get home in early October, so expect a call then. It is my distinct impression we may be able to do one another a considerable service. With kindest regards to yourself and the delightful Louise, whose acquaintance I look forward to renewing.

Forbes W.

Did I really have a bedroom full of whales like a fish tank at the top of the house? Not that I remember, my dear. At least not the way Forbes describes it. Even on paper he could charm the commonplace into the exotic. Louise, you've done us proud.

French bread, smoked ham, Stilton, freshly-ground coffee. But the aroma I am seeking is of dampness slightly tainted by sulphur and tobacco. The smell I want to draw to the very back of my throat is that of a Dundee tram on a dull, frosty morning.

Chapter 10

ALEXANDER YULE and Harry Wilkie climbed on to the platform of the tram for which they had waited approximately five minutes in Perth Road. Above the slate roofs and chimneys of the jute mills, a pale smudge suggested daylight was not far away, but the muffled figures on the pavement went about their tasks in darkness, moving in and out of yellow pools of gaslight like ghosts trailing frosty plumes of ectoplasm. Yule made room on the bench for Harry, and from the folds of his pilot coat that still bore traces of mist produced a pipe and tobacco pouch. Harry Wilkie followed suit, filling the bowl of his little briar with quick, prodding movements of the forefinger. They lit up. Neither man spoke, and though Harry would dearly have liked to ask about the reception he could expect when he applied at the company office for a berth as fireman, Yule, who had pushed his hands deep into his pockets and closed his eyes, was so clearly disinclined to conversation that Harry thought better of it and directed his attention to the window. It was then that he noticed a vaguely familiar figure about to board at the next stop. The man paused to knock the moisture from his coat and hat before climbing aboard, and in the moment he stood bareheaded on the pavement, Harry recognised the foreigner who worked in the laboratory at Dens Mills and who had recently created an uproar in the kirk. But he knew nothing of the connection between Jochen Dau and his sister Ethel, and his curiosity was short lived. Harry pulled his cap down over the bandage on his head and, like Yule, closed his eyes and smoked in silence. In the Nethergate, as the tram shuddered to a halt outside St Mary's Church, Alexander Yule awoke from his genuine nap and Harry Wilkie from his feigned one. They set off down Union Street through a crowd of sombre businessmen and sleepy shopgirls; and if either noticed Mr Jochen Dau crossing nimbly through the traffic in the direction of Tay Bridge Station, he did not think it worthy of mention.

Another tape? Of course, my dear. And while you see to your machine, and Louise clears away, I can decide how best to explain what happened on that dreary November day so crucial to our story. Should we follow Harry Wilkie to the docks, or wait with Jochen Dau at the ticket window? Is it best to take each in turn, or strike out boldly between them as their day unfolds? For the present, we'll leave our would-be fireman on the corner of South Union Street.

Jochen Dau walked down the platform and stepped into a vacant second-class compartment of the eight-thirty Edinburgh train. He placed his hat, stick and briefcase on the rack, and as the compartment filled with the sort of people who travel second class at that hour of the morning, took the briefcase down again and leafed carefully through its contents. Mr Dau was nervous. He was on a mission which, if successful, might considerably improve the fortunes of Messrs Baxter & Co., not to mention his own. Dau had already reproduced the technique of making heatproof oilcloth, for which he had been enticed to Dundee. Several trial batches had been tested and Baxter's management were keen to begin production, but Jochen Dau was not satisfied. A chance meeting with the travelling representative of a printing firm who happened to stay in the same lodgings when he was in Dundee had opened Dau's eyes to a new opening in the market. One evening after dinner, Dau had helped his fellow guest carry some huge, leather-bound portfolios to his room. It turned out they contained linoleum patterns. However, the designs were not printed on linoleum itself, which would have been impossibly heavy, but lithographed on to heavy paper and varnished to form an excellent imitation of the real thing. The company which produced such remarkable work was based in Kirkcaldy, where it did brisk business beneath the pall of boiling linseed-oil fumes for which the town was rightly famous. Mr Dau had shown interest. Cards had been exchanged. Dau had arranged a meeting with a director of the printers by telephone, but had been vague about why he wished to see the process. He had been equally evasive with his colleagues when he announced that he would spend the day visiting a firm in Fife; for in the bedroom in Windsor Street, Jochen Dau had realised that if the same printing technique could be used on oilcloth, not for samples but for the real thing, it would open a whole new world of washable, coloured, patterned cloth.

The train rumbled across the bridge towards the dark coast of Fife. From the window, Jochen Dau peered through the lattice work of the new bridge at the water sucking and swirling beneath it. Twenty years had passed since the previous bridge had collapsed, carrying a whole passenger train into the depths of the Tay, but in the minds of those who lived in Dundee and along the coast of Fife, the story of that dreadful night had, through constant retelling, created a gruesome fascination for that stretch of muddy tideway. Dau had been told the tale almost as soon as he arrived in the city, and watched the water apprehensively until the train steamed slowly into Wormit Station. Green lanterns swung, whistles blew, and with only a slight jolt, the train moved off and continued its journey by way of Ladybank, Markinch and Thornton Junction across the dark and wintry farmland of Fife.

By the time the train stopped for the regulation four minutes at Kirkcaldy, Jochen Dau had read every page of the *Courier*. He had apprised himself of the current situation in Natal; mused for a moment on uncorroborated reports of Russian persecutions in the Caucasus and mentally noted the price of flax. He placed the newspaper in his briefcase and left the train. His appointment was not until eleven. There was time to kill. Prudently he inquired where to find the printing firm in question. It lay within ten minutes' walk of the station, and after strolling around for a while, confirming the size and probity of the premises, Dau set off down a steep wynd which ran along the side of the print works and emerged in the High Street of the busy little town. At first Jochen Dau thought of finding a teashop in which to while away the time until his appointment, but none was to be seen. Reluctant to wander too far, he was retracing his steps to the foot of the wynd when he spotted a sign which suggested even more pleasurable warmth and sanctuary. He hurried across the street towards the red and white striped pole and stepped into the premises of Mr William Adam, whose reputation was second to none in the town. Perhaps a dozen gentlemen were reclining on the upholstered benches, smoking, reading newspapers and waiting their turn to occupy one of the four barber's chairs arranged like thrones before a long mirror. The proprietor nodded genially to Dau and waved him to a seat. In the warm scent of soap and cigar fumes, Jochen Dau relaxed and let his excitement about whether the project would work and whether or not he should keep the discovery to himself subside. He took his newspaper from his briefcase and idly flicked over the pages while the barbers and their customers chatted about the topics of the day. Suggestions were put forward for the relief of Ladysmith. The defeat at Magersfontein was analysed and blame apportioned. The quality of performances at the local music hall was criticised, and the fate of the football team discussed. Steam from the gas burner wafted into the air, and such was the feeling of wellbeing after the bitter cold of the High Street, that Jochen Dau had almost dropped off to sleep when something so surprising happened that in an instant he was wide awake. The second barber from the left, whose chair had just been vacated, turned towards the queue and said, 'You're next Mr Dau.'

That the barber should know his name was disconcerting enough, but when an elderly gentleman in a black morning coat rose and took the vacant chair, Jochen was so taken aback that his newspaper fell to the floor and he gaped at the second Mr Dau in disbelief. His surprise went unnoticed. Five minutes later, another barber signalled that his turn had come, and he took his place in front of the mirror two seats away from his mysterious namesake. The barber who attended to Jochen Dau was the proprietor of the shop. He draped Dau in a sheet, tucked a towel inside his stiffly-starched collar, and with a few deft movements, adjusted the chair to his satisfaction.

'A haircut and a shave, if you please,' said Dau, whose hair was tidy and chin already smooth from an earlier shave before the washstand in his lodgings. He lay back against the headrest while the barber selected brushes, combs and scissors from the marble-topped counter. 'I am a stranger here,' said Dau, 'but somehow the gentleman in the next seat but one seems familiar. Might you perhaps know who he is?' The barber met Jochen Dau's eyes in the mirror.

'He's Mr Dow the undertaker from Hill Street. Comes here every morning.' The barber eyed Jochen Dau's reflection dubiously. 'Where did you say you came from, sir?'

'I come from Germany, but now I live in Dundee.'

The barber ran a comb rather briskly through Dau's immaculately parted hair. 'Well. I doubt you could have met Mr Dow in Germany. As for Dundee, you'd better ask him yourself.'

Dau moved his head for a better view and squinted into the mirror at the old gentleman whose face was by now covered in lather. 'Do you think his family might have come from Germany?'

The barber's powerful fingers jerked Dau's head straight again. He leaned close to Dau's right ear. 'That's hardly my business or yours; but as far as I know, Mr Dow is Kirkcaldy born and bred. There are many people of that name here.'

'Many people,' Jochen gasped, twisting his head till the towel sprang from his collar. 'How many?'

The barber glanced towards the elderly undertaker, whose eyes were shut and head tilted back. 'I've no idea. Dozens probably. It's quite a common name.' He whispered despite the fact that Mr Dow was hard of hearing, and began to tuck the towel back in position. Jochen Dau caught his white sleeve in trembling, excited fingers.

'How do you write it?' Dau asked so loudly there was a sudden hush in the saloon. 'How do you spell that name?'

Convinced he had a madman in his chair, the barber bent his mouth close to Jochen Dau's ear and, in a stage whisper that carried to the furthest corner of the shop, said, 'D-O-W, Dow. If you want to know any more, ask him yourself. Now, do you want your hair cut or not?'

Jochen Dau sat quietly and allowed the barber to continue combing and snipping his hair in petulant silence. When the operation was almost over, the barber took a small bottle of macassar oil and, at a nod from Dau, began to massage it into his customer's scalp. 'I heard tell,' said the barber slyly, 'that in some places in Germany, or maybe it was Russia, they still put bear's grease on their hair.' And he laughed at Dau's startled face in the mirror.

Now let's go back to the street corner on which Harry Wilkie and Alexander Yule stood as Mr Dau set off on his adventure in Fife. 'Take a look at her first,' said Yule, 'in case she's not for you.' Harry had no doubt the *Ultima Thule* was for him, but still felt some apprehension as he turned up his collar in imitation of the older man and set off in his wake along Dock Street. They crossed the damp expanse of cobblestones and railway lines that led to the edge of Victoria Dock, and then Harry saw them. Lying alongside the wharf on the far side of the dock, black-hulled and dismal, were three ships of the Dundee whaling fleet. Tall masts and bare spars rose above the choppy water. In the lee of a shed, Yule jabbed his pipe towards the farthest ship which lay apart from the other two. 'The *Ultima Thule*,' he said. 'And there's the *Balaena* and *Nova Zembla*. I've sailed on them all at one time or other, but the old *Thule*'s as good as any. They trudged round the rim of the dock towards the ships, which seemed more dismal and abandoned the closer they came. As a lad, Harry had often skipped school to cheer off the whalers from the pier head, but now the ships looked much smaller than he remembered, and they seemed almost forlorn among the big iron freighters.

What should I tell you about the ships that plied from Dundee in the dwindling years of the Arctic trade? I couldn't help but notice your excitement when I mentioned the process by which Mr Jochen Dau hoped to revolutionise the oilcloth industry. Can I hope to match it with details of the thoroughly nautical and frankly rather distasteful calling that attracted Mr Harry Wilkie on the selfsame day? Step over to the mantelpiece, my dear. The painting above it, though of indifferent quality, gives a fair idea of how the *Ultima Thule* would have appeared; and if you stroll down to Discovery Point, which no visitor can possibly have missed, you'll find a similar, though much grander ship preserved in full municipal pomp within a stone's throw of your hotel. Like most whaling ships of those days, when the sphere of activity was about to move from the northern to the southern hemisphere and harpooning from open boats was about to give way to the steam whalecatcher, she and her sisters looked decidedly old fashioned. She was barque-rigged, about six hundred tons and wooden hulled to withstand the pressure of Arctic ice. A spindly funnel was mounted almost as an afterthought between her main and mizzen masts. She had a raised poop, and running forward from it was the engineroom skylight, which ended at the funnel casing. On each side of the casing, steps led to the main deck. The bridge, which was little more than a platform protected by rails and canvas dodgers, ran transversely across the skylight forward of the mizzen mast. The double wheel was right aft, protected only by the carved taffrail aft and a dumpy little deckhouse forward that housed the binnacle and formed a cover to the companionway which led to the cabin. The broad waist of the ship and the eight pairs of davits along her gunwales clearly marked her as a whaler, but when Harry Wilkie stood on the quay and looked through the fine mist, no whaleboats hung from the falls. Three lay upturned on deck, the others were lined up under tarpaulins on the quayside no doubt for maintenance. Alexander Yule scaled the short, steep gangplank and Harry Wilkie followed only slightly less nimbly. They made their way forward to where a hatch opened on to the forecastle ladder. Yule whistled with two fingers against his teeth. Scuffling was followed by a fit of coughing and a figure emerged from the hatch and blinked at the gloomy daylight. There stood before them a man of at least seventy years. Beneath the muffler, which he wore like a turban, his face was so scarred and pitted that Harry felt the hairs on his neck tingle and tried to look away. Yule clapped the old watchman on the shoulder.

'This is a new fireman, Willie. I'm going to show him the ship.'

The hole that passed for a mouth moved. 'I'll mak the tea.' The old man disappeared down the ladder. Yule motioned Harry to follow, and soon they were seated on a narrow bench by the forecastle stove on which an enamelled pot steamed ominously.

'Your berth will be in here.' Yule nodded to the four-high banks of bunks that lined the forecastle. 'There are four firemen and three engineers, but the chief has a cabin aft beside the captain and the mate. The sailors live in here as well, and I berth in the tweendecks beside the Orkneymen we pick up at Stromness on the way out.' The watchman was groping about in the forward part of the forecastle. He emerged clutching three tin mugs against his chest. As he deposited them on the edge of the stove, Harry realised that, save for the thumb of his right hand, the old man was quite devoid of fingers. The tea was scalding and sweetened with molasses, but the old man clutched the mug between his fingerless paws oblivious to the heat. Yule glanced at Harry Wilkie.

'Willie got nipped by the frost when the *Resolution* was lost in eighty-six. They walked seventy miles over the ice in Notre Dame Bay after the ship was crushed, but scarcely a man was fit to go to sea again.'

Harry had no chance to find out why the *Resolution* had come to this end, for Yule, fearing that the sudden confrontation with a less palatable aspect of the Arctic fishery might weaken his protégé's resolve, downed his tea as quickly as its temperature would allow and led Harry aft to the stokehole and boiler and bunkers, the tending of which would be Harry's concern should he be accepted for the crew. The light that filtered through the stokehole skylight was scarcely enough to see the boiler. Yule lit a lamp. In its yellow glare, Harry Wilkie moved about, running his hands over the three fire doors, the cold firebars, examining the glass water gauges, the blow-out taps and ventilating grids, getting to know the equipment he'd have to tend in these unfamiliar conditions. Yule, who knew and cared little about marine steam propulsion, stood on the ladder and, after having watched Harry for some time, said, 'D'you think you can manage it?'

And Harry wiped his hands on a rag draped over the water feed pipe and said, 'I'll manage just fine.' Compared to the battery of gigantic boilers in the engine house of Lower Dens Mill, the simple boiler of the *Ultima Thule* presented few problems; or so it seemed with the vessel lying at rest alongside the quay. How Harry would cope at sea in heavy weather only time would tell, but if he had reservations, he kept quiet. He hoped Yule would take him farther round the ship, show him the engines and the cabins where the officers lived, but the specktioneer was keen to be off. 'We must get you a discharge book,' he said, 'then go to the company office.' They shouted farewell down the forecastle ladder and went ashore to deal with the bureaucracy that, even in those days, was necessary to transform a stoker of landlocked boilers into one with the authority, if not yet the ability, to stoke boilers at sea.

I have several examples of these fascinating documents which track, between Board of Trade covers, every voyage of a sailor's career. But the ones I'd most like to posess have eluded me despite many a search through old family papers.

Chapter 11

HARRY WILKIE and Alexander Yule walked up Trades Lane towards the Seagate. The mist had given way to rain, and its iciness contrasted with the steamy, animal smell that wafted from the corporation stables in Allan Street. Deep in his coat pocket, Harry clutched an envelope containing all the documents needed for his new calling. He whistled through his teeth as they turned into Seagate and crossed to a doorway whose brass plate was inscribed 'Victoria Whale and Seal Fishing Company Limited'. The offices were on the first floor, reached by a highly polished flight of stairs which led to a little outer room panelled in wood and opaque glass with a sliding window. A clerk sat on the other side. Yule spoke to the clerk, who opened a door in the partition and let him into the inner office. Harry sat on a bench and waited. In the far corner of the waiting room, on a chair that seemed dangerously fragile to support his bulk, a man sat with a briefcase on his knees. He wore a brown bowler, a checked suit and smoked a cigar from which he had not removed the band.

'Davis Straits again this year?' he boomed to Harry, letting ash drop carelessly to the floor. Harry looked nonchalant and sailorly.

'Probably,' he said, and pulled at the peak of his cap to give it a more nautical angle. The man took out a cigar case and thrust one towards Harry.

'Go on,' he said. 'Help yourself. It's not often I meet one of the chaps who actually catch the beasts.' He wheezed with amusement. 'Hopwood's the name, United Tanneries and Fellmongers. I'm up here to see your Mr Fairweather about walrus hides. D'you think you'll get many this trip?' Harry looked blankly at the Englishman. 'Walrus,' said Hopwood, 'or seahorses if you like. Can't understand why you call them that. D'you think it'll be a good season?' Harry took a puff at the cigar.

'I'm a fireman,' he said. 'I've no idea.' For a moment he thought Hopwood might take back his cigar.

'You don't know why we're so keen to get our hands on walrus hides?' The fat man slapped his hands on top of his briefcase. 'Bicycles. Everyone's wanting them now, and not just the gents but ladies as well. And all these bicycles need saddles. What better to mould them from than prime walrus hide, eh? I declare those old walrus would be fair tickled if they knew where their skins were going to end up. You get my drift?' And he laughed so much that Harry at first failed to notice that the clerk was beckoning him into the main office.

A lady typewriter looked at Harry in amusement as he passed, and he quickly removed his cap; but this exposed his embarrassing bandage and he did not know what to do with the ridiculous cigar. The clerk tapped on a door, pushed it open and stood aside. There were three men in the room which was almost entirely filled by a huge mahogany desk. Behind the desk there sat a man of perhaps sixty years. His grizzled, wedge-shaped beard rested on the front of his morning coat, completely concealing the collar. From Yule's description, Harry knew it was Fairweather, the general manager. A second elderly gentleman leaned on the mantelpiece. He was also in morning dress, though of a rougher, dark material with a black kerchief tied at the throat. His beard was pure white and neatly trimmed. Alexander Yule stood, cap in hand, at the far end of the room. The man behind the desk adjusted his pince nez and looked up.

'Yule tells me ye want tae sign as fireman for next season.'

'Yes, sir,' said Harry. 'I've seen the ship and I think I could manage.'

'Nae doubt ye ken a fire at sea is no as easy worked as a fire ashore.'

Harry made a decision and stubbed his cigar in a brass ashtray on the table. 'I think I could do it.'

'D'ye no like cigars?'

'I thought it might . . .'

'There's no mony firemen throws cigars like yon awa. No these days.'

'What happened tae yer heid?' It was the man by the fireplace who spoke. Harry glanced at Yule, but he seemed to be pre-occupied with something below in the street.

'It was an accident. A sort of fight. But it'll be better soon.'

'D'ye fecht a lot?'

'No. Not at all. It was more of an accident really.'

At last Yule spoke up. 'A woman threw a stane at his heid, Captain Jamieson. It was meant for somebody else.'

'I see,' said the old man. 'Would I be right in saying ye tak strong drink Mr Wilkie?'

'No more than the next man.'

'But what if the next man is me?'

Fairweather spoke up. 'Captain Jamieson, here, is a total abstainer. He disna' expect that much frae his crew, but ony trouble wi drink and ye'll never sail wi him again.'

Harry realised that the final decision rested with the old captain, but he addressed the general manager. 'I never had any trouble in my last job. I can get you references from Baxters.'

Fairweather said, 'Yule thinks highly o ye. I'm prepared tae tak his word, but once ye sign on there's nae goin' back. I doubt ye'll see mony whales, though. The *Thule*'s bound for the sealin'. She sails for Newfoundland at the beginning o February. Ye should mak twa trips out o St John's afore the end o the season. After that ye might see some whales up the Davis Straits, but they're getting scarcer and shyer every season. And maybe ye'll hae had enough by then.'

This seemed to amuse the captain, who rocked back on his

heels before the fire. 'I'll tak him on twa conditions,' he said. 'First, he stays sober. Second, if the engineer speaks ill o him, or he canna dae his job, I can set him to day-work an tak on another fireman in St John's.'

'Ye heard the Captain,' said Fairweather. 'See Dinwoodie in the office about signing the papers. Ye sail on the first o February, but be aboard three days early for coalin ship.'

Harry Wilkie and Alexander Yule sat behind steamed-up windows in Laird's pie shop and scooped broth from brown, earthenware bowls. Harry said, 'Jamieson's got it into his head I'm a right boozer.'

Yule shook his head. 'Don't worry about Pinnacle Tam. He's the same with everybody, but none the worse a skipper for that.'

'What did you call him? "Pinnacle Tam"?'

'Aye. When we're deep in the ice and every man would give his back teeth for a dram, the strongest thing he'll take is pinnacle tea. We thaw pinnacles of ice from the floes, you see. With a good strong brew and plenty molasses, it's better than nothing.'

And then they went their separate ways: Yule to pursue some private business, and Harry Wilkie, whose shift at the mill did not start till ten that night, to the matinee performance at the Theatre Royal. While Harry snoozed in the stalls and dusk fell over the city, Mr Jochen Dau stepped from the Aberdeen express. His briefcase was full of new information from which he could assess the viability of his revolutionary idea, but when he climbed into the first cab on the rank he did not ask to be taken to the laboratories of Baxter's linen mill but to the library of the Albert Institute. While Harry Wilkie watched chorus girls' plump arms and plumper thighs, Jochen Dau sat at a highly-polished table and surveyed the three books the librarian had been pleased to put at his disposal. One by one, he opened the books and selected a page. One by one, he ran his finger down the columns of closely-spaced type.

DOW, Andrew: Shoemaker, Murraygate. DOW A.W.: Drysalter, Panmure Street. DOW, Bernard P.: Sheriff's Officer, Commercial Street. DOW and PATON: Sawmillers, Forfar

Road. He laid aside the Dundee Trades Directory and, with eager fingers, turned to the second book.

Douglas . . . Doull . . . Dove . . . DOW: (Celtic) Of dark complection or hair. English corruption of Gaelic DUBH. The third volume served merely as confirmation.

DOW: Gaelic and Irish 'Dubh' = Black. Anglicised as 'Dow'. A characteristic Gaelic nickname akin to Boyd (yellow haired), Ogg (young) etc. Rapidly Jochen Dau scribbled the details into his notebook, then swept the books from the table and deposited them before the librarian.

'Many, many thanks,' said Mr Jochen Dau. 'You have been of great service to me.'

The librarian smiled a feeble smile and held out a pen. 'As you are not a regular user of the Institute,' he said, 'might I ask you to be good enough to enter your name and address?'

'Of course,' said the most delighted customer he had seen all day. 'My name is Dow, John Dow, but most people call me "Jock".'

No one waiting for the tram in the High Street could have realised the metamorphoses that had overtaken the two young men who arrived, one from Castle Street, one from Commercial Street, to join the queue. No one noticed the contented smile on the face of the young man who watched his reflection in the glass against the lights of Perth Road. He was Harry Wilkie, fourth fireman of the whaler *Ultima Thule*, bound for St John's and the Davis Straits with his papers in one pocket and in the other a letter to the office of Baxter & Co. announcing that he would leave their employment as of Saturday, 25 January 1900 to take up a post with the Victoria Whale and Seal Fishing Company of Dundee.

Anyone who observed the young businessman seated in the corner might well have attributed his evident good humour to the successful transaction he had completed that day. Only the keenest onlooker would have noticed that, despite the jolting of the tram, he spent the entire journey between the High Street and the Sinderins with a notebook spread on top of his briefcase, repeatedly practising a signature the spiky newness of which gave way to a rounded familiarity as the journey progressed.

Oh yes. He passed on the name. Maybe now you see why I want to tell our story in this particular way. How, by coaxing memories into your recorder, I am trying to get to the bones of the relationship that led from an artist's studio to a mortuary slab. Forbes knew all the secrets, or said he did, not that I have ever hidden the fact that this family Dow, far from being of anglicised Gaelic origin, related perhaps to drysalters or sawmillers, takes its name from the whim of a Baltic charlatan who had scant title to it in the first place regardless of how it was spelled. Few except Forbes knew or cared. The clients to whose wills and affidavits I add my name; the police who respectfully asked me to sign a short statement confirming the identity of my late, artistically gifted second cousin, assume my scribble represents the short, unremarkable surname that even now fills a modest column-and-a-half in the Dundee phone book.

You're right, of course. Forbes's numerous and convoluted relationships did produce one brief marriage and even a son. That was upwards of twenty years ago. I met his wife only twice. Both times in London, both times before I was married. As you know, she was Mexican. Stunning, though with minimal English. In their relationship, I suspect this didn't matter. They had met through some artistic connection; perhaps she was on a scholarship. Forbes was captivated by her exoticism. When I next saw her, she was pregnant and Forbes was spending more and more time on the phone to his US dealer. He was about to open his second one-man show in New York. The Guggenheim had shown interest. Nuria, that was her name, was not keen even temporarily to exchange the dank heaths of Hampstead for the windswept canyons of New York. She missed the sun and a different pace of life. Both the birth and the divorce took place in America. On the way here from the mortuary, I dropped into the office. My secretary will place advertisements in the Mexican newspapers; a formality from which I eventually expect a response. Forbes never did entrust me with his affairs. As soon as the news breaks, some City solicitor will start calculating his fees for unravelling the web. But for the time being, the police and the procurator fiscal are quite content, for the purpose of identification, to regard me as Forbes's next-of-kin. I have no reason to believe he didn't think the same himself.

Chapter 12

FORBES Wedderburn, my second cousin, arrived here on the second of November last. Just before he was due, Louise came into the study, her face glowing with excitement. I heard music from the ground floor. I had noticed this endearing little habit before. Whenever we are expecting a visitor, she chooses background music to accompany the arrival. Perhaps she tries to match the selection to the expected guest; maybe she chooses at random. I have never asked her, but I like to think that, in her own way, she is making a quiet comment. She had selected Prokofieff. How chillingly the long, climactic chords evoked mists over the frozen lake.

Louise and I greeted Forbes warmly, showed him to the room that had been prepared and withdrew to await him with whisky in the sitting room.

'My dear friends,' said Forbes, settling into the chesterfield with a large Laphroaig, 'it's great to relax in good company after a journey that's taken me half way round the world and back.' His eyes twinkled. 'How often, in a Tokyo traffic jam or cooling my heels in Taiwan, have I thought of a day like this, when frost and Scotch mist mingle on the breath?'

'It must have been very interesting nevertheless,' said Louise, sliding a bowl of nuts in Forbes's direction.

'It was, my dear, but terribly frustrating. And even more so when I heard what has been happening here during the past few months.' He eyed me over the rim of his glass. 'I refer to the grey seal. You know I'm associated with several organisations which protect wildlife. I was sorry to be out of the country when they thwarted the efforts of Norwegian hunters to cull four thousand pups and nine hundred adults in Orkney. You must have followed events with equal interest. I'm sure your passion for aquatic mammals can't be restricted to the pelagic whale.'

Had his eyes become misty only through Laphroaig? I refilled his glass and said, 'Yes, I was aware of the affair in Orkney. No one could escape the blast of righteous indignation. In the unlikely month of October, Orcadian hoteliers experienced a boom unsurpassed even by the oil as mediapersons matched pound against pound on expense accounts, cast apprehensive eyes towards the sea and waited for a slaughter that never took place.'

'A pity I couldn't make it,' he said wistfully. 'Roger went, and Nicole. Even Claudia came all the way from Paris.' He reeled off the celebrated names as though he was on intimate terms with each of the personalities whose ecological consciences had been pricked by the proposed seal cull. How was he so well informed? Newspapers must have reached him even in that part of the world. 'What was your impression?' he asked suddenly. 'You could not have remained unmoved.'

Louise knelt on the sofa, her legs tucked up beneath her. She was following the conversation with interest and turned in anticipation of my reply. It was then, at that precise moment, I found myself making a conscious decision to take issue with our distinguished guest. This arose neither from deep conviction nor from malice, but more from a wish, which I maybe barely recognised, to pursue an argument with Forbes. To accept, if you like, a brief for the defence. It took only an instant, but from that moment I knew Forbes and I were on opposite sides.

'From a legal point of view,' I said,' I found it unacceptable that servants of an Officer of State should have been impeded by professional protesters while carrying out their lawful duties. In fact the abandonment of the cull had as much to do with awful weather as disruptive activities. But what a field day they all had. What a feast of televisual selfrighteousness. Talk, talk, talk. So much passion, so much emotion; and at teatime, over Welsh rabbit, I watched a pretty young presenter with the legs of a filly and the brains of a rocking horse bait a bewildered spokesman for the Scottish Office till tears welled in her eyes and the producer mercifully ended our ordeal with the touch of a switch.'

Forbes couldn't tell if I was serious. Eventually he said something like, 'I hear the cull was political rather than economic; an easy way to answer the fishermen's complaints about dwindling stocks. Though I was overseas, my friends kept me in touch.'

I imagined tasteful stationery winging its way from Knightsbridge and Mayfair and even the Avenue Foch, sounding the alarm and steeling Forbes for action. 'You've missed the boat,' I said. 'It's all over. Old news.' Forbes removed his glasses. Nimbly his pale fingers swept the handkerchief from his breast pocket to caress the tinted lenses. He stared at me with myopic intensity.

'The first round may have been won,' he said, 'but not the fight. The six-year plan to cull grey seals is still on the table. Twenty-four thousand will be killed. We still have much to do, which is why I'm here. I want your help with a project which will open everyone's eyes to the impending slaughter.'

Forbes knew how to play to the gallery. Louise was squirming with excitement. Maybe she imagined him prolonging his stay or introducing us to his famous friends. I was in danger of becoming trapped, but I offered no resistance and let Forbes drink my whisky and enmesh me in his plans.

You want to know what happened next? All in good time. Before I let you in on the publicity-seeking proposals of my second cousin, I want to set the record straight. I want to take you back to a Thursday in the last month but one of the last year of the nineteenth century. If I switch off the desk lamp and banish misleading reflections in the window, there is just enough daylight left to pick out the silvery line of the shore. In just such light, then, when everything could be seen but might not have been quite what it seemed, when a light powdering of greyish snow dusted the ground, on just such a Thursday at fifteen minutes to four, Samuel Doig rested his feet on the firebox doors and sunk his somewhat uneven teeth into a folded slice of bread which, earlier in the day, his wife had liberally smeared with lard. Samuel Doig was half way through his shift and had time to kill till the signal changed and allowed him to propel his six wagons from the East End Mineral Depot along the Dundee Foundry branch line.

Samuel Doig drove the 'Ink Bottle'. Everyone called it that. When Harry Wilkie was delayed by a slow-moving line of wagons crossing Foundry Lane, he said, 'I was held up by the "Ink Bottle".' When Dr Fraser's horse became difficult to control, he said, 'She's been frightened by the "Ink Bottle".' When Miss Ethel Wilkie's poor wee shifters, with squeaking pencils and thumbs wet with spit drew the outline of a cone on their slates, surmounted it with a squat chimney and placed four wobbly wheels at its base, they told her, 'Please, miss, that's the "Ink Bottle".' For the little engine that pushed and pulled wagons along the mineral railway looked like nothing so much as the type of bottle in which then, as now, it was customary to store ink. Whereas most railway engines worthy of the name carry their boilers in a horizontal posture, the 'Ink Bottle"s was vertical, like a big iron cooking pot. While every engineer knows the proper place for a smoke box is in front of the boiler, the 'Ink Bottle's' sat on top like an upturned pie dish. And though every schoolboy knows the chimney should be placed at the front of a railway engine, the 'Ink Bottle's' emerged right in the middle, exactly like a stopper that one must remove with care for fear of spilling the ink.

Samuel Doig chewed his bread and lard, let the heat from the newly-stoked fire seep through the soles of his boots and gazed across the bleak landscape. Alongside the track ran a tarred board fence, behind which rose the roofs and gables of Foundry Lane. Beyond the roofs towered the great, slab walls of Lower Dens Mill. The Italian bellcote of the Bell Mill rose domed and incongruous on the skyline just where the signal pole cut the horizon with its semaphore arm in the 'stop' position. Though the bleak walls of the mill were so familiar to Doig that, in the normal course of things, they would not merit a second glance, he nevertheless adjusted his position to see more clearly over the tarred fence and peered into the twilight with such concentration that he even forgot to chew his bread and lard. Black against the grey stonework, someone was climbing the vertical iron ladder that ran, five storeys high, up the mill wall to the roof. In the normal course of things, someone making his way, however precariously, up a ladder to a factory roof is unlikely to interest even the most bored engine driver. Linen production is a complicated process, requiring all manner of pagodas, turrets, and slatted ventilators to project from the roof of the building in which it takes place. Periodic, if hazardous, inspections must be made. In the normal course of things, then, Samuel Doig would have paid less attention to the engineer on the ladder than to the signal pole with its arm at 'stop' and much less than to his bread and lard had it not been for one thing. The figure, which by then had reached the top of the ladder and was creeping up the sloping roof to its flat summit, was dressed not in dungarees or workman's overalls, but a tall hat and an Inverness cape, the folds of which flew out in the wind, giving its wearer the appearance of a human bat. The figure stood up on the roof, looked round, then disappeared behind a turret of wood and pipework which jutted on the skyline and emitted a thin cloud of steam. Doig took advantage of the interlude to finish his bread and lard, but before he could lick his fingers, the Inverness cape popped out from behind the cupola, crossed the roof in a leap and a jump and began attacking a huge wooden ventilator using a crowbar brought specially for the purpose. One good turn deserves another.

In the laboratory deep in the mill, separated from the pulleys and looms by four walls of wood and frosted glass, Jock Dow sat at a bench and examined the piece of fabric on which he had persuaded the lithographer to print a sample pattern. He took scissors from the pocket of his coat, and carefully cut the sample into six pieces. Then he gummed a label to each piece. Mr Dow permitted himself a smile of satisfaction, and from his waistcoat pocket withdrew a little ring box. He had bought the ring on favourable terms two days previously; on the very day, in fact, when he had told Ethel Wilkie of his change of name. She had greeted the news with such enthusiasm that Dow was convinced he need only pick the appropriate moment to ask her to be his wife. On the way home, he dropped into a jeweller who augmented his income by exchanging pawns and therefore stayed open late. Dow was so preoccupied by pleasant thoughts that at first he did not notice the laboratory assistant whom he'd sent out for a flask of naphtha. But business was business. Hurriedly, Dow returned the ring to the safety of his pocket, held out his well-manicured hand and accepted the receipt which required his signature. Why did Jock Dow not append his brand-new signature on the dotted line? Why did he not go on to number and classify the samples which were spread on the bench? When Mr Dow applied his nib to paper, only a thin scratch marked the smooth, white surface. When he thrust his pen into the inkwell, it emerged as dry as it had entered. He had run out of ink, and as laboratory assistants should not stand idle, as receipts should not remain unsigned, as labels demand to be filled in, he rose from his seat and walked to the far end of the laboratory where, on the second shelf of the wall cupboard, he knew there was a bottle with enough ink to fill every inkwell in the mill.

But the receipt remained unsigned, the labels stayed blank, for just as Jock Dow reached the cupboard and turned the key, the ventilator designed to extract the more noxious particles of flax from the atmosphere detached itself from its mounting on the roof and plunged earthwards through the mill. The ventilator crashed through the skylight into the top floor. It passed through the fourth storey as if it were not there. The half-ton of wood and iron plunged through the floor of the third storey like an express train, and on the second storey, where Jock Dow's well-manicured fingers were within an inch of all the ink he required, it burst through the ceiling, shattered wood and frosted glass, and in an instant swept away bench and chair, pen and empty inkwell, laboratory assistant, receipt and six samples of oilcloth all crying out for classification straight through the floorboards to the storey below. Jock Dow took down the ink bottle from the second shelf and turned round. His brow wrinkled in annoyance as he surveyed the eight-foot-square hole where his laboratory had been. Carefully, he replaced the ink bottle and brushed the dust from his jacket. Then he fainted.

Outside on the railway track, Samuel Doig watched the angular silhouette of the ventilator topple and disappear through the roof of the mill. He gaped as a cloud of dust rose above the factory and a shower of dislodged tiles rattled into the yard below. He rubbed his eyes as the figure in the Inverness cape, who had prudently stepped back after levering the ventilator from its mounting, picked his way carefully along the edge of the roof and began to descend the ladder. He watched the tiny, bat-like form creep inch by inch down the wall of the mill and disappear behind the tarred wooden fence. Only when the dust had settled on the factory roof, only when the Inverness cape had disappeared from view, only when a bell started to ring deep in the Bell Mill did Samuel Doig direct his attention to the arm of the semaphore signal which had meanwhile dropped into the 'go' position. The engine driver stood up. As his locomotive had been stationary for some time, he opened the cylinder drain cocks and blasted a cloud of steam towards the fence. He gave the regulator a gentle pull and slowly the 'Ink Bottle' moved forward. Smoke and steam flew into the frozen air. Slowly at first, then more rapidly the beat of the engine increased. Slowly at first, then more rapidly the tarred wooden boards passed by until barely twenty yards ahead a goggle-eyed figure in Inverness cape and high felt hat vaulted the fence from Foundry Street in one leap and landed on the track slap in front of the 'Ink Bottle'. For an instant, Doig's eyes met those of the Craigie Ghost; but as Doig grabbed simultaneously for the brake and the whistle control, the Ghost flexed its knees, sprang clean across the track and was gone in leaps and bounds along the mineral railway.

Chapter 13

THE LIGHT has almost gone, but why draw curtains at the top of a house that stands on a hill? I just have time to tell you that many, many years ago, in the overheated bedsitting room to which she had been summoned by a handwritten note, Miss Ethel Wilkie firmly closed the curtains on just such an evening and turned her attention to Mr Jock Dow, who was in bed with shock at his amazing escape. Workmen with a ladder had rescued him from his precarious perch and borne him, still unconscious, to his lodgings, where Dr Fraser pronounced him sound in wind and limb and in need only of a night's rest to recover from the ordeal. He prescribed a sleeping draught to calm the patient, who was by then very wide awake, and a tonic to provide stimulation should the sedative induce prolonged torpor. Having thus anticipated all medical eventualities, the doctor packed his things and left, slipping his invoice beneath a bowl of wax fruit on the sideboard as he took his hat.

But Mr Dow refused to be sedated. Propped on a heap of pillows, he shook his head, rolled his eyes and jabbered so loudly in both German and English that he quite startled his landlady who had been asked to wait by the bedside till he fell asleep. Only when she agreed to send one of her children to Ethel Wilkie's house with a note to call on him at once did Mr Dow become more composed. When Ethel arrived, flushed and anxious, the landlady withdrew to the adjoining room; but she kept the connecting door open and for the duration of Ethel's visit maintained such a commotion with the coal scuttle and hearth brush and fire irons as to leave no doubt of her proximity and vigilance. What happened behind drawn curtains to the music of rattling fire irons? Jock Dow poured his heart out to Ethel Wilkie. He said the disaster at the mill was by no means an accident, that he feared for his life, and that the only way she could brighten his miserable existence was to agree to marry him and to wear the ring which could be found in his waistcoat on the back of the chair. On the understanding that, as soon as he recovered, Jock Dow would speak to her father in the proper manner, Ethel let him slip the ring on to her finger. When the landlady reappeared, she surreptitiously returned it to the waistcoat pocket and prepared to leave. Though Dow made a half-hearted attempt to persuade Ethel to stay, the landlady's expression left little doubt that her departure was overdue. Further embarrassment was saved by the sleeping draught, which took effect so suddenly that the ladies feared Mr Dow had suffered a relapse. When they realised the cause of his unconsciousness, they stole silently from the room.

And so, my dear, my paternal grandmother, Forbes Wedderburn's great aunt, took the first step in the process which would transform her from Miss Ethel Wilkie, teacher at Baxter's Half-time School, into Mrs Ethel Dow, housewife and mother. The incident which had precipitated her decision to cast in her lot with that of Mr Dow soon superseded the wash-house battle as a topic for gossip and speculation in the city. Blame fell on Baxters for failing to maintain their premises in a safe condition; and though they argued that the collapse of the ventilator must have been caused by a deliberate act, they undertook, out of goodwill, to care for the dependants of the laboratory assistant, whose back had been broken and who was unlikely to work again. Inevitably, this act of compassion, which had been most strongly supported by Jock Dow, was generally seen as an admission of responsibility.

Why did Samuel Doig, engine driver and prime witness, not come forward with his story? The answer lay in a very human weakness. At that time Doig was waging a somewhat unequal struggle against drink. He had striven manfully to restrict his tippling to off-duty hours, but was aware that his weakness had not escaped the notice of the manager of the mineral railway yard. Doig could well imagine his reaction to a tale of a man dressed as a bat, who could clear the foundry fence at one leap and whose eyes gleamed with malicious delight. Though he believed what he had seen, Doig chose the path of discretion and said nothing. To clear the company's name, plans were made to bring a case under the Employers' Liability Act, which, at the time, was barely three years old. Entangled in the cumbersome web of the law, the matter soon lost the attention of the locals and, like any nine days' wonder, passed into obscurity.

Jock Dow recovered swiftly. Within the week, he presented himself before Ethel's parents and, with the sober formality that was still part of life, requested her hand in a fitting and proper manner. The Wilkies listened to what he had to say, then gave him a glass of Madeira from a bottle that had mysteriously appeared in the dresser cupboard to seal the bargain. If Ethel's father or mother had misgivings about her choice of partner, they kept them to themselves. I have no reason to doubt that Dow's impeccable and charming manners quite won over Mrs Wilkie, while his excellent prospects sufficiently impressed her husband to counteract any prejudices the old mason might have harboured about his aspiring son-in-law's unusual background. Ethel had set her mind on the match; and when it came to crucial decisions, her will usually prevailed. She was a schoolteacher, after all, and could be said to have made more of her life than either of her brothers. The wedding was to take place the following February on a date to be fixed by the minister of St Mary's Church. As Dow took his leave, he promised to pay frequent visits to the Wilkie household to cement his friendship.

Have I gone too far? Have I suggested that Ethel Wilkie really believed her prospective husband's life to be in danger? Nothing was further from the truth. I have no evidence that Ethel did not put down Dow's accusatory ramblings to shock and the effects of Dr Fraser's sedative; and as he never mentioned the subject again, we can assume that in the excitement of wedding preparations, she soon forgot the incident. Only one trivial event might have caused her to reflect on the matter. Some three weeks after her engagement, Ethel was making her way down Sea Wynd. It was early evening and she was in a hurry. Under her arm she carried a carefully wrapped length of material which she had promised to deliver to Mrs Dalgleish, the dressmaker in Nethergate, as soon as it arrived from Edinburgh. Measurements had been taken and already preparations were well advanced for the construction of a wedding dress in the latest fashion. Miss Wilkie's thoughts were preoccupied with lace trimmings and Irish crochet, so when she came upon a dozen or so people in the middle of the alleyway, her impulse was to squeeze past in annoyance. Something in the awestruck appearance of the crowd made her stop. The people were bunched around a makeshift platform of luggage and instrument cases. Enthroned on this stage sat the yellow-haired German woman, and on either side, holding their instruments but not playing a note, stood the other members of the little band. Behind the musicians, Kaspar the bear stood on all fours at the end of his chain, thinking bear thoughts with his muzzle close to the ground. His keeper also seemed preoccupied. He paid scant attention to the blonde woman who was holding forth in thickly accented English, from time to time peering at the palm of a little working girl which she grasped tightly lest the girl escape.

'She's tellin fortunes,' said a labourer with coal dust on his face and whisky on his breath.

'Mary Philp,' said the woman. 'Who is this I see running after you? Maybe he is a ghost!' The girl squealed, then giggled in excitement.

'Have you seen a ghost, Mary Philp?'

'Aye, she has, Missus. We both saw one, Missus.' Harriet Todd, flushed and wide-eyed, squealed from the front of the crowd. The woman peered more closely at Mary Philp's palm.

'I think this is not a ghost,' said the woman. 'This is a young man, a very nice young man. Do you often get chased by young men, Mary Philp?' The audience laughed. The woman released the girl and turned her attention to a corpulent little man in post-office uniform. 'Think of a number between one and four.' The postman wrinkled his brow. 'Tell me the number you thought of.'

'Three,' said the postman.

'Please lift this guitar case.' On the bottom of the case, the figure three was scrawled in white chalk. The audience gasped and craned forward to verify the incredible fact. Involuntarily, Ethel was propelled to the front of the crowd. When she tried to push back, it was too late. The keeper of the bear was looking her straight in the face with such intensity that she clutched her parcel to her bosom and stood rooted to the spot. There was no malevolence in the gaze, more an impression of scornful curiosity as if Ethel had intruded at a private function to which she had not been invited. The keeper, whom we must call Dau, stepped over to the blonde woman who was preparing to go among the crowd with her collecting box. He spoke rapidly in his own language, whereupon she resumed her seat on the makeshift stage. Motionless, Ethel stood before the heap of trunks and instrument cases, breathing in the frozen air. When the woman spoke, she looked straight ahead. Her voice was so soft that some people thought the show was over and turned to leave. But Ethel knew better. She had no doubt at whom the whisper was directed.

'No one can hide behind a name,' said the woman, 'for bears understand no names but their own, no matter how they are spelled.' Ethel brushed aside the collecting box which the leering woman thrust beneath her nose. Frau Bella Niemcewicz turned expectantly to the keeper and held out her hand. The man we must call Dau dropped a gold coin into her palm, then slowly began to erase a chalk mark from the back of his violin case. It was the figure four.

When Ethel Wilkie left the dressmaker's, it was too late to visit her fiancée without upsetting his landlady. She reflected on the incident with the fortune-teller as she rode home in the tram. The likeliest explanation that came to mind was that the Germans had somehow heard of their countryman's change of name and decided to make a joke of it. Hadn't Jochen said they were good for nothing? The matter went completely from her mind when she reached home and discovered an unexpected scene in the kitchen. Beneath the elaborately draped gas lamp, Harry, Alexander Yule and her father were seated round the table, which, in addition to the remains of supper, held an uncorked whisky bottle. Though the lamp was turned down, there was no mistaking the good-humoured glow on her father's face.

'Your mother's awa tae her bed,' he said. 'Help yersel tae some supper, lass. We're just bletherin about the whalin wi Harry's friend here. But I think you've met my dochter, Mr Yule.'

'I have that, sir,' said Yule, winking over his glass. Ethel put some cold meat and pickle on a plate and sat down at the end of the table.

'You've changed your tune,' she said to her father. 'Not so long ago, anybody who thought of going to the whale fishing was daft.'

'I just din'a want Harry daein something he might hae regretted,' the old man said. His face became even redder.

'Quite right, Mr Wilkie,' said Alexander Yule. 'We all know the whaling days are numbered, in the Arctic at any road. The only real money to be made now is out of the bone, but you can sail for weeks without seeing a right whale. That's the one with by far the best whalebone in its mouth. The Norskis get blue and fin whales round the Faroes, but they work with steam catchers and a shore station to flens the fish. It's a different matter with rowing boats and wee guns like ours. Still, last season there were some fish up the Straits, very shy and hard to get, mind, but plenty. And I hear the Italians are paying up to twenty-three pounds a ton for oil.'

'There's the sealing as well,' said Harry, lifting a pickle from his sister's plate. 'There's still plenty money in that.'

'Harry's right,' said Yule. 'And remember, now the lad's got his discharge book, he can sign on any ship he wants. If he doesn't like the whaling, he could be off round the world like Wiggy Bennett.' Both he and Harry shook with laughter. But old Mr Wilkie's eyes, glistening with whisky and enjoyment, were set on other horizons.

'I've often seen seals round the mouth of the Tay,' the old man murmurred, 'but I've only ever seen one whale. That must be nigh on sixteen year ago. Harry and Ethel will mind it, though they were just bairns. It came ower the sandbar after sprats and couldna get out o the river. Crowds went down every day tae see it. When it died, they sold the carcass and put the skeleton in the museum.'

Ethel began to clear the dishes from the table. She said, 'You'll have grand tales to tell when you get back.'

'And maybe a pair of fine sealskins for you,' said Yule. 'I hear you're getting married in the new year. You'll have to be patient till I can give you a wee something as a wedding present.' Ethel busied herself about the sink.

'You've done quite enough for me already,' she said without looking round. 'Did I tell you, father, Mr Yule rescued me when I got stuck in the Blondin Car?'

But her father was miles away from the partially completed bridge at Stannergate. Old Mr Wilkie was dreaming of great seas and whales that blew and sounded between grinding floes of ice. 'Mr Yule is in charge of every harpooner in the ship,' he said. 'Next to the captain, he's the most important man there is.'

'Oh, I'm quite sure of that,' said Ethel and hung the dishcloth over a brass rod in front of the range.

And there, perhaps, we'd better leave it for today. No doubt you've heard the phone ringing and my recorded voice echoing in the cupola above the stair. Little scope for privacy in Arts and Crafts houses; even decadent ones. Still, the news is out. It wouldn't be right to leave all calls unanswered. Genuine expressions of regret may well have been received, and I shouldn't wonder if Inspector McCreath has left a few suggestions or demands. Don't worry. You're the only journalist with the remotest chance of getting to the truth. In that respect, you'll find I keep my word. Tomorrow, my dear, you'd better phone before you show up. We can't have you waiting in the cold like a common hack.

Chapter 14

WERE YOU surprised when I suggested we meet in your hotel this morning? Inspector McCreath wants a word in his office at noon, and this saves you the trip out to West Ferry. There was no sign of the press when we left, but the telephone started to ring while we were still in bed. No, thank you. I had three cups at breakfast. No doubt Louise will welcome a coffee when she picks me up, so I'll wait till then. You said your editor had been in touch. I appreciate his anxiety to get things down in black and white now that Forbes's demise is beyond doubt. The flurry of reports in newspapers and on the air must have convinced him that a scoop was slipping from his grasp. But have no fear. What I heard last night and read over my third cup of coffee fell well short of the mark. Simply speculation fuelled by those same tired faces whose opinions may be had at the press of a button. This morning, let's give your man something to calm his nerves: a hint, maybe, of what led Forbes from the arts page to the obituary column. Set down your wee machine among the crumbs. The people in the corner won't give a second glance, and if you slant it this way, my voice might just prevail over the scandals of the Monifieth Ladies' Curling Club.

'It is my intention,' Forbes said when I had poured his third glass and Louise had gone to dish supper, 'to create in minute detail a sculpture which will reproduce exactly the slaughter of a baby seal. The moment of impact, when the executioner's club crushes fur and bone, will be shown with such clarity that I defy anyone viewing the work to remain unmoved. I've outlined the plan to several influential friends. They'll take care of publicity when the work's complete. Then I'll take it on tour: Westminster; Brussels; then on to Norway and the Northern Isles.'

I listened to his plan with some surprise and said, 'I still don't see how I can help. But if you need a donation, perhaps . . .' Forbes laughed till tears glistened behind the tinted lenses.

'I don't propose to construct this work by myself,' he said at last. 'Recently I have come more and more to the belief that the true role of the artist is that of organiser. An impresario, if you will, who brings together such talents as are necessary to enable him to realise his grand design.' His expression took on an almost pious sincerity. 'In the past, I have employed the services of a fibre-glass moulder and a constructor of waxworks. Now I intend to add those of a taxidermist. Each shall have his task: the duplication of a slab of tide-washed rock; the more-than-human likeness of the hunter, clad in authentic garments; and at his feet, the innocent, wide-eyed quarry. Rest assured, our creation will be shockingly lifelike, but one aspect still concerns me. Despite considerable research, I can't decide what's best. As you know, the contractors employed by the Scottish Office favour the high-velocity bullet to execute both young and adult seals. In Canada, however, where the equally iniquitous slaughter of harp seal pups causes annual outrage among conservationists, the favoured instrument of death is a blunt-nosed club. You must see my dilemma. Should I, for authenticity's sake, try to juxtapose a hunter with a rifle and his helpless victim, or should I settle for the less accurate but sculpturally more satisfying arrangement of a hunter in the very act of clubbing his victim to death? While a club is sure to stimulate the desired emotions in the viewer, criticism might be raised that I am deliberately distorting the facts by equating seal-culling methods on both sides of the Atlantic. In this regard, I humbly seek your advice. You have lived too long with your harpoons and flensing knives to be indifferent to the subject.'

There was no denying a grain of truth in what he said. As my career has progressed, I have acquired the habit of putting aside from time to time a modest amount to indulge my collection. At first I bought from junk shops and curio dealers. Now, as you know, I negotiate with specialists. Some men have a passion for swords or firearms, or for memorabilia concerning golf, but whereas their collections arouse general interest, mine is of a more specialised nature, capable of being appreciated only by the true enthusiast. I'll never forget your expression when first you set eyes on my study. Your gaze roved in astonishment across the walls, and though you were too polite or bashful to say, I could see your amazement at the profusion of weaponry. But now that it has taken on significance in our tale, I shall indulge myself by giving you a brief description of my collection. You must have a camera in your bag. When next you visit you could take a photograph, just for reference, or maybe as a little supplement to your article. As you recall, fixed above my fireplace are hand harpoons of both double- and single-barbed varieties. On the opposite wall, a selection of gun harpoons is arranged like the spokes of a wheel, each labelled with approximate date and place of manufacture. Beneath them are displayed various flensing knives in excellent condition. Did you know that, whereas the knives commonly used in the Antarctic fishery to strip blubber from the whale's carcass had crescent-shaped blades, their earlier counterparts in the Arctic were straight, with blades reminiscent of a medieval poleaxe? In neat racks, intended for nothing more lethal than billiard cues, I keep my killing lances and blubber spades. You have already inspected my collection of largely transatlantic scrimshaw. In short, Forbes Wedderburn's request for guidance was not as unusual as it might have seemed. I pondered the matter after supper, when Louise went to bed, leaving Forbes and me alone.

Of course you know Forbes's uncanny ability to create, from a variety of everyday materials, disturbingly lifelike images. I have already described his failure: the *Bear as Washerwoman.* Although inspired by a bizarre and baffling imagination, the work was astonishingly convincing in detail. If Forbes, for whatever reason, decided to re-create a seal pup at the moment of slaughter, I did not doubt his ability to pull it off. But just as I had been antagonised by his blanket condemnation of the seal cull, his supreme confidence that a plastic charade of blood, fur and bone would influence future policy on seal hunting annoyed me with its conceit. Nevertheless I was flattered that he had chosen to consult me. With the vanity of the amateur, I refilled his glass and led him up the staircase with which you are already familiar. Did I notice his eye wandering to the strip of light beneath the bedroom door behind which Louise would already have disrobed? While I unlocked the bookcase, selected the necessary reference books and spread them on the desk beneath the reading lamp, Forbes, with almost religious reverence, surveyed my collection. His hot fingers passed nervously over shafts worn smooth by years of handling in the Arctic Sea.

'What a fearsome armoury,' he murmured. 'Such gruesome instruments of death.' I took him to task.

'You are holding a flensing knife.* No more an instrument of death than the carving knife in a butcher's shop. The lances to your right, however, and the harping irons† you see above you must, in their day, have put paid to a fair tonnage of cetacean life. See how that harpoon shank‡ has twisted in the body of the whale.' Forbes shuddered and approached the desk.

'These photographs, taken in Newfoundland, clearly show the type of club you describe as "blunt-nosed". To my mind, it seems nothing more than a baseball bat, which must be imported in copious numbers to supply the tiny recreational and considerable criminal demands in this country. I'm sure you must have seen countless similar pictures, each outdoing the other in portraying callous cruelty. Let's look at it in a different light. Observe the solid stance of the hunter, legs astride, arms raised to support the strong perpendicular line of the club. Even a layman can see the sculptural possibilities. If the action of slaughter can be aesthetically pleasing, I submit we have an example here. And remember, the Canadian authorities maintain that the club has been found to be the most effective way to render the seal

* Flensing knife: a longe-handled, long-bladed knife used to cut the blubber from the carcass of a whale.
† Harping irons: old-fashioned hand harpoons.
‡ Harpoon shank: the part of a harpoon between the barbs and the whale-line.

instantly unconscious.' Before Forbes could object, I pointed to a second picture. 'Here we have a seal hunt using rifles. The photograph was taken in the twenties, but the method remains the same. I appreciate the detachment of the hunter and the quarry pose considerable problems from the sculptor's point of view.' Forbes bent over the yellowing photograph.

'Distance is the problem,' he said. 'All immediacy is lost.' I closed the book and picked up the third, ancient volume, already open at the place.

'Then let me suggest a compromise. Where more appropriate to seek a solution than in the pages of Scoresby, that unique amalgam of whaleman, explorer and scientist who ended up in holy orders but not before producing the bible against which all serious accounts of the Arctic fishery are judged? He has provided us, in volume two of his *History of the Arctic Regions* with detailed drawings of all the traditional whaling implements in use during the first part of the last century. Here we have the killing lance; here the "pick-haak";* here the krenging knife† and here, between harpoons of varying pattern and purpose, the seal-pick, designed and made in Britain specifically for killing young seals. In years of searching for relics of the Arctic trade, I have never discovered a seal-pick, but there is no doubt they did exist. A reconstruction will be necessary. Scoresby has supplied the drawing. All we need is a craftsman in metal to follow the pattern of the master. For me, Scoresby's seal-pick will be a token of the golden age of Arctic fishery; for you a symbol of man's inhumanity to beast. Do you know that in a museum in Hull, beneath suitably angled fluorescent lights, one may inspect a complete collection of whaling implements reproduced in miniature with the precision of surgical instruments? What exquisite pleasure to examine those masterpieces in ivory and silver with a constant background of whale voices thoughtfully transposed to loop-tape.' Forbes held the valuable volume to the light, scrutinising the delicately engraved illustrations.

* Pick-haak: a tool akin to a boat hook, used for handling blubber etc.
† Krenging knife: a short-bladed knife used by the krengers, who remove muscle and fat from the blubber.

'Brilliant. I knew you'd have the answer. What more poignant indictment of man's age-old exploitation of the seal? I'll inquire about a toolmaker.'

Why didn't I modestly accept his approval and lend him the reference material he needed? Out of pride (or had I realised I had already gone too far to disassociate myself from Forbes's scheme?) I said, 'I have a chap who repairs railings and helps out with a little restoration work from time to time. I'm sure he'd be able to knock up something convincing.'

'Then I'll leave it entirely to you.' Forbes smiled and passed me the Scoresby, which I returned with the other books behind plate glass.

Yes, my dear. It was my first collaboration with Forbes and, depending on how one looks at it, my only one; for subsequent events can just as easily be seen as extensions of his grand project as steps towards catastrophe. Excuse me if I stretch out my legs. My toes are prickling. This morning I took only half the prescribed dose of painkillers on the grounds that I'd need a clear head for Inspector McCreath. Now I'm beginning to regret it. I told Louise I'd walk from here to police headquarters. It isn't far, but she insisted on picking me up after shopping and driving me there. What a sensible woman she is, despite a certain weakness for celebrity. Do you know, on the second day of Forbes's visit, she approached me furtively in the hall with a crumpled piece of paper from the wastebasket in his bedroom? Despite the twice-weekly visit of a cleaning lady, she had taken it upon herself to char for him in person. It turned out to contain line upon line of titles: popular songs; classical pieces; folk music; verbal excerpts, even effete 'mood sounds' (London traffic; birdsong), each either marked with a spidery asterisk, a question mark or a tentative and regretful scoring out.

'No mention of a book or a luxury,' Louise whispered, her eyes bright with pride. But now, before she comes to whisk me into the inquisitive clutches of the law, I just have time to tell you in a sketchy, general sort of way, what happened here not really so very long ago.

In Scotland, the last Christmas of the nineteenth century

passed amidst strong winds and blustery snowshowers. Often the snow lay for days on end. On warmer shores, in Mafeking and Ladysmith, the beleaguered garrisons settled down with Yuletide hymns and Lenten fare to await belated relief in the next century, and in Dundee, where plans were already well advanced for the marriage of Miss Ethel Wilkie and Mr Jock Dow, Christmas was celebrated in the manner most typical of Scottish religious festivals; that is to say with conspicuous lack of interest or ceremony. Mr Dow presented his fiancée with a necklace of amber set in silver, a Baltic heirloom which his ageing parents had sent from New York on hearing of his engagement. In return, he received boxes of expensive cigarettes and an invitation to Christmas supper, which, as I have implied, differed little from normal supper save for a bottle of Madeira on the table.

After this subdued, Presbyterian affair, Ethel drew Jock aside and broached the subject of a honeymoon. Wouldn't it be lovely to sail to Germany? Jock must miss his homeland, and he was entitled to a fortnight's holiday. As for Ethel, she would legally be required to give up her teaching post on marriage, so had all the time in the world. Dow had other plans. At first, he teased her by saying he could not afford the time off work. He became mysterious and asked whether her studies had included French. Then he came out with it. Despite the shattered laboratory, which had been hurriedly enlarged and rebuilt in another part of the mill, his experiments had borne fruit and, for the last three weeks, Baxters had been capable of producing on a commercial scale, heat-resistant oilcloth in a range of full-colour patterns. To launch this unique commodity, it had been decided to send a representative to the 1900 World Exposition in Paris. There was no doubt who was best suited for the task. Furnished with promotion and a considerable bonus, Jock Dow was charged with launching Baxter's remarkable product, which had been imaginatively named Tayline (pronounced tay-leen), on the unpredictable waters of the European market. With understandable pride, Dow announced that he and Ethel would travel to France at the end of April and spend four weeks in Paris while he finalised the details of the firm's modest display in the Palace of

National Manufactures. Furthermore, he would be obliged to return to Paris later in the year when the exposition was at its peak. Ethel could also accompany him then. She was delighted. She had been disappointed in the lack of grandeur of the wedding. Save for his landlady and a colleague who had agreed to be best man, no one represented Jock's side of the union, and in order to spare embarrassment, she had limited her list of guests to the very minimum to form a respectable congregation. Now any fears that her wedding might not be sufficiently impressive were immaterial. The honeymoon made up for all of that. What news to tell her friends.

Thus the Wilkie family approached the forthcoming nuptials in great good humour. Even the inconvenient coincidence that Ethel's wedding and Harry's departure for the Arctic fell on the same day scarcely dispirited them. So when the happy couple were being toasted both in best Scotch whisky and Danziger Goldwasser, a bottle of which had been specially procured by the invaluable Mr Gruber, Harry was bracing himself unsteadily over a basin of tepid water in the forecastle of the *Ultima Thule*, attempting to remove from his nostrils and eyelids and fingernails the encrusted dust that is the badge of a fireman on any steamship afloat.

Some weeks earlier, three days into the new century, when most of the population had recovered from their New Year celebrations, the German band suddenly quit their lodgings, trundled their hand cart to Tay Bridge Station, and with their luggage and instruments and dancing bear boarded the first train for Edinburgh. They found some difficulty in persuading the guard to let the bear called Kaspar travel in his van; but the bear's keeper, who had Kaspar's interests at heart and sovereigns to hand, soon ensured a snug, straw-lined berth for both himself and his charge. The train steamed slowly out of the station and, to the best of my knowledge, the German musicians were never seen in the city again. Who remarked on their departure? Mr Gruber certainly did, with considerable relief. Perhaps one or two children who, on their way to school, passed the departing band felt a pang of regret that the bear would no longer be around to amuse them. For all I know, days may well have passed before Jock Dow or Ethel Wilkie realised that the German band was no longer in Dundee. If Ethel remembered the curious warning, and there is no reason to believe that in all the bustle of setting up home she did, I suspect she regarded the incident with amusement. And if her fiancée's mind dwelt from time to time, as I'm sure it did, on a man who never spoke, who led a dancing bear and who reproached the world through steel-rimmed spectacles, he kept his own council and said nothing.

I have heard it said that about this time a group of foreign musicians, one of whom had a performing bear, appeared around the waterfront at the Port of Leith. They were looking for a ship to Hamburg, and, until one was found, lodged at a small commercial hotel near the docks. The keeper of the bear (some said he was Russian, but opinions varied) caused considerable interest by painstakingly inquiring in remarkably good English of every possible informant whether, numbered among the several corpses recovered from the water in recent years, there had been that of a cobbler whose passion for drink was exceeded only by his love of clocks.

Ah, here's Louise. Have we time for coffee? Perhaps not. Pass me the stick, my dear, if you please. While I submit myself to the tender mercies of Inspector McCreath, why not stroll down to the river and take a look at *Discovery*. Though it differs in virtually every detail, there's nothing better to give you an idea of the type of ship on which Harry Wilkie set sail. Besides, you seem particularly pale this morning. Maybe the breeze will do you good. Let's say seven at the house this evening if I make good my escape.

Chapter 15

No, my dear. Not exactly trying, more tiring really. The inept probings of one middle-aged functionary confronting the inept obfuscations of another. We both knew the game we were playing, though I suspect McCreath's patience will not last. Someone apologetically snapped a photo on the steps. In any case, turn on the tape. The time may be approaching when I must devote my attention to less pleasant things than the story which, I'm sure, will make your name.

I left Louise imagining a desert island and found Forbes in the dining room. He had started before me, tucking into bacon and eggs, and as I entered the room he rose and beamed in my direction, still clasping his knife and fork.

'I was saying to Louise: tonight you are my guests. I've booked a table at the Steading. We'll do things in style.'

'Fine,' I said, 'but not too early, I hope. I must show my face at the office. Don't expect me till after seven.'

'Fine,' said Forbes. 'Maybe you could drop in on your blacksmith friend on the way. The sooner we get things moving the better.'

At the office, I found work had mounted up. I occupied myself steadily with deeds, indentures and memoranda all day. I ate sparingly at lunchtime in anticipation of the coming feast and, towards evening, remembered to ask Miss McWhirter to make a photocopy of the relevant pages of Scoresby's *Arctic Regions.* The original was much too valuable to be left lying around a workshop, and I replaced it in my briefcase before setting off through the damp streets to where my car was parked. Neon signs and showroom windows reflected on the pavements and everywhere there seemed to be determined, grim-faced people hurrying on errands, their shoulders hunched against the wind. I had left early and was surprised how busy it was, then I remembered that most shops stayed open till eight that evening. Perhaps to avoid the crowds pressing towards the main shopping streets of the city, I turned down a quiet back street that led roughly in the direction I wanted to go. It was some time since I had been along the narrow street, which, since student days, I had associated with seedy little shops and public houses. But times had changed. Renovation and pedestrianisation had played a part. Properties had become desirable. Values had risen. The display windows of boutiques, craft shops and fashionable jewellers turned the flagstones to a strip of silver. Cars and delivery vans were everywhere, flouting the regulations. I hurried on, avoiding window shoppers and straggling children, and was about to turn up a lane to the carpark when I suddenly stopped and crossed to the other side of the street. My attention had been taken by a girl in the window of a tiny corner shop, or more precisely by what she was pinning to a cascade of ribbon to form the centrepiece of a premature Christmas display.

I assure you it's pure coincidence that tonight is my wife's stress management class, but the matter of which I speak is perhaps easier to explain, particularly to another woman, without the presence of Louise. Don't be alarmed, please. There's absolutely no need. The shop door bore the words *le Boudoir* engraved in tasteful copperplate. I pushed it open, and as I entered, a bell chimed softly. The girl in the window, who had been holding some pins in her mouth, removed them and said, 'I'll be with you in a minute.'

'Don't hurry on my account,' I replied. 'I have plenty of time.' I made this remark solely out of politeness, for I was already uneasy in such uncompromisingly feminine surroundings. It was as if an interior designer had taken the shop's name as a theme, but had been incapable of knowing when to stop.

Silken drapes bedecked the walls, interspersed with full-length mirrors of pink glass that filled the little shop with dappled, rosy light. Added to that, the racks of lingerie, the glistening show-cases of diaphanous, lace-trimmed garments and the young woman's cloying perfume combined to give the impression of having stepped into an extravagant, nineteenth-century brothel which had been temporarily deserted by its inmates and their well-to-do patrons. The gilded chairs seemed dangerously fragile, so I stood in the centre of the carpet till the girl completed her display and stepped, with a careful whish of thighs, out of the shop window.

'Can I help?'

'In passing, I happened to notice the garment in your window and it occurred to me to buy something along these lines for my wife.'

'You mean the white basque, sir.'

'Indeed. The white basque. The one with the boned front panels. I wonder if it is too much to suppose that such a delightful name finds its inspiration in the Basque whalers who chased the Biscay right whale for its superlative bone?'

The girl regarded me with an expression not altogether unlike your own. She crossed to a shelf piled with multi-coloured boxes. 'May I have bust and waist measurements, please?'

'Thirty-six C,' I said crisply, 'But the waist . . . I really don't know.'

'Then how about these cami-knickers,' she said, holding up by its flimsy shoulder straps something which reminded me, disturbingly, of my mother.

'My wife's a good bit younger than I am,' I muttered in the face of this matronly garment. The girl pouted and picked up something which, had it had any substance, might have been a miniature, backless swimsuit.

'This is a body,' she said. 'Very popular. It's unboned, you see, so it's sure to fit. And it can be worn under anything.'

'You don't understand,' I responded rather sharply. 'The boning is precisely what attracts me. I have a particular interest in whalebone.'

She looked at me with amused astonishment mingled, I suspect, with a hint of apprehension lest a fetishist or, worse, an ecology freak had found his way into her cosy boutique. 'Whalebone has not been used in corsetry for years,' she said primly. Her accent hinted at expensive education; no need to work for money. 'Modern boning consists of fine-gauge spring steel. Apart from silk, which is, after all, scarcely part of an animal, we pride ourselves in stocking no garments made from animal substances.'

I picked up the creation of fine-gauge spring steel and non-animal substances from the counter, tested the pliability of the boning and read the little label which, as it happened, said 36C. 'At the height of the Victorian passion for corsetry,' I said, 'many ladies had a set of whalebone stays cut to size and transferred them from one bodice to another as required. Hardly surprising when you consider that, latterly, unprocessed whalebone was fetching almost three thousand pounds a ton on the open market. How much do you require for this little concoction?'

'Fifty-nine pounds ninety-nine,' said the young woman hurriedly. 'Cash or credit card?'

Driving home, I was so preoccupied with my purchase and how amusing it would be to ask Louise to wear it at dinner with Forbes that I almost forgot about the seal-pick. I remembered as I was about to turn into Ellislea Road and only just got back into the stream of traffic hurrying towards Broughty Ferry. The person I had in mind, whom Forbes had grandly termed 'blacksmith', plies an erratic and mysterious trade from a shed on the edge of Broughty Ferry basin. As I expected, the doors were shut and bolted, but Muirhead's shabby Saab was nearby and I knew exactly where to find him. The low-ceilinged, old-fashioned bar was already busy with fishermen and financial advisers, lifeboatmen and lecturers who inhabit the narrow, shoreside lanes. Muirhead was throwing battered darts at a board on the whitewashed wall. He seemed to be alone.

'Mr Dow! What brings you in here?' I bought him a drink and crossed to where he was yanking the darts from the pitted cork.

'I want you to make something. Here's a wee drawing.' He threw the darts: four, nine, double-five, and eyed the drink.

'Not having one yourself?'

'I'm driving. And my wife and I are going out to dinner. I'm late as it is.' He took the drawing and held it up to the shaded lamp above the board.

'Very nice,' he said in a voice that could be heard by half the bar, 'going out to dinner with the wife. I used to play darts with mine . . . until her head went blunt.' The landlord spluttered and lumbered off into the next room. Muirhead jabbed a grimy thumb at the photostat.

'What's it for, then?' I cast an anxious glance lest any customers, hoping for another bon mot from Muirhead, were listening to our conversation. Apparently not. I decided on the truth.

'It's what they used for killing seals. I've been looking for an original for years, but no luck. I want you to make a replica for my collection.' Muirhead scented money. He laid the drawing on a table and very slowly rolled a cigarette.

'It looks a wee bit like a pick,' he said at last. 'Maybe I could cut down an old pick head and flatten out one of the tines. How would that do?'

'I'd prefer if you copied it exactly. The measurements are on the drawing, and while I remember, the shaft must be made of spruce.' Muirhead exhaled a pensive jet of smoke.

'You'd be better off with hickory. It looks just like a pick-axe handle. Hickory's the stuff for that, not spruce.'

'But it's not a pick-axe handle. It's a historic reconstruction. On board ship, such items were invariably made from spruce.' Muirhead shrugged, folded the drawing and stuffed it into the pocket of his shirt.

'It'll take a couple of weeks.'

'Absolute maximum. And the cost?' Muirhead sucked air through his teeth.

'Hard to say. Could be a couple of hundred, maybe more. It all depends.' I took three ten-pound notes from my wallet.

'Something on account. Give me a ring when it's ready.'

'Whatever you say, Mr Dow. Not having one for the road?'

When I got home, Forbes was reclining in the lounge with a copy of *Musical Times*. He looked pensive. I hurried upstairs to change. Louise was already in the bedroom. She wore heated rollers and a huge, towelling dressing gown. On the bed she had spread out the dress she intended to wear. Now I have no intention, my dear, of revealing to you or your readers intimate details of my private life. However these events are important, for in my view, they typify the contrasting emphases with which Forbes and I approached the project even at that early stage. Louise's reaction when I presented her with my gift caused unforeseen embarrassment and annoyance. At first she was full of curiosity, pulling open the extravagant carrier bag and folding back the tissue paper. But when all was revealed, when my gift lay in its splendid, whalebone (I prefer the term) rigidity, she gave a gasp and collapsed on the bed with laughter.

'Really,' I said. 'You're crushing your frock. We must dress or we'll be late.' Louise swung her legs on to the carpet and sat on the end of the bed. She seized the corset and held it against her trembling torso.

'I really don't see what's so funny. I came across it in a little shop near the office. It would be nice if you could wear it tonight.'

'You old devil,' said Louise. 'So your palate needs a touch of stimulation. We'll have some fun while Forbes listens through the wall.' She jumped up, kissed me on the nose and continued to dress in her usual manner.

'But the corset,' I said in frustration. 'I want you to wear it now, when we go out. What more natural dress for a lady when discussing seals and whales and mammals of the Arctic Sea?'

Louise put up resistance. 'I've nothing to wear that would suit it. Look, it needs stockings. I haven't had a pair in the house for years.' She waggled the elastic suspenders at the base of the Basque and let it drop on the bed.

'Louise is a little late,' I told Forbes, pouring a whisky for him and a sherry for myself. 'I asked her to wear something special.'

'Never tell a woman what to wear,' said Forbes. 'It's always an anticlimax.'

With sinking heart, I sipped my drink and listened for my wife's footfall on the stair; but when Louise appeared in the doorway, Forbes's astonishment was exceeded only by my delight. For the moment, the unfamiliar rigidity beneath her silk dress remained a secret. Forbes was oblivious to the unnaturally jutting bosom. He ignored the hint of suspender buttons on the silk-sheathed thighs. His complete attention was focused on the coat which Louise had draped, almost casually, round her shoulders. It was out of fashion, bought years ago, I remembered, to celebrate a particularly successful legal transaction which happened to coincide with our wedding anniversary. Its cut was dated, but Forbes ignored unfashionably wide sleeves and scalloped collar. He saw only the soft, sleek pelts of three baby seals.

The Steading, as its name suggests, is a converted farm building. It sits in a fold of the Fife hills and has been turned into a restaurant of distinct culinary pretension. Louise and I seldom go there. I prefer simple food and begrudge paying high prices for delicacies whose effect is lost on me; but plenty are happy to pay. When the taxi Forbes had ordered drove into the carpark, there was scarcely a space. We were ushered through the smoked-glass door. Only two tables were vacant. Forbes had phoned ahead to make it clear the Steading was being favoured with his presence. From the moment we set foot in the place, we were attended not only by the unconvincingly matey proprietor, but by a waiter and a waitress, whose knowledge of contemporary art was unlikely to be extensive, but who constantly addressed Forbes by his Christian name in the most irritating manner. Within moments, every diner was aware of his presence, and we took our places in that embarrassing void that precedes a babble of inquisitive chatter.

Louise and I ordered sherry. Forbes chose a viscous, yellowish drink of some sort. Forbes wiped his spectacles and looked at the menu. The proprietor provided a chorus of explanations and recommendations. Forbes made suggestions which Louise accepted and I chose to ignore. Louise had avocado. I chose plain onion soup. Forbes ordered eel soup, marked on the menu as a speciality of the house.

'The soup,' said the oleaginous owner, 'is prepared from salted eel, thinly sliced; peppers; carrots; leeks and parsnips; and sprinkled with chopped parsley.'

'I am in your hands,' said Forbes. He beamed at me and said, 'I have eaten only two memorable eel soups: one in the Gironde, the other, and by far the better, on the Baltic, in Stockholm to be exact, where a succulent purée of Baltic eel is served with dill and peppers. A dish not unlike those found on the southern coast of the Baltic, with which your grandfather must surely have been familiar before his sudden arrival on the shores of the Tay.' Louise looked mildly quizzical. Though I have never hidden the unusual origin of that portion of my family, it was rather touched on in passing and must almost have slipped her memory. Forbes went on, 'I wonder if he passed on any favourite recipes from his homeland?'

'Alas, as I remember, my grandmother's cooking was good but unadventurous,' I said.

'In contrast to her life,' he whispered, and turned his attention to the wine list. 'What luck. You may be surprised by what I recommend here, but in the more modestly priced section you'll find a Rioja Imperial. I know it's Spanish. I know your legal eye will go at once to the safe old clarets. But choose the Imperial and you'll taste a wine made exactly as it was in Bordeaux more than a hundred and fifty years ago, when several wine-growing families crossed to the Ebro valley after the French vineyards were devastated by phylloxera.'

'Fascinating,' said Louise, leaning forward so that her shoulder brushed his. Forbes's eyes left the wine list and he realised, I'm sure, that my wife's figure was confined by a garment more exciting than customary feminine underpinnings. He slid his arm behind Louise's back and held the list towards her. I guessed the gentle, almost accidental pressure of his hand confirmed what his eye had already told him.

The first course arrived. Chardonnay was poured. We started to eat. But while Louise and I contended with mayonnaise and croutons, Forbes talked. He talked about his visit to the Far East. He talked about efficiency and corruption, dynamism and collapse. From Taiwan, he had flown to Hong Kong. His suite for the handover had been booked years in advance. Everyone had been there. And while he reeled off several stories at once, without losing the thread, his brimming plate of eel soup emptied as if by magic and he drummed his chubby fingers on the damask, impatient for us to finish.

'I can't tell you how useful Gilbert has been already,' Forbes said to Louise and turned to me. 'No false modesty. He solved the problem right away. You really have quite a husband, my dear. I hope to be able to repay him very soon.'

Boeuf à la Bourguignonne arrived for Louise; stuffed trout for me. Rioja Imperial was splashed. Forbes had tried to persuade us to eat Entrecôte aux Huitres with him. ('A grave mistake. Nothing can be more satisfying. The sensation of swallowing a cool, fresh oyster after a mouthful of steak smothered in piquant, fiery sauce is quite indescribable.') But the very thought of this exceedingly risky combination, which seemed to include the most hazardous foods around, was quite enough to discourage us. By the way, my dear, have I warned you against eating the crab and lobster round these parts? They're perfectly healthy, but the thought of the diet on which a few have recently been feasting rather repels. It's silly, but you'd never know if the tasty crustacean on your plate was actually the one. So I'd give them a miss this season. But where was I?

Forbes launched into a description of the tableau he hoped to construct. Louise was intrigued, and I had to listen while he described every detail of his preposterous scheme.

'My taxidermist is working on the animal element already. Such a very young man to spend his time among furs and formaldehyde. He simply leaped at the opportunity to work on a sizable cadaver. These days, he must content himself with nothing larger than a prize salmon or the occasional capercaillzie.'

'Where did you get the seal?' I asked, suddenly curious. Forbes let the last oyster slip over his gullet before replying.

'Canada. Thousands are killed every year. I had one deep-frozen and flown over. Conservationist friends helped.' Louise shuddered. 'Unpleasant, I agree. But we have the old chestnut of omelette and eggs. Think how the finished work will help the cause. Critics will argue; children will weep; but most important of all, newspapers and television will carry the message over Europe and across the world. Incompetent bureaucrats, supported by the most dubious and disputable scientific evidence, can no longer let this ecological crime continue. The senseless killing must stop.'

I wondered if Forbes's sudden intensity was for the benefit of Louise or for our fellow diners, who had fallen silent when the great man raised his voice.

'They are working quite within the law,' I said rather softly, and caught a glint of anger behind the tinted lenses. We completed our meal in that forced atmosphere of bonhomie which so easily arises between friends at the first hint of fundamental disagreement. As we rose to leave at last, amidst solicitous flourishings from the staff, Louise plucked discreetly at her dress where the bodice passed under the arms.

'I must loosen this bloody thing,' she hissed. 'Wait in the bar.' As she turned towards the powder room, Forbes slipped his hand, as if by chance, from the constricted waist to the pliant bottom.

'Take your time,' he said. 'We have lots to chat about.' Surprised to find us still on the premises, the owner insisted we have another cognac on the house. Forbes, of course, had Armagnac. The driver, who had been waiting twenty minutes already, wandered off for a smoke. I asked Forbes what he had to say which was of such great interest, but clearly not for the ears of my wife. But the proprietor, who had by then promoted himself to a member of the company, stood between us, glass in hand. For once, Forbes chose discretion, and we indulged in the smallest of small talk until Louise reappeared.

My memory of the drive home is blurred by wine and the lateness of the hour. As we crossed the long, almost deserted bridge and the sodium lights flashed hypnotically across the dark interior of the taxi, I remember Forbes saying something like:

'When the time is right, I'll tell you something that will change your whole view of life.' The sentence, if I've got it right, was so innocuous and inconsequential, despite its portentous sentiments, that I immediately classified it with all Forbes's other momentous announcements. Besides, Louise had fallen asleep and was close to revealing, beneath her ever-upward-riding hemline, something I'd much rather Forbes did not see. I rapidly changed the subject and drew his attention to the beauty of the reflected illumination of the city, which, despite its use as a diversionary tactic, I still recommend as one of the finest views of Dundee.

Later, I sat in our bedroom as Louise undressed. In the belief that I had made her wear the basque for its erotic potential, and inspired, I suspect, by an uninhibiting intake of sherry, Chardonnay, Rioja and cognac, she undressed with studied languor, humming a little tune through half-open lips and letting her dress fall round her ankles. (Never over the head.) To enhance the effect, she had kept on her shoes, which normally would have been kicked under the bed. She looked breathtaking.

'I thought you didn't have any stockings.' She stepped behind me and put her arms round my neck.

'I cut the top off some tights. I'll buy proper ones next time I'm in town.'

'Really, there's no need.' I smelt brandy as she laughed. 'Do you remember the old amber necklace that belonged to my grandmother? Put it on.'

'But I'd have to look for it. I don't know exactly where . . .'

'Put it on. For me.' A hint of annoyance crossed her brow: an indication, perhaps, that I had broken the spell. Still, she rummaged in the dressing table and at last produced the necklace of tarnished silver and held it to her throat.

'I've never liked it,' she said. 'It so badly needs cleaned and there's always been a piece missing from the front.' Nevertheless, she let me fasten the old-fashioned clasp behind her neck and even gave a little gasp of surprise as I drew her to her knees on the carpet.

You seem anxious to go, my dear. I had hoped to tell you all about what happened to Harry Wilkie, but it can wait till tomorrow. Though your hotel was convenient, I'd rather we met here. My library's to hand to reinforce my tale of a journey into the ice.

Chapter 16

LOUISE? I LAST saw her in the conservatory, fussing with the *Chorchorus Capsularis.* Anyway, she's around. When we're settled in the study, I'll ask her for coffee. Lead the way. If you'd stayed a little longer last night, I'd have remembered to ask whether you took a look at *Discovery.* You did? Perfect. What I want to say into your little machine today concerns what happened to Harry Wilkie in the first year of this soon-to-be-extinguished century. He set sail on a ship different in every detail but identical in broad terms to the unhappily situated relic you saw stranded like a beached whale amid paving and plate glass. I'm familiar with the brochures, thank you. Coffee's on its way. Let's begin.

Harry Wilkie, fourth fireman of the auxiliary steam whaler *Ultima Thule*, my late great-uncle and, as you'll no doubt have worked out, grandfather of Forbes Wedderburn, braced himself on the iron gratings of the stokehole, narrowed his eyes against the heat and, for the seventh time that watch, retched in the direction of the gaping firedoor. For the seventh time, a mass of vomit rose from his stomach, caught painfully in his gullet, then spewed from cracked lips across the red-hot firebars. It sizzled and bubbled for a moment and was gone. There was a muffled roar from the back of the furnace and he just had time to raise his shovel before a blast of flame belched from the door. Wicked tongues of fire flicked round the shovel Harry held before his face, then died. Tom Bell had shown him the trick of dealing with blowbacks which bedevilled the ship whenever she met a powerful headwind. Harry scooped a dipperful of water and oatmeal from the bucket wedged between the iron ladder and the hull and splashed it towards his mouth. He passed the back of his hand across his forehead, smearing a patch in the tears, sweat and coal dust, then, pivoting on the unsteady deck, heaved another shovelful of grade-two steam coal into the fire. Normally Captain Jamieson shut down the engines on clearing the sand bars at the mouth of the Tay and beat up the east coast under sail. But a new piston ring had been fitted during the lay-up, and the necessity to test the engine took priority over conserving fuel for the Atlantic crossing. So all the way past the Bell Rock, past Lang Craig and Scurdy Ness, Harry Wilkie stoked and retched as the *Ultima Thule* set her bluff, reinforced bows against the lumpy sea at a steady six knots.

From the moment he stepped aboard, Harry's world had changed. At first, with the exception of the old ship-keeper, the firemen had been the only crew on board. Harry was the only green hand among them. He accepted their coarse humour at his expense. Not one of them could understand what would persuade a man to give up a reliable shore job for a berth in the forecastle of a whaler.

'Ye'r runnin awa frae a wumman,' said the third fireman, whose name was Munro.

'Frae her faither, mair like,' said Bell, the second fireman, heaving his kit bag on to a narrow bunk.

'I hope he can dae his job,' said the first fireman. He was a west coaster called Hector Robertson. He waved Harry towards a cramped berth close under the deckhead. It was more like a shelf than a bunk, with a fixed bunk-board to stop the occupant falling out should he ever manage to squeeze into the narrow slot in the first place. Harry put his hand into the dark space and felt a straw-filled mattress perhaps eighteen inches wide. This was to be his home for the next eight months.

On the second day, the first mate, the bosun and the chief engineer had arrived. Twenty wagons of coal had been shunted along the wet quayside and a sullen gang of day-labourers had drifted up just in time to start loading the coal into baskets which the bosun swung aboard. One after another the baskets poured their contents into the waist of the ship where Harry and the other firemen toiled with shovels and wooden scoops to force the fuel through the circular coal holes into the bunkers that enclosed the boiler-room on three sides. As he vomited into the fire for the eighth time, Harry reflected that not even sea-sickness was quite as bad as the misery of coaling ship for twelve hours solid in constant, driving sleet. On the third day, the remainder of the crew had begun to arrive: the captain; the third mate; the six seamen who worked the ship under sail; and all the tradesmen whose services were need on an Arctic voyage. The carpenter for maintenance. The cooper to knock together barrels for the hoped-for oil. The blacksmith to forge new harping irons and sharpen killing lances. Only the men who actually caught the whales left it till the last minute. The harpooners, line managers and boat steerers, who were to join the ship at Dundee, strolled, staggered or hurried up the quay together with a number of spectators who, even at this late stage in the history of Arctic whaling, had made their way to the dock to 'see the Greenlanders awa'.

'In the old days,' the second fireman had said as they watched the crowd on the pier head from the lee of the engineroom skylight, 'we always left on Dundee spring holiday. The ships were full of visitors as far as the outer locks and many a time we had to anchor off till enough men sobered up to put to sea. But it's all changed now, what with leaving early for the sealing.'

When Harry Wilkie at last emerged from the stokehole and stood unsteadily on the glistening deck, it was already dark. A north-east wind whipped the crests of the short, choppy waves across the bulwarks in a constant, icy spray. As the old ship rolled her way northwards, Harry tasted the salt, let the freezing wind beat against his brow and, for the first time since leaving the Tay, felt a little better. Save for the faint glow of the binnacle light which outlined the muffled figure at the wheel, the only illumination was a horizontal yellow slit where the deadlights over the engineroom skylight met the coaming. With its help, Harry picked his way forward. The main and foresails had been set to increase speed, but as the speed increased, so did the rolling, and he barely kept his footing as far as the forecastle companionway, which he descended into a malodorous haze of warm tobacco smoke. Harry thought of finding Alexander Yule, but he was apprehensive about wandering about the unfamiliar ship into accommodation where he might not be welcome. He splashed tepid water over his face from a can near the stove, then ladled himself a bowl of stew from the iron pot that sat in a ring above the glowing hot plate. Without removing his clothes, he fell asleep in the tiny bunk before the gravy had congealed on his lips.

The first time Harry saw Yule since leaving Dundee, the specktioneer was standing on the forecastlehead, the collar of his coat pulled up to his ears against the freezing drizzle that swept fitfully across Stromness bay. At first light on the second day of the voyage, they had passed from the Pentland Firth through the Sound of Hoxa; shortened sail in Scapa Flow, and ploughing north of Cava by way of Bring Deeps, dropped anchor just as the gulls were beginning their daily uproar from Stromness fish quay. Stromness was not unlike other fishing villages Harry had seen on the mainland, but here, the little black-roofed houses at the water's edge actually stood with their foundations in the sea while boats rode at their moorings outside the parlour windows. The harbour was full of fishing boats and little cutters that traded between the islands. As the *Ultima Thule* entered the bay, one of these cutters had put out from shore and tacked slowly towards the whaling ship under a drab, brown sail. They watched it approach while Yule filled his pipe, taking care no rain should get beneath the fold of his walrus-skin tobacco pouch.

'I heard you were sick,' said Yule, clasping his unlit pipe between clenched teeth.

'A bit,' said Harry, 'but it didn't keep me from my work.'

'Well,' said Yule, 'you'll be over that now. If not, the Atlantic will cure you.'

Harry set about lighting his own pipe as if to prove the strength of his stomach. The tobacco tasted peculiar. Perhaps it was the salt air mingled with the smell of seaweed from the anchor cable.

He blew a cloud of smoke into the drizzle and crossed to the rail to watch the Orkneymen coming aboard. There were under a dozen sitting with their boxes and kit bags in the little cutter in the lee of the ship's side. Of these men, the majority seemed middle aged, even elderly. The balance was made up of boys in their teens, many of whom must have been going to the Arctic for the first time. Yule watched as they climbed the ladder one by one. Now and again, he'd nod as a familiar face appeared over the bulwark, but Harry sensed the specktioneer was not entirely happy with the new recruits. One man, past fifty, seemed to be the spokesman, if not the leader, of the Orkneymen. He came over and shook Yule by the hand.

Yule said, 'You've brought me a poor-looking lot this trip, Mansie.'

'There's no sae mony as wants tae go tae the Straits these days, Mr Yule.'

'Where's Flett?'

'He thocht after last year he'd try the fishin. There's an awfu lot at the winter herrin this season.'

'And Foubister?'

'The same.'

'What about Tulloch?'

'His wife's just had a bairn. He disna want tae be awa that long, so he's shipped for the Baltic on a timber boat. Fine, easy work and back hame in twa month.' He gathered his gear and dragged it towards the ladder that led to the tweendecks where the Orkneymen made their quarters. Yule watched him go, then spat a jet of tobacco juice in a long, contemptuous curve over the ship's side. It floated for a second and was gone.

Captain Jamieson went ashore in the cutter to see to some final business and dispatch the customary telegram to the owners, telling them that the *Ultima Thule* would sail for St John's on the tide. Already the sailors were clearing the decks for the long Atlantic crossing, lashing down gear and making sure the boats were securely stowed. Harry retired to the forecastle out of the way, and soon heard the sound of the steam winch overhead and the anchor cable rattling into the chain locker. He lay on his mattress alone in the yellow lamplight and gazed at the rows of deserted bunks like empty pigeon holes; not unlike the pigeon holes in Mr Dow's laboratory which had been smashed to matchwood. Ethel would be married by this time. Her choice of husband had surprised Harry. Of course, he knew Yule's sudden decision to promote his own nautical career had hardly been selfless. The specktioneer had made no secret of his interest in Ethel; but if Harry thought his sister's marriage to the German surprising, he would have regarded the possibility of Ethel accepting the overtures of Alexander Yule with utter disbelief. In Ethel's world, and he had lived with his sister long enough to discover a little of her character, anyone whose business was messily dispatching aquatic mammals was likely to come fairly low on her scale of acceptability. As Harry listened to the water rushing beneath the bow of the ship, he wondered why Yule had still taken him on the voyage despite the announcement of Ethel's engagement. There had been plenty time for Yule to engineer his exclusion from the crew list, yet here they were, bound to co-exist for eight months. Rocked by the motion of the ship, with confused thoughts tormenting his tired mind, Harry Wilkie drifted to sleep, only to wake with a start as Munro's grimy hand shook him back to consciousness to stand the middle watch in the stokehole.

The *Ultima Thule* sailed into the north Atlantic with a fresh south-easterly wind astern and very heavy snow squalls. Despite the ship's heavy rolling, the captain was reluctant to shorten sail as every day gained meant more time fitting out in the yard at St John's. On the fourth day, the wind increased to a whole gale. Jamieson was obliged to reduce sail to a reefed mizzen and main topmast staysail. The engines were slowed down also, and for those who fed the fires, there was a short respite. As Yule had predicted, Harry's sea-sickness diminished as the passage progressed. But the fireman was still weakened by being unable to keep down food in his stomach, and spent almost every moment of free time in his bunk. As they tracked north on the great circle route, the cold intensified. Ice formed on the decks and in the rigging and had to be chipped away by deckhands muffled to their eyes, with breath like white mist before their faces. Under such conditions, a fireman's job had advantages, and when, after a watch on deck, the sailors tumbled into the forecastle, beating the frost from their coats and holding their fingers to the stove, Harry was glad he worked below deck. On the afternoon of the eighteenth, they sighted the first ice-fields and soon were nosing through the half-melted grey sludge that marked the edge of the floe. It would not normally have been necessary to approach this close to the ice, but the old captain wanted to take a good look at the formation of the pack and gain an advantage over the Newfoundland skippers, who would have had no chance to inspect the possible location of the seals.

While I freshen your coffee, my dear, cast an eye over the pictures I looked out last night. Surprisingly few exist of commercial sealing at that time. The impressive snowscapes of ships and ice you'll find in museums were usually taken on expeditions which could afford the luxury of a photographer. They show rather different men from those who set out into the ice every year to earn an increasingly precarious living.

When at last the ship was slowly piloted between the cliffs that guard the entrance to St John's harbour, Harry climbed the stokehole ladder and pulled himself just far enough out of the trunkway to see the land. There was a lighthouse on one headland, and opposite it, on the right, a signal station was sending a flickering message over the mastheads that crowded the harbour. As the *Ultima Thule* headed upriver, the city of St John's gradually unfolded over the shoulder of the hill. Row upon row of weatherboarded houses spread across the lower slopes of the icy buttress of rock which enclosed the town like an encircling arm. Now and then, the roof of a more prominant building, a warehouse or church or courthouse, would project above the uniform rows of gables. But St John's was a new community, still in the process of acquiring those grander architectural manifestations said to bestow dignity on a capital city. Harry observed as much to Tom Bell when he regained the warmth of the stokehole.

'Rubbish. It's new because they keep burnin it down.' Bell spat in the fire. 'When I was here in ninety-two, in the old *Esquimaux*, the whole town caught fire. We were lucky tae get hauled awa frae the quay. Ships were burnin at their berths. And when we went ashore, folks were saying it was the third time a fire like that had happened.' Harry threw a shovelful of coal into the furnace and let the door shut with a clang.

The remarkably similar sound you hear from the kitchen is Louise conducting a symphony on pots and pans. I asked for an early lunch, for today we have much ground to cover. You must stop me from departing at too oblique tangents, my dear, but you'll have gathered this part of my story is one which I tell with particular pleasure and authority. Forbes knew the tale well, but he always relied on me to furnish the precise detail.

Chapter 17

As WAS the custom, the *Ultima Thule* berthed opposite a yard that had been prepared for her by the Newfoundland agent of the Victoria Whale and Seal Fishing Company. The yard, which amounted to an acre of muddy slush running down to the waterfront, bounded by a board fence and with a lean-to shed along its farthest perimeter, was of vital importance to the Dundee steamer. Here, its whaling equipment was unloaded until it had completed the trip to the sealing grounds, and on its return, the seal oil and skins which were to be shipped home could be safely stored until the whaling was over. The day after the ship berthed the transformation began. All the whaleboats, except two for emergencies, all the barrel staves and hoops, all the stores of rope and whale-line* and harping irons were lifted ashore and stowed under tarpaulins. Planks of rough timber were brought aboard and, with the help of day workers hired by the agent, the carpenter began sheathing the decks and bulwarks and cabin floors with an extra layer of wood. Temporary bunks were set up in the tweendecks and everything that could possibly be dispensed with without hazarding the safety of the ship was dismantled and stored in the yard. By the end of February, when St John's began to fill with men looking for berths with the sealing fleet, the *Ultima Thule* had metamorphosed from a neat, albeit elderly whaling steamer into a

* Whale-line: the rope between the harpoon and the whaleboat.

floating barracks-cum-storeroom ready to receive the three-hundred-or-so hunters the captain signed on at the gate of the compound. Who were the Newfoundland sweilers* Harry Wilkie watched filing into the yard? They were men who made their normal living in small boats at sea or on harsh little farms. They were powerful yet stoical, with little of the high spirits one might expect at the start of such a venture. They were dressed like fishermen, and possessed little more than a bedroll, a kettle, a knife and a wooden club or bat that was the sole implement of their calling. They wore boots of untanned sealskin, double-soled and spiked with iron nails to grip the ice, which was why the decks had wisely been sheathed.

In those days, no ship could leave for the sealing before 2pm on 10 March. Fines for breaking the rules were so large that few took the risk. The sealing itself was not allowed to start before the fourteenth, so there was great rivalry among the captains to be first off the mark in the race to the ice. When the tenth arrived, steam was raised by noon and, to the excitement of the crowds lining the wharves, the *Ultima Thule* hauled out into the middle of the stream where she dropped anchor to await two o'clock. Harry, whose watch had finished at noon, stood on the forecastle and gazed at the seven or eight ships lying ready in the roadstead, their decks packed with men. Already he could see the bosun making ready to weigh anchor. The mate stood on the afterdeck with the Newfoundland scunners, whose job it was to stay night and day in the barrel at the top of the mainmast to scun the ship through leads in the ice towards the seals. There were four scunners, each in charge of quarter of the sweilers, who respected their authority partly through family ties but also because the scunners organised the summer's cod fishing on which most of the men depended.

Harry made his way aft, pushing through the close-packed mob whose eyes were now on the signal station waiting for the flag. He found Yule at the bottom of the after companionway, unchaining rifles from their locker for inspection.

* Sweiler: a Newfoundland seal hunter (from 'Sweil' = seal).

'You're going to shoot them as well?'

'Some of the older ones if we get the chance.' Yule slid home the bolt of a 355 magnum. 'The sweilers club the pups, but now and then we get a shot at a cow that's a bitty slow off the ice. And there's sometimes the odd walrus, though we're more likely to see them on the land ice up the Straits.'

'I met a man in the office in Dundee. He wanted walrus hides for bicycle saddles.'

'They're paying one and six a pound for walrus hide,' said Yule, 'but I doubt we'll see many. They say there are herds near Franz Josef Land. A few ships tried it three years ago and only *Balaena* made anything of it. You'd better get forward; we'll be away in a minute.' As he spoke, the clatter of the capstan resounded through the bulkheads. Simultaneously, the ship's whistle blew a series of long blasts which were multiplied as the other ships signalled their readiness to leave. Harry scramble up the companion ladder just in time to see the flag break from the yardarm of the signal station and stand out in the stiff, westerly breeze. Then, before the anchor was even secured in its tackle, the *Ultima Thule* was moving up the harbour to cheers from the ships, the wharves and the hundreds of men that crowded her decks. Behind her, the *Neptune* and the *Aurora* swung into the stream, while ahead, the *Terra Nova* passed swiftly between the headlands and was first into the open sea.

Shortly after the fleet had left port, thin fingers of fog began to spread across the icy water. It was patchy, insubstantial fog, which seemed to prove no hindrance to the majority of ships who ploughed ahead under steam or sail, sounding their whistles in the frozen mist. Only the *Ultima Thule* reduced speed and, as if her old captain was afraid to enter the fog in company with so many targets for collision, dropped back until only the slowest of the Newfoundland sailing ketches remained astern of her. From the expression of those sweilers who had remained on deck, Captain Jamieson's action hardly met with approval. As evening wore on, they became progressively more restless, and before darkness fell more than one Dundee officer had voiced doubts that discipline could be maintained. Going on watch, Harry met the chief engineer at the top of the stokehole ladder.

'Looks like an easy night,' said Harry. 'We're barely making half speed.' The officer pulled himself on to the deck and stood aside to let Harry pass.

'Dinna be sae sure, Wilkie,' he said. 'Mr Jamieson ken's what he's doin all right.' Suddenly they became aware of the ship coming round to port, altering course from north-east to north. By then it was almost pitch dark. Not even the steaming lights of the other ships were in sight. The engineer looked round with satisfaction. Before heading for the warmth of the officers' cabin, he leaned over the hatchway and shouted, 'See, Wilkie. What did I tell ye? He's given them a the slip.'

When dawn came, had Harry been awake to see it, they were alone on a pale-grey plane of ice-strewn ocean with not another vessel in sight. All that day and into the next, the *Ultima Thule* held her course northwards, butting through the rotten pans of old ice that littered the seaward approach to the floes. By midday on the thirteenth, she was in the ice-field, forcing her way up the leads between the floes at a steady five knots. Any trace of mist had long since disappeared. The white icescape, silent save for the churning of the ship's engine and the creak of ice against her reinforced hull, was lit by a watery sunlight that cast oblique shadows on the uneven surface of the floe. There was continual coming and going in the barrel at the top of the mainmast. At least once a watch, old Jamieson would relieve the scunner who was on duty and take a spell as lookout himself. Latterly, he spent almost his entire time there, descending only for food and sleep.

The restlessness of the sweilers had been checked by reaching the ice-field so soon. Now they watched the captain's every move to catch the first hint that seals had been sighted. As in every profession where mysterious skill is involved, Jamieson employed his fair share of showmanship to keep them guessing. Half way through the eight-to-twelve watch that night, the order came to throttle back the engine. Even Harry Wilkie could sense the expectancy among the hunters as they stamped their feet in the frozen darkness or squatted by the bulwarks with billy-cans of pinnacle tea. Despite his tiredness, Harry was reluctant to turn in.

Eventually he lay on his bunk fully dressed. He slept fitfully, waking at the slightest sound of feet overhead or ice against the hull. Then it happened all at once. A shout followed by wild whoops from above and the instant clatter of hundred upon hundred spiked boots on the timber sheathing. Harry rushed on deck. Ice-fields stretched all round bathed in the grey light of dawn. And over the ice, leaping from outcrop to outcrop, ran the black figures of the sweilers. For on either side of the *Ultima Thule*, and stretching ahead of her as far as the eye could see, were thousands of young seals. Alexander Yule was standing on the gunnel, his arm crooked through the starboard foreshrouds. Harry pushed through the few remaining sweilers not yet on the ice and joined him.

'Sly old beggar, Pinnacle Tam,' said Yule, his face glowing with good humour. 'Put us right in among them in the middle of the night. When the sweilers looked out this morning, you'd have thought the seals had dropped out of the sky from the looks on their faces. That'll teach the Newfies a thing or two.' Harry watched the men on the ice already wielding their clubs and knives on the edge of the vast colony of animals.

'It doesn't take them long to get started,' he said. But Yule grinned and shook his head.

'They're not hunting in earnest yet; just getting some nice fresh livers and flippers for breakfast.'

Now let's have lunch. You seem positively chilled by so much talk of ice. Louise's hotpot will put colour back into your cheeks. For the record, seal meat is rich in protein and akin to brisket in flavour, but more robust. Not even Forbes, with his wide gastronomic experience, had tasted seal, though I did suggest that with a whole deep-frozen animal at his disposal it was capricious not to try the meat, which, after all, was superfluous to the taxidermist's requirements.

When we first met, I recall saying my work seldom took me outwith the city. There was an exception. In London, save for the financial rewards, the oil boom has no doubt passed unnoticed. But Dundee has benefited, or rather oil-related work has formed a glitch in our declining employment pattern which will no doubt prove as transient as that in your revenue figures. In any case, a client, keen to diversify, hit on the idea of importing the special mud used to cool the drills in the North Sea. Business boomed. The Norwegians showed interest, and I found myself in Stavanger for a few days as the token lawyer on his negotiating team. We flew directly from Dundee Airport in a little chartered plane with our luggage on our laps and our hearts in our mouths. I'll spare you the technicalities of wrestling with mud; suffice it to say that on the second day I managed to slip away for a couple of hours. I wandered the streets of the expensive, uninspiring little town in circles which always led back to my hotel. Then it occurred that the answer could probably be found there. On hearing my request, the hall porter regarded me in much the same way as the young woman in the boutique; but twenty dollars soon produced a compliments slip with a sketchy map and a hastily scrawled address. The biroed cross, it turned out, represented a long, single-storey shack set in a waste of container trucks and four-by-fours. In a queue of giants in quilted jackets I was served whalesteak on a white enamelled plate. It was accompanied by dumplings, pureed carrot and a glutinous brown sauce, which, astonishingly, tasted of chocolate. The meat was as appetising an entrecôte as I'd seen. The knife passed through it like butter, refuting the belief that whale meat is tough. The first bite (I had carefully scraped off the sauce which the beautiful but sloppy cook had poured all over) had the flavour of the best grass-fed Aberdeen Angus; but as I continued to chew, an unsettling aftertaste began to emerge. You are much too young to have been subjected to the daily dose of cod-liver oil recommended to maintain children's health in the grim, post-war days. But as I ate my way through the slab of meat amidst raucous, unintelligible conversation, I was transported to the kitchen in Dudhope where my mother, with varying success, would force an oily spoonful between my lips. The necessity of the sauce became clear. Alcohol was not available. I washed down the mixture of meat, oil, chocolate and dough with mineral water, which I later worked out cost five pounds. Luckily my part in that afternoon's negotiations was not great. I dreaded the effect on my colleagues when I opened my mouth; but I didn't regret the experience for a moment. Of course you may visit the bathroom, my dear. You know the way.

Chapter 18

FORBES LEFT us the next day. Several phonecalls to London had convinced him that his presence was required. Now that he, or rather I, had formulated the composition of his sculpture, the studio beckoned and he was anxious to be gone. His flight left from Edinburgh. I offered to drive him there, but he insisted on taking a taxi. As we waited while the driver stowed his cases in the boot, I said, 'I'll call you when the pick is ready, then send it down by post or courier.'

'Pay us a visit,' he said. 'See how things are progressing. I owe you that at least.' I started saying something about pressure of work, but Louise had appeared in the doorway, smoothing her skirt. It was clear she had overheard and was anticipating a trip to London. Strangely, though I retained a vague memory of the important announcement Forbes had promised but failed to deliver the previous night, neither of us broached the subject. Handshakes. Embraces. And for a lingering moment, Forbes Wedderburn was merely a blurred smudge with a pale hand waving from the receding cab window.

Yes, my dear, we did visit London. I see how your interest has quickened at the mention of something closer to home. But before we step into the leafy streets of Hampstead, we must follow Harry Wilkie on to the ice. How can you hope to comment on Forbes's project without first having a flavour of what he hoped to depict in wire and wax and fur?

Once or twice, Harry went on to the floe with the sweilers.

When there was nothing much to do aboard, all the sailors used to take turns on the ice. And it wasn't easy crossing broken loose ice, for some was thick and some was quite thin and you had to jump over the leads from ice-pan to ice-pan. If anyone fell into the water, they had to get back to the ship right away. This wasn't so bad if the ship was nearby, but there were well over two hundred men on the ice, and the farther ones would easily be a mile from the ship. If you got soaked out there, you were in real trouble. There was noise everywhere: the sweilers shouting to each other; the seal cows calling as they deserted their pups and headed for the water. Trails of rich milk smeared the ice where nursing had been interrupted. On the edge of the group, the specktioneer and harpooners tried to shoot as many cows as possible, but it was dangerous with so many men on the ice, and most cows got safely into the water. But what did they leave behind them? Thousands of pups, fat as barrels. So fat they could hardly move to follow their mothers into the icy water. The pups lay ready all across the ice: yellowish-white torpedoes with black noses and glazed eyes. Some had already been abandoned before the arrival of the sweilers. It was time they took to the water and learned self-preservation; for the sweilers were passing among them now: the first human beings in their lives and the last. The pups' nostrils twitched. Their eyes looked all round. There was something new on the ice, something wet and sticky that was not a patch of lovely, protein-rich milk, something unknown, something warm and red. They sniffed at it with their snouts, then it was their turn. A sweiler stepped among them in his spiked boots. He needed a firm foothold. A display of skill and exertion was about to take place. The sweiler held his club in both hands. Some of them already called it a bat, but the sweiler had never seen baseball. He had no intention of hitting the longest home-run. He sucked the frosty air between his teeth, then smack, the club found its mark. Smack, another blow. The next pup has caught it. On spiked, sealskin boots, the sweiler moved on. The little seals writhed, twisted from side to side then, no longer conscious, just lay there on the gently rocking ice. Were the sweilers after the pelts, or did they want the whole carcass to render down for oil? It was making twenty-three pounds a ton, you know. The birds wondered. The shower of mollies and dovkies and plain white gulls that could never get enough soared and dived over the black figures on the ice. Already two men had scrambled across to where the young seals lay so deeply unconscious they were barely alive. They both had knives sharpened on stones which they carried in the pockets of their pilot coats, knives that were not too long, handy knives that fitted into sheaths of sealskin. Slash, slash they thrust them into the throat. One stab, so as not to damage the pelt. And with the blood, the last flicker of life seeped on to the ice. Its warmth condensed in the frozen air, mingling with the breath of the sweilers as they leaned over the fat cylinders of fur. The knives flashed. They opened up the animals like a bag. Evisceration must take place. Putrefaction must be avoided. Who knew how many days the skins would lie in the hold of the *Ultima Thule* before being handed over to the curers? The birds wheeled and tumbled in the Arctic air. A thousand airborne eyes watched the sweilers drag the pelts away from the steaming entrails across the gently rocking floe to where a hundred sealskins were piled round a yellow flag. There were fifty flags, each with its pan of seals, each bearing a black number and the initials *UT*. Location must be ensured, ownership established. If fog should descend, the captain could tell by the numbers on the flags how far away from the ship the gangs of seal hunters were working, and send warning blasts on the whistle across the plane of ice. But there was not a trace of fog; only the faintest hint of refraction on the horizon impaired the purity of the light. The birds hesitated just long enough for the sweiler to move on, select another target and raise his club, then, like great, rapacious snowflakes, they settled on the heap of reeking flesh, biting, tearing, clawing, smothering its startling redness in a white blanket of feathers. Later, but not much later, when their feathers were as red as their beaks, the birds rose and lazily glided above the floe. Beneath them, more and more furry bags spilled their tasty contents on to the ice. The gulls swooped silently now, too gorged even to cry out their greed. Before they resumed their feast, they spewed the bloody contents of their gullets through wide, retching beaks. And on the fringes of the flock, the smaller, more timid birds flapped about in the mush of blood and ice, excitedly swallowing the warm sputum.

The *Ultima Thule* took thirty-four thousand five hundred seals. So many that they had to throw thirty tons of coal overboard to make room for them, and even then, the old ship was loaded right down to her marks. They were first back to St John's, thirty-six hours ahead of *Terra Nova*. Everyone reckoned they had done so well because 'Pinnacle Tam' had seen the state of the ice on his way across the Atlantic. But skill and luck had a lot to do with it. When the sweilers got ashore and their money was shared out, they went crazy. The crew worked round the clock unloading the seals at the yard. There was still time to make another trip to the ice, but so many sweilers were missing they sailed with only a third of their original complement of hunters. The older ones had gone home to their farms and the youngsters were legless with drink. Harry Wilkie, who had not set foot ashore since they tied up, so pressing was the need for steam, watched as the lights of the town and the tinkle of pianola music from the saloons faded and the *Ultima Thule* passed between the headlands once more into the open sea.

Some air, my dear? Of course. Should I open a window or would you prefer a few moments in the garden? We could even take a turn down to the shore. It's not far.

That's good. There's nothing like a breeze to raise the spirits, though from the water, you'd think there was scarcely a breath of wind. The Tay is deceptive; take my word. Yes indeed, there was a footbridge here when they chased the Craigie Ghost along the railway line so many years ago. Fishermen used it to reach their boat-houses on the shore. This one's a bit later, I think; stinks of shit instead of herring. It's a handy shortcut for dog-walkers, so watch your feet. Things don't change all at once. The picture shifts so gradually. Would Ethel Wilkie recognise the bridge at Stannergate, smoothed out and widened and straightened? Now it's no more than a bend in the road. I bet not one driver in ten knows a bridge is there. No, my dear. We're too low down to see the sand bar, but if you look towards Broughty Ferry, just landward of the lifeboat, you'll see the gable of Muirhead's shed. And there's the castle, full of Arctic remains. Of course you may talk to Muirhead if you wish. He's a minor player, yet the deus ex machina of our story. You might get on together. I'll steer clear, if you don't mind, till things are settled. I'd rather know if I must face Muirhead from the dock before I face him in a bar.

Oh, yes. He came up with the goods. No more than a fortnight after Forbes left I was surprised to get a call from Muirhead at the office. He said, 'Your what d'you call it's ready. Had a bit of spare time. Got on quicker than I expected. Let's say two hundred for cash.' I left early and drove down here. I found him in the usual muddle of lathes and acetylene cylinders and half-dismantled outboards talking to a chap who half-heartedly worked one of the few lobster boats in the harbour. Muirhead barely acknowledged my presence and continued his conversation which involved much pursing of lips and shaking of heads. I was obliged to kick my heels and look interested in the litter of nautical debris until the customer wandered disconsolately away; preferable, I dare say, to having Muirhead's creation revealed before inquisitive local eyes.

If Muirhead had modified the head of an ordinary pickaxe, he had done it so well that not a trace of its original form remained. The weapon he produced from beneath an oily workbench was an exact copy of Scoresby's drawing. The tines were of precisely the right length: one ending in a hammer, the other in a vicious spike. A second spike, which protruded from the top of the shaft, had been forged separately and served to stop the pick-head flying off in even the most violent use. The shaft, I suspected, was of hickory rather than the spruce I had specified, but so cunningly had Muirhead treated the wood, anyone but the most tenacious forensic investigator would have been convinced that the seal-pick had seen season upon season of severe use on the Arctic ice. I took the weapon in my hands. What sensual pleasure in the roundness of the polished shaft and the weighty balance of the metal head. Pale light from the open doors reflected on the pick as I raised it above my head and brought it down in a great, sweeping arc to within a few inches of the concrete floor.

'Magnificent,' I said. 'How on earth did you make it look so old?' Muirhead rubbed his nose with a finger, the nail of which was like a black rivet.

'Wee trick of the trade,' he said. 'Knew a bloke who made antique furniture once. Kists and dressers. Dead simple stuff. He'd bury the wood for a couple of days in the garden, then hit it with a bag of chains and polish it with Brasso. Sold them to the Dutch every time, no problem.' A drink, of course, was called for, and it was some time before I extricated myself from the pub, leaving Muirhead with a third large scotch before him and ten twenty-pound notes tucked safely in the huge paper-clip which was his wallet, business account and filing system. Louise was less impressed with the pick than I'd expected, but the prospect of visiting Forbes excited her so much she insisted I phone him right away with the news.

Frankly, I could ill afford time away from the office. For reasons I'll shortly make clear, I had instituted some legal investigations of a particularly personal nature in France. The results were expected any day, so once more I suggested to Forbes that we send the pick down by courier and visit him later when his sculpture was finished. He disagreed. We left the situation unresolved and the next morning Louise and I were wakened by a man from a travel agency with two business-class air tickets and a reservation for two nights in Brown's. I took the line of least resistance. At check-in, the seal-pick, incongruously wrapped in Christmas paper which was all we had in the house, was consigned to the hold beneath haughty, disapproving eyes. It emerged unscathed. Forbes had left a message at the hotel suggesting I visit his studio next morning and that we all meet up for lunch. I suspect Louise was disappointed to be excluded so pointedly from seeing the great man at work. She was also miffed at not being invited to stay in Forbes's house; but the sumptuousness of the hotel and the prospect of shopping in Mayfair cheered her up. As things turned out, it was sensible not to be all under the same roof. Forbes had got it right again.

Well, here we are. Muirhead's workshop's over there. The doors are closed. His car's still here. The pub's not open. There's only one more possibility. If we go down the side of the lifeboat shed, we'll see the harbour basin. I'd rather not step into full view. There he is, sculling out to that yacht in his punt. From the tool-boxes I'd say he may be a while. Your chat will have to wait. Still, you know where to find him. We'll take the quick way home: through the town and along the main road. The wind's quite icy now. Not unlike the chilly winds which blow across the Ile-de-France at certain times of year. I assume, my dear, you are familiar with Paris.

Chapter 19

JUST SUCH a wind gusted over the damp cobbles of the Place de Roubaix, raising eddies of dust on the flagstoned floor of the Gare du Nord customs hall. It was seven in the morning and already the passengers who had disembarked from the Calais boat train had been waiting half an hour. Mr and Mrs Jock Dow stood amidst the disgruntled travellers, anxiously watching the porters and *octroi* officials moving about behind the counters of the hall in which the examination was to take place. Their fear was not that contraband might be unearthed, but that one of their many items of luggage might have been mislaid. Dow was particularly concerned about the book of Tayline samples he had brought to help select the most appropriate patterns for the space allotted to Baxters at the exhibition. The book was as big as a table, bound up in leather. When at last it appeared on the counter, he rushed to claim it, provoking comments about damned foreigners who would not wait their turn. Dow paid no heed. He dealt rapidly with the sulky *douanier*, unbuckled the portfolio to prove nothing suspicious lurked between its bulky leaves, and strode purposefully from the station followed by a porter burdened with luggage and a wife burdened with embarrassment.

'In Germany,' he said, 'there is only one examination. In France two. Always the same. Always so complicated.'

In the courtyard, the cab driver squinted at the slip of paper Jock Dow passed up to him, let his chin drop almost imperceptibly and flicked his whip over the back of his bony steed, which, as if guided by telepathy, set off down the Rue du Faubourg St Denis, where the proprietors of shops and cafés were opening their shutters for the day. Ethel had never been abroad, not even to England. Scarcely anything, however trivial, escaped her notice. I like to imagine her keeping a diary and recording her impressions as mile upon mile of railway track distanced her from the familiar coast of the Tay. It would not have been out of character, but if such a book existed, it has long since gone. I am certain, however, that when the cab turned into the Boulevard Poissonnière and pulled up at the door of a modest establishment bearing the inscription *Grand Hôtel Beau Séjour*, both travellers were grateful their journey had come to an end. The hotel was clean, cheerful and well kept. It was thoroughly French in its management, though curiously the majority of guests were Germans. Far from revelling in this discovery, which he made when inscribing J. Dow, businessman, and spouse, nationality Scottish, in the register, Jock Dow seemed disenchanted and hurriedly called for a boy who led them to the couple of rooms above the entresol which had been reserved in their name. The rooms were prettily decorated but very small; one was fitted out to resemble a salon with a leather sofa and armchairs, the other filled with two little beds and a vast wardrobe which must have been in vogue when the first Napoleon was alive. There was an iron balcony overlooking the boulevard. Before he withdrew, the boy threw open the window and at once the room filled with the roar of steel wheels on cobbles, the rattle of omnibuses and the hum of the city going to work. Ethel took off her hat and coat and laid them across the sofa. She bent and unfastened her high-buttoned boots, then stepped into the adjoining room and flopped down on the bed. The ceiling was duck-egg blue, with cherubs moulded into the cornice, and somehow, these plaster figures caked by dozens of ill-applied coats of paint, typified for Ethel all the foreignness of the country. She shut her eyes and listened to the traffic. There was a bump of wood against metal. Jock had shut the window. He had taken off his jacket and his celluloid collar was in his hand. I like to imagine it was there, under the most intimate of circumstances, that my grandmother announced she was expecting a baby, that all was well and that he (she had no doubt about the sex) would be brought up as a Scotsman.

For the next few days, Ethel was escorted round Paris like a queen. Dow outdid himself in husbandly concern for my grandmother and her important cargo. When she wished to go out, a cab was always there. When she stayed in, only the most important matters were allowed to disturb her. On the second day, a ladies' maid appeared and took charge of even the most trivial of Ethel's tasks and Jock Dow, any idea of economy forgotten, regarded his wife with a thoroughly proprietorial air, though no hint of her condition showed to any eye but his. Only repeated assurances convinced him it was safe for Ethel to see the sites of the Great Exhibition. They took a cab to the Cours la Reine to visit the Topsy-Turvy House, where everything was upside down and spectators walked along little gangways fixed to the 'ceilings'. At the Meorama on the Champ de Mars, they stood on the deck of a ship while around them the optical illusion was created of visiting exotic foreign ports. Dow insisted his wife be given a seat lest she be overcome by *mal de mer* though the floor was absolutely steady. And when Ethel asked to ride on the Revolving Road, a moving walkway from the Chicago Exhibition, only the most profound assurances of its safety would persuade Dow to permit the journey.

Every day, Jock Dow visited the Palace of National Manufactures, where he measured the space allotted to his exhibit, selected appropriate patterns of Tayline and wired Baxters for so many square yards of this and lengths of that. When he asked about a reliable decorator to stain the woodwork and emulsion the walls, an official handed him a slip of pasteboard engraved:

Gaston Pietri et Fils
Sq. Montholon 26
Paris 9

'I shall call there tomorrow,' said the representative of Tayline.

'Go early,' said the official. 'By eight, they're already out at work.'

At exactly seven-thirty next day, Jock Dow and his wife left the hotel in a closed hackney carriage. It was a magnificent spring morning. Ethel had insisted on coming because the decorator's shop lay in the direction of Montmartre and the maid had told her the very best view of Paris was from the Butte. As her husband expected to be detained only a few minutes, it was a chance to kill two birds with one stone. As they drove, Ethel explained the aphorism and Jock wrote it down in his notebook. The cab rattled up Rue du Faubourg Montmartre. Shops and cafés were bathed in sunshine. Most were already open, and early shoppers threaded their way between piles of vegetables, gossiping tradesmen and little *blanchisseuses* hurrying along with baskets of fresh laundry. Once, they had to stop to let a huge furniture van back into a courtyard. At the Rue de La Fayette, the driver turned right and presently pulled up beside some black iron railings. Square Montholon was a cobbled rectangle set back from the main street, with a dusty little garden at its centre in which lime trees were just coming into bud. From the farthest corners of the square, two streets ran diagonally in opposite directions. To the left, Rue Mayran led towards Montmartre, while Rue Baudin climbed steeply from the other end of the square in the direction of the Gare du Nord. Jock Dow stepped down from the cab and peered at the numbers painted on the buildings. One hundred and seven; one hundred and five. The premises of *Pietri et Fils* were at the other end of the square. He turned to beckon the cabby, but Ethel had already alighted and the cab was moving off. He took her arm.

'We must cross to the other side. Number twenty-six, you see.'

They walked along the pavement. Outside the Café St Bertrand workmen were already drinking coffee or an early glass of marc. Jock and Ethel Dow stepped carefully across the gutters, down which water was cascading from the slope of the Rue Baudin. Jock stopped and looked at the shop sweepings and old newspapers, sawdust and pieces of sodden cardboard swirling towards the gaping culvert of the municipal sewer.

'Don't you see?' he said to Ethel. 'The water carries everything away.'

But Ethel didn't see the sawdust and sodden cardboard. Ethel leaped across the gutter with no regard for footwear or dignity. A huge, two-horse water wagon was careering down Rue Baudin out of control. Did Ethel close her eyes or did she stare in horror as a dozen foreign voices screamed at her husband above the thunder of iron wheels? Very slowly, so slowly you could count the heartbeats, Jock Dow raised his eyes from the fascinating stream of municipal water. He gazed up the hill with a puzzled smile, a look of bewildered recognition as though an unexpected friend had crossed his path. And as the hooves drowned out the screams, he removed his hat and brandished it towards the commotion, as if a pearl-grey fedora might just ward off a team of stampeding percherons.

When the water wagon came to rest there was no sign of Jock Dow. The workmen who came running from the Café St Bertrand found him wedged between the rear wheels and the splintered iron railings. A gentle stream of water sprayed from the sprinkler on to his shirt front, washing away the blood where a broken railing protruded from his chest.

My grandmother, so far as I can tell, witnessed nothing of the immediate aftermath of the accident. Before the breath of the foremost horse met Jock Dow's astonished brow, Ethel swooned into insensibility on the pavement. Before bystanders carried her through the doorway of the Café St Bertrand, the stream of water had dislodged several hairpins from her rich, auburn locks. A damp stain had spread over her elegant fichu. When Ethel came to, she found herself in the company of a doctor, who slipped the contents of a twist of paper into a glass and held it to her lips; a Brigadier of Police, who repeated questions in halting English; and a representative of the British Consul who had happened to be at the local *mairie* and had hurried to the scene. At last a cab was called and the Consular official escorted the widow Dow to her hotel.

After a Gallic display of grief and a flood of genuine tears, the ladies' maid led Ethel into the bedroom and closed the door. She folded back the covers on the bed and helped unhook Ethel's bodice. While the maid busied herself with a stone hot-water bottle, Ethel slipped out of the rest of her clothes and pulled a starched linen nightdress over her head. Before she dropped her underclothes into the basket, Ethel examined the linen which had lain closest to her skin, and after the maid had gone, took the plump bolster that had so recently supported her husband's head and slipped it beneath her hips till her pelvis rested at an angle of forty-five degrees. My grandmother needn't have worried. Neither the shock of the accident nor the violent vomiting she suffered as a result of the French doctor's therapeutic powder was sufficient to dislodge the germ of life within her. Two days later she returned to Dundee in a first-class compartment paid for by the directors of Baxters. Her husband's place was taken in Paris by the ageing representative who had first recognised Jock's talents under another name in the Baltic. Tayline enjoyed a slow but steady increase in market share until the First World War dashed all sales predictions. In the apse of St Mary's, a simple service was held in remembrance of Jock Dow, whose remains had been returned to his adopted home by express freight. At Ethel's request, the Scottish version of his name was used on the headstone in the Eastern Necropolis, and six months and twenty-one days later, she gave birth in her father's house to a perfectly unremarkable male child of nine-and-a-half pounds in weight. When the midwife had laid the little Cancerian in his new cradle, she placed a damp cloth on Ethel's brow.

'His name will be John Montholon,' said the new mother, 'and he will dress in black.'

Except for his first year, when his black baby clothes and unusual middle name aroused matronly sympathy, my father spent an utterly conventional boyhood. Brought up in the dust and clamour of a mason's yard, he naturally saw his future in construction. And just as his grandfather had followed the path from master mason to proprietor, my father, who was very much a man of the new century, enrolled as soon as was financially and academically possible in an Edinburgh college that offered a reputable diploma in civil engineering. When he returned to Dundee he did three things. He steered the family firm away from traditional stonecraft towards the lucrative field of municipal housing, which was just beginning its inter-war boom. He married Miss Heather Kinloch, a librarian and fellow Savoyard who had often added her refined soprano to his robust baritone; and early in 1939, when his only son was barely a month old, he accepted a commission in the local Territorial unit of Royal Engineers. Long before hostilities commenced, he had his title amended to 'Captain J. M. Dow' on the stationery of Wilkie & Dow Ltd. Building Contractors.

What's that, my dear? Ethel never remarried. After a specially-convened meeting, the young widow was allowed to return to her teaching post, which had been temporarily filled by a pupil teacher. She stayed till the First World War and more stringent labour laws brought an end to half-time education. And Tayline? What an interesting question. It enjoyed a steady if unremarkable popularity till it was discovered that, printed in a camouflage pattern and fitted with various flaps and eyelets, it could form a crude but serviceable anti-gas cape. What Mr Dow would have thought of his invention being used to ward off the more sinister attacks of his former fellow countrymen can only be imagined; but as always, Baxters didn't lose out.

Chapter 20

LET'S CROSS here when there's a chance. The traffic never seems to slow on this road, though you often find police waiting with their little radar guns. I'm glad my brief, if tragic Parisian excursion was of interest. Forbes knew the facts, of course, but like you, I can't call to mind any work which might have drawn inspiration from the calamity in the Square Montholon. Crazed Percherons and fountains of municipal water don't figure in the Wedderburn oeuvres.

As I said, Forbes made the right decision lodging us at Brown's. While Louise soaked away a hard afternoon in Bond Street, I sipped gin and watched with some interest a programme which dealt, not without levity, with the Turner Prize. I wouldn't have been surprised to see Forbes beaming forth his opinion from the screen, but for once he wasn't asked. Over dinner, I mentioned to Louise what I'd seen. She showed mild amusement, but soon was engrossed in the metropolitan company of our fellow diners, whom she observed with Dundonian shrewdness.

Next morning we took breakfast in our room. I left before Louise had dressed and promised to let her know where Forbes had picked for lunch. The porter caught my eye. I waved away his offer of a cab. He also caught a glimpse of the seal-pick, which I had tucked under my arm rather as old military men carry rolled umbrellas when the martial spirit is particularly strong. Later I noticed that the sharpest tine had pierced the wrapping, which perhaps accounted for his curious gaze and the ease with which I found a seat on the tube. Of course, my dear, I'd forgotten you'd know Forbes's studio: the high wall in the lane of select houses and the little lychgate that leads straight to the staircase, bypassing the house. He bought during the property boom. Not on the first wave, as I had recommended, but rather close to high-tide, when I doubt his investment would be fully realised. He didn't care. His voice answered the intercom so swiftly he must have been waiting by the door, and I made my way up to meet him. Forbes hurried towards me, hand outstretched. He gave me a glass and retrieved his own from a corner table.

'We usually take a wee sherry at this hour,' he said. 'Just say if you'd like coffee or tea.' Sherry at eleven isn't my habit, but I took the glass and let Forbes lead me towards a rather precious young man in denims who extended a languid hand. Have you any preconception of taxidermists as a breed? I had imagined those who stuff and mount the spoils of field and stream to resemble the sportsmen who supply their curious trade. I saw the taxidermist as quite accustomed to moor and heath and long hours watching his prospective subjects in the wild. Despite, or maybe because of, the fashionably shaven head and glistening, new tattoos, there was something insubstantial about Dennis Summers. Save for a camouflaged waistcoat which he wore regardless of the heat, he struck me as more suited for dressing shop windows than eviscerating carcasses. Forbes's eyes lit on my parcel.

'The club,' he said reverentially.

'The seal-pick,' I replied. He stripped away the gaudy wrapping and, with an expression of deepest awe, carried the pick to one of three tall windows which pierced the north wall of the room. Flat, November light glistened on the cunningly timeworn shaft and cruelly pointed tines. When Forbes spoke, emotion choked his voice.

'Brilliant. Just brilliant.' He motioned towards the far end of the studio where there stood among a clutter of artist's debris an angular object maybe six feet high draped in a paint-smeared dust cloth. 'Dennis, do the honours,' said Forbes, and the young man plucked at the sheet. More and more he reminded me of a window dresser unveiling a mannequin. Then I saw it. The culmination of their efforts. The super-tableau set to wring the heart-strings of animal lovers the world over. And as I looked at the bizarre fusion of wax and fur and contorted metal, there arose from deep within me an utterly uncontrollable gale of laughter. I laughed till my sides hurt, till drops of sherry fell from my shaking glass to the parquet floor. I laughed at the taxidermist's outrage and Forbes's consternation. There was an embarrassing silence while I caught my breath and Forbes tried to regain his composure.

'All right,' he said testily. 'All right. To the untutored eye, the structure may seem somewhat mannered. Besides, it's not finished. We're waiting for the clothes. They're being flown across from a store in Newfoundland.'

The structure was incomplete all right. The seal was there, of course, and as stuffed seals on polystyrene ice floes go, I dare say it passed muster. Mr Summers had even given a cunning twist to the upper body, as if the little animal were offering its head for a friendly caress. Implanted behind it, far enough to ensure a firm stance, were two calf-length sea boots, and from the boots, like a contorted scarecrow, there emerged a construction of chicken-wire and steel armatures roughly in the form of a human body. At its extremities, the scarecrow became flesh. A waxen head surmounted the spinal armature like a toffee apple on a stick. The face, it seemed, bore more than a passing resemblance to a photograph of Forbes's maternal grandfather in his youth. But the waxen cheeks were so puffed up with exertion, only the closest family member would recognise the subject of Forbes's inspiration. Each spindly arm ended eerily in a perfectly-moulded waxen hand. Two powerful waxen thumbs and eight waxen fingers, callused from dishonest toil, hovered in mid air awaiting what? Surely the chicken-wire spook had no need of an expensive seal-pick with tines sharpened to cleave through fur and bone. There was only one object that could possible fit between those eager fingers. The pursed lips and ballooning cheeks were crying out for fulfilment. I turned to Forbes, who was holding the seal-pick defensively across his chest.

'It doesn't need a pick, Forbes,' I gasped, 'it needs a saxophone.'

Don't think for a moment that I had planned this unwelcome reaction to Forbes's sculpture. My laughter was quite involuntary; in fact frighteningly so. Of the three men who stood in the silent studio, I suffered the most lasting embarrassment. The skinheaded taxidermist, after a look of speechless outrage, lapsed into pique and contributed nothing more to the occasion. Forbes, when the shock had subsided, lowered the seal-pick and carefully propped it against an easel. He hastily drained his glass and went at once to refill it. He tipped some sherry into mine and led me firmly to a sofa that ran the whole length of the wall opposite the windows. It was made in sections of padded canvas and metal tubing. I sat in the middle and dabbed my eyes.

'Hell,' said Forbes. 'I know it's asking a lot of you to visualise it before the clothes are ready. They'll make all the difference.' He raised his voice so that Dennis Summers could hear. 'You know the saying about not showing fools or bairns half-done work.'

'Well, you've tried it on a fool,' I replied. 'Don't bother testing it on bairns. No amount of genuine Newfoundland oilskins will convince even the most imaginative child it is looking at anything but a charade. Your little pup with its glass-marble eyes will have no more effect than those rigid rabbits Mr Summers's predecessors were so fond of inserting between the talons of petrified eagles in our municipal museums.'

'Nonsense,' said Forbes. 'Dennis studied dozens of photographs. It's exact in every detail. What would be the point of going to such trouble with the club if the seal wasn't perfect?'

'None at all,' I responded. 'for the club is alive. It's a real, functional weapon that has no place among stitched fur and chicken wire. You can never instil terror into a glass eye.'

Forbes moved uncomfortably on the canvas sofa. He said, 'Be reasonable,' and at that moment, I remembered the programme I had seen in the hotel the night before. How could Forbes be so detached from the world he professed to lead?

'Constructive criticism,' I said. 'Nothing more. You're behind the times, gentlemen. Events have overtaken you. Already Damian's sliced-up cows and sheep are commonplace. To match him, you'd have to pickle a real sweiler in formaldehyde. Weren't you on the panel this year, Forbes? Action is the watchword. The image must move, even if it is a row of unconvincing policemen trying not to. Your tableau, or whatever you call it, is lifeless. It gathers dust. We're in the age of motion. People don't want a monument. There will be no contributions for a seal memorial. Or are you thinking of the "Unknown Seal" – a furry national shrine for the tender hearted? You'd face stiff opposition from that island in the lake. You, of all people, must know the score. We've heard you over the years. "Rationalism was the principle of the Italian Renaissance . . . No finer Fauve image can be found than Derian's *The Pool of London* . . . Lautrec, more than any artist, shows the contrast between being and appearance, between everyday life and dreams . . ." I watched them all, Forbes. Over Louise's shoulder. When it came to the Moulin Rouge, you weren't content with focusing on the posters of the midget genius; you were right in among the greasepaint and sweat and German tourists. I remember your hand passing in one sweep from the painted form of Cha-U-Kao to the plump, naked back of a modern dancer to demonstrate the subtlety of the master's line. Come on, Forbes. You know the tricks of the trade. Your cuddly fluff-ball cringing before its wax scarecrow falls short of the mark. People expect thrills, action, sensation.' I paused to catch my breath. My fingers were trembling and Forbes had gone very white. For once I had taken the wind out of his sails, but what was the use of constructive criticism if not to point the way ahead? 'Think of the *Rainbow Warrior* fighting to save the whale,' I said. 'And the brave Canadian protesters who meet the sweilers face to face on the ice. Maybe one of them deep-froze a seal for your crony to turn into a cuddly toy. Even in Orkney, where they're quite justifiably culling the grey seal, protesters have daubed the fur of likely candidates for the bullet with green dye to make the pelts valueless. An eccentric gesture, but worth three columns in anybody's newspaper and half a page if the picture is right. Your battle shouldn't be fought in a studio, but on the high seas. Surely you can see the ultimate answer.'

Forbes shook his head. He passed the back of his hand across his brow. I stood up and he tried to catch my elbow. When I seized the seal-pick, Dennis Summers flattened himself against the studio wall. When I lifted the hickory shaft, Forbes moved more swiftly than he had done for years. He leaped towards the sculpture fearing, I suppose, that I was about to put paid to its chances of completion once and for all. His upset glass rolled across the floor. Forbes need not have worried. I intended to destroy something much more substantial than a bag of stitched fur. Slowly I raised the pick and, taking it by the metal tines, held the handle invitingly towards him. Like a visitor unwilling to linger at a sickbed, I stepped out of the studio on to the landing. I stood before a painting, *Gulls in the Eye of a Typhoon*, and from the door behind me, which I had not bothered to close, there came the satisfying sound of steel demolishing chicken wire.

When Forbes at last emerged, several minutes after the whey-faced taxidermist had rushed past me and down the stairs, his expression was as serene as if nothing more unsettling had occurred than a spilled glass of sherry. We called Louise as planned, and set off through the quiet, empty streets, in which leaves had been raked into regular, neat bundles. Having destroyed his original plan, I was keen to help with the solution to the task he had set himself. I watched keenly as we walked for any hint that Forbes's resolve might need boosting, but it seemed he was already quite committed to the idea of direct action.

I said, 'Let me take care of the details. I know the perfect place, and someone who can fix us up with a boat. He won't ask questions. As for the other side of the operation, you know the business so much better than I do. It would be best to organise your own camera work; shoot the killing at your leisure and edit it the way you want. The last thing we need is a fleet of reporters bobbing about after us like at the Boat Race.' Mention of the press brought the first hint of doubt.

'But the consequences. I'll be asked to resign from every organisation I'm trying to help.'

'Think of the good you'll do,' I replied. 'Think how many canapés will hit the gallery floor, how many TV dinners will end up on the Wilton when Forbes Wedderburn, three times life size, appears and bashes out the brains of a seal pup before their very eyes.'

'Maybe I'll be prosecuted.'

'All the better. There's no finer platform than a court of law for airing your views. Call it awareness through example. And don't worry about the charge. The Scottish Office agriculture and fisheries people might try to nail you for killing a seal without a licence, but I doubt any procurator fiscal would entertain a charge of cruelty. He'd be playing straight into your hands. I'll represent you free, though you'd maybe prefer a big name for the sake of publicity.'

When we arrived at the restaurant, Louise was already there. I remember catching Forbes's eye as we approached the table and saying beneath my breath, 'In the pub and in the barbers, never talk of ships and harbours.' An unnecessary caution, it turned out, for Louise had so much to tell us we scarcely got a word in during the meal.

That evening, it was the opera. Frankly, my taste has not even reached the level of Gilbert and Sullivan, which so preoccupied my father and inspired my mother with my Christian name; but Louise's delight plus the prospect of reinforcing, however subtly, the secret pact I had with Forbes was enough to fill me with anticipation. Forbes was late. He had the tickets, but mention of his name was enough to let us take our seats. For the life of me, I can't remember what was playing. The audience was rich and urbane. There was a stir beside us. Forbes had arrived with a dark-haired young woman he called Inez. Another manifestation of his penchant for the exotic. There was no chance to talk, and at the interval, Forbes was so intent on greeting and being greeted, it wasn't till we were in the taxi that we discovered Inez was from Argentina and a photographer. Come to think of it, you may well have met.

They came into our hotel for a nightcap. We were taking the early shuttle, and I was ready for bed, but I didn't want to let Forbes out of my sight. It was then I noticed he was carrying a slim black portfolio; nothing more than a posh folder for A4 paper. He laid it on the arm of his chair, and when the women left to fix themselves up, tapped it slowly with a finger.

'You've been a great help,' he said. 'Now let me help you.' I could see by his expression that he didn't want to be overheard. 'I've been trying to find a way to let you know something I discovered some time ago quite by chance. I almost told you after that amazing meal in the Steading, but somehow the moment slipped by.' I was becoming uneasy. Forbes had once more recovered some of the air of complacency which my morning's work had tried to dent. He cast his eyes towards the lobby and said, 'I thought it would be best to let you see for yourself. Don't read it now. Mull it over on the plane. We can talk when next we meet.' He leaned over and handed me the folder, and at the same time, patted my knee with an earnestness I was glad no one had observed.

At that moment, the women returned. Inez and Louise were deep in conversation. Louise was saying, 'Forbes will be visiting us again very soon. You must come too. Everyone's pleasantly surprised by Dundee.' For an instant, I thought Forbes might lose his cool.

Chapter 21

COFFEE, PLEASE, Louise. We're back.

I'm glad our walk did you good, but you still look a little off-colour. Too pale in the cheek and pink around the gills. I hope you're not going to come down with something. We don't have long to finish my tale, and there's nothing worse than being ill in a hotel room miles from home. Ah, Louise, I think this young lady could do with a couple of paracetamol with her coffee. I'll try not to keep you this evening, my dear, but I'm sure you'd like to hear what Forbes had so mysteriously handed me in the lobby at Brown's. I've made you a copy to read at your leisure, but , for the sake of completeness, I'd be happy to read it out. Of course I didn't wait to mull it over in the plane as Forbes had suggested. I read the pages of neat, italic script as soon as we reached our hotel bedroom. As I remember, Louise wore the basque and some real stockings in the hope, no doubt, of metropolitan excitement. She hung around for a while in a state of exotic undress before at last heading for a shower and bed. I felt rotten disappointing her, but you'll understand my distraction. Is the tape running? Good.

As soon as I read it, I doubted it was authentic; and in my calling, you develop an instinct for the truth. In essence, Forbes had given me a transcript of what purports to be a conversation he had had with Harry Wilkie, his maternal grandfather, sometime in the late sixties when Forbes was, as he put it, 'In that phase every young man goes through of seeking his roots'. Be that as it may, what I read in that room in Mayfair, oblivious to Louise's whaleboned blandishments, did not look thirty years old. The paper was fresh and the ink unfaded. It still is.

Maybe I should tell you a little about Harry Wilkie's later life. Help you put things in context. Without unduly anticipating my story, let me say Harry didn't stay with the Victoria Whale and Seal Fishing Company. His first trip was his last; but though he understandably lost his appetite for Arctic hunting, he kept a love of the sea. He sailed as a fireman with several merchant companies, and, well before the First World War, was to be found in the uniform of Chief Stoker aboard a succession of battleships and cruisers preparing for inevitable action in the North Sea. It was during his naval days that Harry must have married his first wife. Forbes's mother was born towards the end of the war. Though the first Mrs Wilkie was much younger than her husband, she also died comparatively young, when Harry, who had at last left the sea, was eking out a living as a boatman and general handyman in Camperdown Dock. Within a year, Harry Wilkie married the widow of an engineer with the Dundee, Perth and London Shipping Company. This lady, I don't have her name, we never met, hailed from Kent. Just as Hitler was marching into Prague, she fell heir to a modest legacy which included a corner shop in Chatham. She and Harry went south to meet this new challenge, leaving their daughter, who was already walking out with one Duncan Wedderburn, to pursue a short career in the order department of Keiller's jam factory. Harry Wilkie never returned to Dundee. The interview Forbes had so carefully recorded must have taken place in Chatham, when his grandfather, by my reckoning, would have been at least eighty-six. This alone aroused suspicion; but judge for yourself.

Gilbert Dow Esq.
Personal and Confidential

We visited my grandfather very seldom when I was a child. I suspect my mother didn't approve of his second wife. In my last year at college, I was invited to apply for a place at the RCA. The visit to London was a chance to re-establish contact and patch up old misunderstandings. I stayed an extra day and took the train to the Kent coast. As it turned out, my apprehension about seeing the old man after so many years was unnecessary. He seemed to attach so little significance to the coolness between his daughter and himself that I wonder whether he had been aware of it at all. When I asked him to cast his mind back to New Year 1900, however, he became quite enthusiastic. He told me the name of every shipmate aboard the *Ultima Thule*, reeled off the exact figures of the catch (lots of seals, disappointingly few whales), and mixed it all with funny little stories. But he didn't want to talk about Alexander Yule. Whenever I mentioned the specktioneer, or recalled his sister's marriage to the ill-fated Mr Dow, he changed the subject or pretended not to hear. Only once did he come out with anything, and that was late at night when we had both been drinking a lot of whisky. He could still put away an astonishing amount. I had asked him about Ethel earlier. He had avoided the issue and the topic had been forgotten about for hours when, out of the blue, he told me the strangest story. The damnable thing was that I didn't have my notebook. I knew that if I went to get it, he'd clam up or lose his thread or simply fall asleep. He'd had a lot to drink, but I swear he wasn't drunk. Come to think of it, I've never seen old Harry drunk in my life. That night, after Harry had finished his story, we had reached the stage where the only thing to do was go on drinking whisky. At last, he fell asleep in his armchair and I managed to escape to my bedroom where I poured some water over my head, grabbed the notebook and scribbled down as much as I could remember of what he'd just said. Next day, on the train back to London Bridge, I tried to expand it a little, to put it in order. But my memory was confused by the whisky. I wrote out the notes again. Here they are. Sit down before you read them.

HARRY: Something happened just afore I went tae the sealin that made me right wild.

FORBES: What would that be?

HARRY: I had just said cheerio tae the lads at the boiler house and was walking back home along Victoria Street. I had my dungarees with me and other bits and pieces I thought I might need on the voyage wrapped up in a bundle on my shoulder and, though I say it myself, I likely had twa or three drinks in me an a, for there's aye a bottle o' beer tae be found in a boiler house. At any rate, I came tae Victoria Brig but before I could cross it, Peter Pye appeared and caught hold of me by the elbow. He must have been waitin beside the brig.

FORBES: Who did you say it was?

HARRY: Peter Pye. He was an idiot. Clean aff his heid. In fact he would have been put away years afore if it wisna for his faither. He was a bit of a toff and had a jute mill up Lochee way. Any road, Pye got hold o my airm. Do ye think I could make him let go? He kept pullin me round intae Dens Road doon the side o the coolin ponds and sayin he had something to tell me. He was slaverin and mumblin that much I could hardly mak out a word he said, but I followed him doon tae the side o the ponds out o sight o the road.

FORBES: What happened then?

HARRY: Pye kept laughin and slaverin and I couldna get any sense out o him, but at last he said he had something tae show me. He held up his haun under my nose and opened his fist. He had on thon woollen gloves wi nae fingers in them, and at first I couldna make out what he had in his haun what with it gettin dark an a. But then I saw it was a wee piece of amber shaped like a teardrop with a wee silver catch on the end of it. Right away I realised it belonged tae the necklace the German lad had given our Ethel for her Christmas. I tried tae tak it frae the fool, but he shut his haun and stuck it back in his jaiket. Then I asked him whaur he had found it. Ye ken what he telt me? He said it must hae fallen aff when Ethel was gettin mounted like a yowe beneath the arch on the Jawbanes Road the other night. Pye was lyin amang the gorse on the Law. It was a good place. A grandstand seat. And then along they came, all lovey-dovey, airm in airm on thon wee path. When they reached the arch o bones they stopped. And then he pulled her down on to her knees. She had her hurdies up in the air. The man was gruntin and she was makin noises too and Pye had seen naething like it in his life.

FORBES: What did you . . .

HARRY: I was that wild I rushed straight at him, but I still had my bundle of claes and he was expectin a fight and managed tae jink round me and run intae one of the ponds. It was only knee-deep at that time anyway. And then he did something I'll never forget till my dyin day. Afore I could get hold of him, he bent doon and put his hauns under the water doon about his feet, then he jumped right out of the pond and ower the wall intae Dens Street in one loup.

FORBES: In one jump?

HARRY: Clean ower the wall intae the road. I could hardly believe my een, but what he said had made me that wild I ran through the gate and chased him towards the harbour. I caught up with him in West Whale Lane and got him up against a wall wi the topmaist lair of stane in the sma of his back. 'I'll teach ye tae cry doon honest folk,' says I, and I knocked the wind out of him wi my knee.

But 'Na , na,' says he. 'It's a true. I swear it. I was just tellin ye so ye could maybe speak tae her and let her see the error of her ways.'

I took hod o his throat. 'Wha was wi her' says I. His face was bricht red and his een like tae burst oot o their sockets.

'Dinna kill me,' says he. And then I remembered and grabbed at his pocket and the hale front o it cam awa in my haun and the wee bit amber fell on tae the cobbles and landed in a puddle. We baith just looked at it, and him rubbin his throat.

'Wha was it?' says I, and I picked up the jewel. He was slaverin again and shakin like tae hae a fit.

'Yule the whaler,' says he. "Wha else did ye think it wid be?'

And ye ken this? I didna kill him. I didna lay another finger on him. I just let him limp away towards the Seagate. And I turned and walked to the dock, under the Royal Arch and over the dock gates and straight out tae the end of the pier at the tidal basin, past a the ships and cranes, as far out as I could go. And I took the wee bit of amber wi the silver catch that I still had in my haun and flung it as far intae the Tay as I could fling. And frae that day tae this, I've never telt a soul about it.

Forbes Wedderburn

I got little sleep that night, I can tell you. The unsavoury information which Forbes had so cunningly introduced turned over and over in my mind. You see, my dear, despite the pretentious prose, despite the phoney Scots, despite the utter improbability of an eighty-six-year-old man revealing such an embarrassing and intimate secret to a youth of barely twenty whom he seldom met and, as far as I can tell, did not particularly like, there was just enough detail in Forbes's tale to set alarm bells ringing. Might it not just contain a grain of truth?

The conical hill which rises in the centre of Dundee is called the Law. These days, the city surrounds it; but at the turn of the century, when Peter Pye's shocking encounter was said to have taken place, it sat surrounded by fields on the edge of the seventh ward. A few country roads ran out from the edge of the city. The widest, and that in best repair, led past the Kinnaird Allotments to disused quarries on the Law's northern face. A footpath circled the base of the hill. Its various sections had no official names, but several local ones depending on whether the users were weekend strollers, roving schoolboys or dogged walkers who exercised their pets in the lee of the Law. There's no record of what the courting couples who found seclusion on the Law's grassy slopes called the paths by which they reached their haven. I doubt if they cared. But something stuck in my mind. The track that wound along the southern edge of the hill towards its lower slopes was, by some people, called the Jawbones Road. As a child, I remembered wondering at the ancient arch, moss green and weathered as rotting timber, which straddled the path at the hill's southernmost point. Regardless of the numerous standing stones surrounding the base of the Law or the vestigal fort which my father would point out on its sumit, my four-year-old eyes could not wait till the sinister archway came into view. As we passed on our Sunday afternoon walks, father would strike the rotting posts with the stick which, even then, he carried in anticipation of a rifle, and tell us that the great, curved beams that formed the arch were not made of wood, but were the jawbones of a gigantic whale. I suppose I believed him. I believed most things told me as a child; but by the time my passion for whales had developed to a point where I sought out such rustic curiosities, the archway had been removed or maybe, taking my father's example, had simply disintegrated; though in fairness, my father spread himself to the winds with the assistance of a 150mm shell from a Sturmpanzer IV *Brummbaer*, hastily deployed by General Model to cover his withdrawal from a rapidly diminishing bulge in the Ardennes.

At the turn of the century, the Dundee whaling trade was facing inescapable decline, but it is not hard to imagine the arch being raised during the years of plenty from the jawbones of Balaena Mysticetae discarded once the valuable whalebone had been stripped to support the skirts and clinch the waists of mid-Victorian womanhood. What more fitting a place for a specktioneer to take his pleasure than under an archway of whalebone? Too fitting, I thought. Too perfect. The pathway beneath the Law was secluded, but not deserted, even at night in winter. And in those days, would a schoolteacher ever have consented? And could such an impromptu coupling be managed easily, if at all? And would a man over eighty years old bottle up such a story for sixty-odd years only to blurt it out to a grandson in a moment of unguarded drunkenness? I resolved to make inquiries. When I got back to Dundee, I did.

Ten minutes with the *Courier* archivist showed that, in February 1900, the weather in these parts was not as inhospitable as you might imagine. It was reported as: 'Muggy, giving place to a dryness which was quite acceptable. Very welcome after the recent snow.' What more bracing an atmosphere for outdoor philandering? As for the technicalities, one mention of Forbes's name brought me into the presence of the head librarian of the art college. To be honest, I had thought of asking Louise to undertake this rather delicate task; but I would have been as embarrassed to broach the subject with her as I was to face the earnest young woman in person. With the hint of a smile, the librarian whose steel-grey crop belied her age and, I feel, her nature, disappeared into the stacks. She returned with an armful of books ranging from scholarly texts to fashion catalogues. I followed her to a table.

'To answer your question,' she said without a hint of irony, 'I doubt if the new-fangled "closed" knickers would have found their way into the wardrobe of a Dundee schoolmistress of 1900. Frank Harris, if anyone can believe him, writes of his distress at discovering them on a young woman of fashion and wealth about that time, but as late as 1907, an advertisement for D. M. Brown's ladieswear department makes scarcely a mention.'

So you see, my dear, Forbes had planted a dángerous seed. Despite myself, I imagined a sudden glimpse of lace. Hot breath mingling in frosty air. Six indentations left in the light powdering of snow, which, I grant you, may well have covered higher ground at that time of year. Four knee marks, two and two, then two shallower marks where Ethel's hands, or more likely her elbows, to save her kidskin gloves, had sustained her against regular thrusts of the harpooner's lance. Have no doubt, our grandparents could manage such matters every bit as skilfully as we can.

To put it plainly, my dear, I was wracked with doubt. Time and again I reflected on the story Forbes had remembered from a night when 'we had both been drinking a lot of whisky'. My instinct was to dismiss it out of hand as an absurd attempt to embarrass me; in revenge, no doubt for my criticism of his sculpture. But how could he have known about the piece of amber missing from my grandmother's necklace? Forbes had planted the harpoon of doubt in my mind. I shall carry it with me always. Here's coffee. I'm glad you feel better. Of course I'll tell you more later if you feel up to it.

Chapter 22

TIME AND again since visiting Forbes in London, I found myself computing minimum and maximum gestation periods; counting the days of January 1900 most favourable for conception. I got my secretary to do some research and provide me with a neatly-typed calendar for 1900. I started by assuming that my grandmother would not have chosen a wedding day when she was likely to be incommoded by her natural functions. It seemed equally unlikely that, if she could avoid it, any young woman would embark on married life knowing that, within the first, precious, balmy days, she would fall victim to that bodily inconvenience. Physical probability, therefore, suggested that on the day Alexander Yule was purported to have achieved a coupling beneath arched jawbones, Ethel Wilkie would have been a thoroughly unsuitable target for such advances.

No sooner had I convinced myself of the logic of the physical approach, than I began to doubt its validity. Maybe avoiding such nuptial inconvenience had not been a deciding factor in choosing the wedding day. At that time holidays, even for senior employees, were few and far between. The promise of an extra day's leave might have been enough to tip the balance in favour of the first week in February. Or maybe the day was decided by the minister to fit in with other functions of the church. Speculation was futile. I turned to more tangible evidence. Like every family, the Dows possess photographs taken over the years and kept for no better reason than no one has thought of clearing them out.

In our case, the custodian of the archives is my mother. She's very old, but can quite readily remember the relationships of the men and women who gaze from pasteboard-mounted sepia paper. She has never quite got round to arranging her collection, preferring the informality of a large biscuit tin to a proper album. Shortly after we returned from London, Louise and I paid an overdue visit to the twilight home in which my mother lives. While Louise helped with tea, I was allowed to rifle the battered tin, which was so worn that only a vestige of the King's head remained on its surface. I was in search of evidence which might show that my father's features were not composed entirely of a blend of Wilkie and Dow.

I said my mother made no attempt to classify her collection. I was wrong. On prising off the lid, I discovered that a very basic and telling demarcation had been made. On top of the heap of photographs and postcards, there lay a plump, yellow envelope which, according to its markings, had conveyed the December 1937 edition of the *National Geographic Magazine* from Washington DC to one Miss H. L. Kinloch, King Street, Dundee. The address, which must have been where my mother lived before she married, meant nothing, but the contents of the envelope, when I spilled them on to the polished coffee table, revealed that at some time in the past, mother had segregated the photographs of her family from those of ours. The yellow envelope was stuffed full of Kinlochs. Standing, sitting, male, female, old, young, four generations of Kinlochs presented their features in upright and landscape format for my inspection. But who could spend time on the Kinlochs, whose stolid countenances belied any possible suggestion of a skeleton in their cupboard when, beneath the transatlantic envelope, the Wilkies and the Dows cried out for closer examination? Quickly, I sorted through the bundle. To save confusion, I chose only the prints that showed my father clearly either in profile or full face. There were surprisingly few.

The earliest, taken when he looked about nine, had an intriguingly nautical flavour. For a background, the photographer had chosen a painting of the Tay Bridge, rising above boisterous, white-capped waves designed to give the impression that the young John Montholon was adrift in a boat on the river. My father was even holding a ship in his hands; not, alas, a vessel fitted out for Arctic whaling, but a crude model of a 'B' Class destroyer. Neither was he dressed in a sailor suit, which in these days would have been all the rage and an ideal costume, but in a tight-fitting tweed jacket, matching knee-breeches and a little round cap with the peak pulled over his brow. His features displayed the plumpness of childhood, though a certain seriousness round the eyes already suggested to those who recognise such things, a thoroughly level-headed view of life. A view, in fact, most commonly achieved through a theodolite, which was to become my father's favourite optical instrument. I have been told that he was calmly surveying a ruined bridge through just such a device when the fatal shell fell.

The second photograph which had captured enough of my father's features to stand comparison must have been taken in the mid twenties. In this picture, he was not alone. He was one of a group of four young people posed beside a heavy, open touring car of the day. I had no difficulty in identifying it as an Alvis, and I knew the car belonged to him, though the photograph left ownership in doubt. For the benefit of the photographer, the group had formed an amusing little tableau round the vehicle. While one young man took the wheel, my father stood on the running-board and pointed to the two girls who were posed by the roadside a little way in front of the car as if thumbing a lift. The girls both had limp canvas rucksacks, though it was clear that as soon as the snap was taken, they'd toss them back into the car. One girl, a pretty little thing with dark hair, had daringly lifted the hem of her pleated dress to catch the motorist's eye with a shapely knee. My father's face was leaner. Lines of character were beginning to form. I laid the print aside and picked up the third photograph.

A stage photograph this time, half-plate format, slightly retouched and set against a theatrical background of windswept clouds. Father was in uniform: high-collared tunic; breast plate; crested helmet held stiffly in the crook of his arm. To emphasise the military aspect of the occasion, he had assumed a bristling, artificial moustache, which, together with false eyebrows, had been dusted with powder to bestow on a still youthful face the grizzled appearance of an elderly officer. His right hand rested lightly on the shoulder of a lady I have no hesitation in calling my mother, though she was well-nigh hidden by a huge bouquet of carnations. The caption, which had been professionally lettered at the bottom of the photograph identified the happy pair as: 'Patience and Colonel Calverley, 1933'.

The fourth and last photograph of my father continued the military theme. The uniform was decidedly less grand. The gold epaulettes and flashing breast plate of the Savoyard had given way to the drab battledress of a reserve captain. The shoulder flashes identified him as a Royal Engineer. He was standing self-consciously before a blackboard on which he was about to draw a diagram of vital military importance, but in the interests of security, the picture had been taken when only the words: 'Annual Camp, Camberley, 1938' had been chalked at the top of the board. By this time, my father had cultivated his own moustache: a clipped, austere affair in no way resembling the Victorian luxury of Colonel Calverley, but doubtless more fitting for the grim days that lay ahead. As far as I know, this was the last photograph ever taken of my father. I laid it beside the others and eagerly sorted through the older prints in search of the two likenesses which had come together to form his distinctive, if uninspiring features.

In the earliest photograph I could find of my grandmother, she was not alone. She was pictured with her class of twelve-year-olds, some of whom looked suspiciously young to be embarking on half-time education. A formal, institutional picture, designed not to flatter but to record for all time the thirty-two faces of Baxter's Class I 1896. Rather than diminish her importance, the sea of grubby faces that surrounded her emphasised her position at the centre of the children's world. She rose above the rows of puny artisans like a bold figurehead above the waves. Her dress was appropriately severe: full sleeves, high in the shoulder and stretching over the backs of her folded hands; a sombre, tight-fitting bodice relieved only by some modest frogging on the bosom and a wide, heavy skirt reaching to within an inch of the dusty schoolyard. In full command of the situation, Miss Ethel Wilkie showed no trace of the timidity frequently exhibited by women in those days when faced by the photographer's lens.

Alas, in the next photograph she had retreated behind a mask of conventional decorum. The wistful, modest smile showed nothing of her strength of character. Why had she adopted the supporting role? The answer stood behind her with his left hand resting on the shoulder of her silken dress. For the first time they were pictured together. For the first time she was Ethel Dow. The photograph must have been taken shortly after the wedding and been produced in sufficient numbers to send to friends and relations as a memento of the event. Although it was still virtually unknown for pictures to be taken at the church, the vogue for studio photography was at its height and it was not unusual for a couple to interrupt their wedding day for a visit to the photographer's shop. On the sumptuous mount, the words 'Thomsons Dundee N.B.' were embossed in gilt letters. What expression had the recently renamed Jock Dow adopted to match my grandmother's wistful femininity? He appeared a masterful blend of strength and compassion. The brilliant clarity of a glass negative revealed masseter muscles tensed into a firm jawline, while a short, vertical crease between pale eyebrows suggested a distant, almost tragic nobility. His moustache, too, was fair and only slightly upswept at the corners of his mouth. Soon he would experiment with patent waxes. This may well have been the only photograph taken of my grandparents together. If they stepped jokingly into any of the numerous photo-booths at the Paris Exhibition, the results have not survived.

In the next picture, she was cradling a baby on her knee and was already a widow. Both she and my infant father were dressed in black, but despite the pitifulness of their situation, there was no doubt her face bore an expression of insuperable self-confidence. On the other hand, the pale blotch that signified my father's tiny face among the folds of enveloping bombazine was so blurred that I didn't consider it a likeness at all. He must have squirmed during the prolonged exposure.

Only two other pictures of my putative grandfather existed. Both had been taken long before his metamorphosis, when he bore the name Jochen Dau and pronounced 'this' as 'ssis'. The earlier print could be distinguished by the wording 'Jantzen u. Biernatzki, Koenigsberg, O. Preussen'. Jochen, in sporting attire, posed amid low, rolling dunes that stretched, we must assume, to the Baltic. He was holding an old-fashioned, upright bicycle, and had already placed one foot on the pedal ready to mount. Why he should have chosen to cycle in such impractical terrain is a mystery, although the openness of his expression suggested the features of my father beside the blackboard. Were the similarities positive proof of paternity or simply coincidental?

No sooner were my hopes raised than the final photograph cast doubt on my assumption. It was a simple studio shot of Jochen Dau standing beside an ornamental pedestal with his right hand resting on its edge and his left holding a rolled parchment scroll bound with a silken ribbon. The sepia print had been detached from its mount, so there was no photographer's name to identify where and by whom this curious picture had been taken. Whether or not the scroll, which he held against his waistcoat roughly at the height of the watch chain, was a genuine diploma or merely a photographer's prop was impossible to tell. Similarly, the utter anonymity of background gave no clues. But something in Jochen Dau's guarded expression led me to think that here was a man with a secret. Here was a man who knew, even as he adopted an academic pose before the open lens, that elsewhere another man was masquerading in his stead. Herr Jochen Dau had hooded his eyes and struck a suitably serious expression, but he could not conceal the guilt. He refused to look the lens in the eye. I have absolutely no doubt that while one Jochen Dau was trying to convince the camera of his absolute soundness of character, another Jochen Dau, who had been invested with the name Lorentz and a five-digit serial number, was facing the prospect of an unexpected and tragically short life at sea. Perhaps the picture had been taken at Memel, before Dau presented his credentials to the kindly linen manufacturer who took him under his wing. To compare the honest frankness of my father's face with this image of deceit was to compare chalk and cheese. As I gazed at the two little rectangles of pasteboard, there seemed to me every possibility that the owner of the name Dau, the name I bore myself regardless of spelling, had been my grandfather in name only, and in a borrowed name at that. The real title had been stolen by a man named Yule, who had sealed the bargain beneath the jaws of a whale.

A comparison was needed. But how could I compare the features of Mr Jock Dow in both Teutonic and Caledonian mode with my putative grandfather when not one likeness of Alexander Yule resided in the biscuit tin? Despite the deep impression Yule had made on the Wilkies, the evidence suggested that he had passed from their lives without leaving a single photograph to be remembered by. One by one I showed the pictures that remained in the tin to my mother. One by one she put names to the sepia images. But not one name was Yule. I borrowed such photographs of the Dow family as were necessary to make a fair comparison and took my search to the banks of the Tay.

In an anteroom in Broughty Castle (you really must make time to see it) the assistant curator of the whaling museum offered me tea and biscuits and expressed polite interest in my investigation. There were indeed several photographs and glass negatives in her possession showing officers and crews from the whaling days, but few of them were captioned, if I didn't mind her saying so, when it came to the lower ranks. Not, of course that a specktioneer was necessarily a lower rank, but on the whole it was not usual to have such a person named on a group photograph. Not in her experience. Adopting another tack, I asked if the museum possessed any photographs of ships' companies for which there were also crew lists in existence. Files were opened, cross-references made. The assistant curator, who was really quite pretty despite her spectacles, let her tea grow cold and at last assembled on the baise table-top, a series of photostatic copies of crew lists and pink file cards to represent the corresponding photographs. Eagerly I scanned the list of names. *Terra Nova* 1895, Capt. M. McKay, 1st Mate R. Kilgour, 2nd Mate P. Deuchars . . . *Balaena* Capt. Murray, 1st Officer A. Henderson, 2nd Officer Wm Smith,

3rd Officer J. Bryce, Specktioneer Wm Laurenson . . . *Esquimaux* Capt. Yule . . . a red herring. Our specktioneer had no interest in high command. *Ultima Thule* c. 1896 Capt. T. Jamieson, 1st Mate Wm Robertson, 2nd Mate J. Seath, 3rd Mate A. J. Milne, Specktioneer A. Yule . . .

I handed the file card to the young woman. Seven-nine-six stroke two. Unfortunately there would be a delay. The suffix 'two' denoted a glass negative. A proper print would have to be made and that would take time. But if I cared to leave my address together with the appropriate fee. I told her to forget postage. I was planning to spend quite some time at the harbour and would call to pick up the print when it was ready. Fine. Perhaps another biscuit before I left? It had all been most interesting. Most out of the ordinary, so to speak.

A week or so later, when I was maybe half way through Muirhead's impromptu and expensive course in small-boat handling, but more of that later, I looked into the castle to pick up the print. My first reaction was disappointment. I had expected a haunting, sepia-tinted picture like those of Ethel and Jock Dow. When I slid it from the envelope, taking care my grubby fingers held only the edges, the starkness of the glossy black and white image shocked me. But why should the municipal photographer have wasted time adding a purely cosmetic tint? Glass negatives never lie. It was all there in black and white. The officers and petty officers of the *Ultima Thule* had been pictured not as I had expected in Arctic wastes, but lined up along the quayside in Dundee with the ship's hull as the backdrop on which the worn letters *Thule* were just visible. Sunday best had been the order of the day. Curiously, not one of the eight men in the photograph was wearing what could properly be called a uniform. The captain, whose rank was evident by his position at the centre of the composition, had chosen a black frock coat and top hat which, even for c.1896, must have been behind the times. In his huge, square hand, he held a walking stick which I at once recognised as a narwhal's tusk. I placed him around sixty: a good twenty years ahead of the next oldest of the group. This man I took for the chief engineer. He wore a tight-fitting, single-breasted jacket with dark piping on the lapels and a matching bowler hat cut much lower on the crown than is the fashion today. Something in his dress suggested a man who had acquired a little style, which would accord with someone who had served a long apprenticeship in the city and travelled the world before settling for the position of Chief aboard a whaling ship. Only one other member of the group was easy to identify. Standing second on the captain's left was a burly gentleman in a Norfolk jacket looking exactly as if he had stepped off a grouse moor to join the little party. Without hesitation, I put him down as the ship's surgeon, likely a recently-qualified doctor who had decided on a season of adventure before settling down to medical life. Whaling ships seldom carried the same surgeon for more than one trip, but there was never a shortage of recruits.

What of the other characters in the line-up? The fellow on the captain's right I took to be the first mate. He was bearded and held his bowler as if unaccustomed to such an impediment. To the left of the captain stood a lad barely twenty years old. He wore a pilot coat buttoned to the throat, and from under his arm there protruded the patent-leather peak of a steaming bonnet. He must be the third mate, newly made up from apprentice. At the extreme left of the line was the only man in working clothes. He was clearly a sailor, with an oilskin smock and white canvas trousers. My guess was that the bosun had been asked to come down from the deck to make up the party, which left two unidentified figures and a deep dilemma.

I assumed that the remaining two men were the second mate and the specktioneer. But which was which? Both seemed in their early thirties. Both were soberly dressed in dark suits. Both wore heavy moustaches and, though one had a considerably thicker head of hair than the other, it was quite impossible to say which was Alexander Yule. In fact both looked disconcertingly similar to the photograph of my father as Colonel Claverley. Time and again I compared the two faces in the old picture with my father at different stages of his development. Now I'd see a resemblance to one of the men, then to the other. For example, though my father retained a fine head of hair till the end, my hair line began to recede early. Such characteristics can skip a generation. If my research could be said to have achieved anything, it was that the visual evidence had convinced me that my father was just as likely to have been engendered by either of these seafaring men as by the cosmopolitan inventor of oilcloths. And this, more than anything else, filled me with the determination only a nagging doubt can provoke. On the edge of Broughty Ferry harbour, as I gazed at the brutal, black-and-white print of the ancient negative, I finally resolved to play Forbes at his own game and to beat him.

And now, my dear, let's call it a day. I'm afraid our walk has set my feet tingling. Maybe we went too far, but I enjoyed it. Of course you can borrow the photographs. I would have shown you them now, but I returned them to my mother as soon as I'd done. You know how old folks worry about losing things. I doubt if your readers will want to see a motley crew of Dows when you must have so many shots of Forbes on file, but you know best.

Chapter 23

SORRY YOU had to wait. My left foot's playing up, and on a morning I'd have preferred to stay in bed, Inspector McCreath and his worthy constable paid us an early call. He didn't say what he was after. Just a few general questions. Raking over cold ashes. Someone had given him a chart and tide tables which we looked at for a while, but my memory refused to jog. He also dropped a few hints about the post mortem. Nothing unexpected. A report, as they say in these parts, will go to the procurator fiscal. It will take a while.

Today I want to tell you how Forbes and I made our plans. As always, Forbes pulled the strings. I became so busy I had to take time off work. I went to college. Three days a week, I sat in with students a third my age and learned about video. Night classes would not do. Forbes prescribed a crash course and I was welcomed to the School of Visual Communications with courtesy and apprehension.

The waterborne skills were up to me. I picked a night when Muirhead was working late. When at last the lights went out and he emerged to close the doors of his shed, I stepped from the shadows and offered to buy him a drink. I steered him to a quiet corner and came straight to the point. Muirhead is not an easy man to disconcert, but when I outlined my plan (I made no mention of Forbes for the moment) I came closer to dumfounding him than anyone had in years.

'You want to hire a boat?'

'And to learn to handle it.'

'But not a sailing boat?'

'Something fast and reliable that can take me well off shore.'

I imagined all sorts of suspicions entering Muirhead's mind where they would be no match against the prospect of ready cash. He lit a cigarette and scrutinised me through the smoke.

'What kind of a boat? Is it for fishing, maybe?'

'I'll leave the boat up to you,' I said. 'Something you can teach me to handle in a couple of days. Something that won't sink.'

Muirhead adopted pensive, calculating mode. I could have predicted his words.

'Going to cost you, Mr Dow.'

'I know.'

'Give you a bell next week.'

The bell duly came and I drove to the harbour. Muirhead was deep in conversation on his mobile phone, so I strolled over to the edge of the tidal basin and tried to spot an unfamiliar boat. There was only the usual mixture of day boats and laid-up yachts. Then Muirhead appeared. Without a word, he led me round behind his shed. On the shadowy wasteland stood a heavy, four-wheeled trailer; and on the trailer was a long, low, grey, sinister, rubber boat. With a few swift movements that scarcely disturbed the ash on the end of his cigarette, Muirhead unfastened a tarpaulin at the after end of the boat and drew it back to reveal two huge outboards mounted beneath a sort of tubular framework. He stepped back, awaiting approval.

'It's rubber,' I said.

'It's a RHIB,' he said tetchily. 'Rigid hull inflatable. Navy use these. SBS. You name it. You'll get well over thirty knots no bother. And it's just like driving a car.'

'Fine,' I said hurriedly. 'If you think it will do the job.' In the half-light, I noticed an oil-company logo inexpertly blocked out with grey paint.

'If you knew the trouble I've had getting this.'

At that point I gave up counting money. Muirhead had scribbled down a list of essentials. There was a towbar for my car, which was just about powerful enough to pull the boat and trailer. There was the question of clothing. A wetsuit? A drysuit? Muirhead looked me up and down and finally suggested the sort of survival suit worn by oilmen in the North Sea. Roomy enough to work in, but insulated and with built-in flotation. He had a source.

'You'd better get two,' I said in an off-hand sort of way.

'Don't need one.'

'I may want to take a friend. Much the same build as me. A few inches taller; a few pounds heavier.'

Muirhead was right about the boat. Within days, I could steer it slowly out of the harbour, then open the throttle and roar across the river in a sheet of spray and petrol fumes. Astride the pilot seat, behind the tiny, perspex windshield, it felt closer to riding a motorcycle than driving a car. Dials showed the state of the engines. There was a compass beneath a perspex dome weathered to near opacity. Other holes in the console were masked by plastic sheeting.

'No VHF,' said Muirhead. 'But a mobile should work from where you're going, and you won't be sailing in the dark.'

Muirhead crouched beside me in his drysuit, now and then yelling instructions into my ear through a cupped hand. I was exhilarated. My survival suit kept out the bitter cold, but my face and hands soon became weatherbeaten to a nautical brick-red, which led to inquisitive remarks from my fellow students and a half-serious inquiry by Louise about visiting sun-bed parlours. My secret fear of sea-sickness never materialised. Concentration drove it from my mind. Day after day, my confidence increased. There was a setback when I entangled the propellers in some floating mooring lines coming into harbour, but in two weeks, Muirhead had to concede there was nothing more he could teach me. But his curiosity would not die down. He wanted to know what I was up to. So did other people who pottered around the harbour and had noticed the big rubber boat thrashing the water and making the yachts dance and strain at their moorings. I decided to tell some of the truth.

'A friend wants to make a video out there at the mouth of the Tay. He asked me to help him. Arrange a boat and so on.'

Muirhead looked far from convinced.

My fellow visual communicators were curious too. They

couldn't work out why I was so keen to know how to use a camera, but showed no interest in editing. I often interrupted the instructor with questions.

'How do you maintain focus if the subject is moving about? How do you keep things in frame if you're shooting from a moving platform like a boat, say?'

The young man explained gyroscopic mounts. 'Expensive, but well-nigh foolproof. Are you hoping to do some action work? Nature, or sport maybe?'

'Maybe.'

We took a camera into the streets. In groups of three, we roamed Dundee recording faces, incidents, townscapes. Where I might meet colleagues, or worse, clients, I pulled up the hood of my anorak and hoped for the best. Then came a little project. By chance, but not surprisingly, my group was given the *Discovery*. We spent a damp day recording queuing children; bored faces, glistening rigging. Everyone wanted to be the director. Jason wedged himself beneath the companionway. He wanted legs descending into the cabin. He got a mouthful from a teacher who spotted the electronic eye focused on her knees. Sam couldn't keep her eyes off the crow's nest. She wanted to shoot from the barrel at the top of the mast. Despite the warnings, she set off up the slippery shrouds. She didn't make it. Her legs were too short or the ratlines too far apart. Maybe she lost her nerve. She froze about fifteen feet up, and to save face, shot the heads of people filing past below. She shot the attendant who shouted at her to come down, and Jason who shouted not to drop the camera. It took her ages to climb down and she was covered in grease and tar. Her hair was plastered to her head. She told Jason she wished she'd gone with the other group to the Verdant Works. A jute mill turned into a museum. Boring but indoors. While they argued, I gently asked for the camera and took a few shots on deck. Whenever I could, I turned towards the river, focused on the waves, tried to experience their movement. My young colleagues were frustrated. I knew the ship inside out. While they scrambled over the famous relic, looking for angles, embarrassingly getting in the way, I tried to come to terms with motion through a viewfinder. It didn't last. I soon surrendered the camera once more. I thought of borrowing Jason's mobile, but didn't want to spoil his concentration. My office was ten minutes away, but in the end I called Forbes from a payphone in the tearoom.

'I think I'm ready. Time for a dummy run.'

He was less excited than I expected. I heard tango music in the background. He could not come north for ten days. I explained the technical difficulties.

'We're going to need a gyro-mount. The college doesn't have one. Even if they did, they'd never lend it. It's so expensive.'

'It's all taken care of. Fax a list of anything else you need. I've got contacts in video-hire.'

'Couldn't you hire a cameraman as well?' I said. Forbes laughed. There were people talking in the background.

'This one's between you and me,' he said. 'You'll do just fine.'

The unexpected delay let me go back to work. News had reached my partners that I was spotted zooming around Broughty Ferry bay. Eyebrows were raised. Ad hoc explanations called for. I repeated my tale about helping with a wildlife video. Eyebrows were raised further. In the mail that had accumulated during my absence, I found a letter which my secretary had marked 'Personal?' She knows me well enough not to ask questions. I have it here. Yes of course, my dear, I'll read it into the microphone.

Copeland, McArthur Ltd
Searchers of Public Records
Edinburgh

Mr G. H. Dow BL
Scrymgeour, Dow and Chalmers WS,
Dundee

Dear Mr Dow,

<u>Peter Hamilton Pye</u>

In accordance with your letter of 17th inst., we have pleasure in enclosing the following information on the late Peter Hamilton Pye of Dundee.

1. The death certificate lodged at Register House states that Peter Hamilton Pye, son of Robert Maxwell Pye, factory owner, and Euphemia Hamilton died in Springfield Hospital, Springfield, Fife, on 3 November 1934. Cause of death is given as pulmonary pneumonia combined with corybantism. (The latter is an outmoded medical term describing a condition characterised by constant morbid involuntary wild dancing movements. It was frequently attributed to syphilis.)

2. A search of the records of Springfield Hospital, which at the time was the chief lunatic asylum for north Fife, shows that Mr Pye was admitted on 20 July 1913 and remained there until his death. His previous address was given as c/o the Parochial Hospital, Dundee. Further investigation shows that the admission date coincides roughly with the removal of Robert Maxwell Pye and his wife from West Ferry, Dundee, to Strathkinnes in Fife, presumably on his retirement from business. There is no record of the personal effects of Peter Hamilton Pye either at admission or at the time of his death. We could find no reference to any particular footwear in his possession.

3. At Register House, we consulted the records of Peter Hamilton Pye's parents and discovered that the death of his last surviving parent (his father) occurred in June 1922. No further relatives of any sort could be found. Under the circumstances, it is puzzling that nowhere in any records we could find is a *curator bonus* appointed for Peter Hamilton Pye. As for business interests, records show that Pye's jute mill, which was known as the Jupiter Works, was wholly purchased by Cox & Co. in 1912. We await your further instruction should you wish us to investigate the disbursement and subsequent history of any funds involved in this transaction.

4. With regard to any possible convictions sustained by Peter Hamilton Pye, we examined the records of Police, Burgh and

Sheriff Courts in Dundee, Cupar and Edinburgh for the years 1899 to 1913 inclusive.

During this period, only two persons with the surname Pye were convicted. The first, John Silas Pye of Colchester, was convicted of stealing a suitcase on Waverley Station, in July 1902 and sentenced to one year's imprisonment by Edinburgh Sheriff Court. The second conviction was of Bertram Pye (or Pie), seaman, of Liverpool for breach of the peace in a public house in Leith on 5 May 1906. He was fined £5 at Leith Police Court. The fine was paid by the captain of his ship. We are sure that neither of the above cases concern the subject of your inquiries.

Drowning of Shoemaker in Leith between 1880 and 1899

1. We have researched police reports submitted to the procurator fiscal concerning bodies recovered from the water in and around the Port of Leith during the above years.

   A total of 79 corpses were recovered, of which 69 were identified. Of that number, none is listed as being or having been employed as a cobbler or shoemaker. Of the unidentified corpses, five were those of children, two were women and one was a male negro. The two remaining males were described as being approximately 25 and 70 years old respectively.
2. No police records of missing persons are extant for the period you specify. We researched back numbers of the local newspapers for the years in question, but no shoemaker is reported as having disappeared.

It would, of course, be possible to research the death of every shoemaker listed as being in business in Edinburgh and Leith between the above dates, but as this would be a costly and time-consuming exercise, we await your instructions.

As you request, we shall submit our note of fee for this commission under separate cover and mark it for your personal attention. Assuring you of our best attention at all times, I remain,

Yours sincerely,

Walter P. McArthur
Copeland, McArthur Ltd

As you say, the Craigie Ghost was laid to rest. I had never expected corroboration of Forbes's tale from the only other eyewitness; but in my profession, I have found evidence in the strangest places. Who was to say there might not have been some notes or diaries among his perhaps numerous and sadly unrecorded effects? One trail was cold, and I held out little hope of success in the other line of inquiry I had set in motion. Continental members of the legal trade are even more notoriously slow than we are. I went back to work. Made up lost time. Buried myself in deeds and affidavits. The rubber boat lay on its trailer outside the house, gathering water in the intermittent showers. I drained it regularly by means of a rubber plug. Louise knew something was afoot, but she believed I had simply borrowed the boat at Forbes's request. She was excited at the prospect of seeing him again so soon, and accepted the impediment in the driveway without complaint. Once I heard her tell the postman it was going to be used for some artistic event on the water, which came uncomfortably close to the truth.

But enough of that. Before we open the throttle and plane across the far-from-silvery waters of the Tay, I must take you into the ice. To understand what happened only days ago, you must hear what took place around seventy-two degrees north almost a hundred years before.

Chapter 24

SET FIRM in the pack of the Davis Straits, the *Ultima Thule* thrust her bare yards against the Arctic wind and drifted westwards with the ice at a steady two knots. To the north and west, great fields of frozen floe stretched to the pale horizon, which, by day, formed a fluid mirage of refracted light. By night, the looming illusion gave way to a flashing rim of light, which, had the skyline not been blotted out by frequent snow-squalls, might have blossomed into aurora borealis. From the barrel high on the mainmast it was just possible for the lookout to spot tiny points of yellow light that showed where the whaler *Esquimaux* lay far to the west. Both ships had taken the pack together just north of Disco Island and had stayed in contact during the slow passage across the Straits. But in the last few days, the distance which separated the two ships had been widening. The ice surrounding the *Esquimaux* must already have been yielding as she approached the western edge of the pack. Two days earlier, they had watched with envy from the *Ultima Thule* as a sudden smudge of smoke on the horizon showed the other ship had started her engine in the hope of forcing her way out through a lead in the ice. From that moment, the distance separating the two ships had increased, and although the gales and freezing sleet had threatened both ships with equal fury, the crew of the *Ultima Thule* became more and more despondent the closer their rival came to clear water.

After her second visit to the sealing grounds, they had

refitted the *Ultima Thule* in a frenzied fortnight at St John's. The makeshift barracks and messrooms for the sweilers had been dismantled. The wooden sheathing had been stripped from her decks and a fresh coat of paint slapped over her battered topsides. Then the steam derrick lifted aboard all the whaleboats and tackle, all the harpoons and Greener guns* and flensing knives and all the staves and hoops for barrels that had been stored in the compound when the ship was hunting seals.

While in Nethergate, Ethel Dow accepted Mrs Dalgleish the dressmaker's, heartfelt condolences and chose a cut of mourning that allowed for expansion, her brother Harry, unaware that his recently acquired status of brother-in-law had been rapidly superseded by that of prospective uncle, sweated along with the few remaining day-workers to load coal from the procession of horse-drawn wagons that slogged through the mud to the ship's side in the relentless Newfoundland sleet. He was glad when the last bag was tipped down the hole and the cast-iron cover was heaved into place. They sailed at dawn.

It would be amusing to imagine Harry and his shipmates defying Pinnacle Tam and spending their last night ashore in one of the grim little saloons. Not a patch on the Barbary Coast, but well worth a yarn back in Tommy Allen's bar. Would Alexander Yule have been invited, or was there already a distance between Harry and the specktioneer? Days at sea are perfect for working a loose fibre of doubt into a tight knot of suspicion, no matter how preposterous the source.

With her company reduced once more to those who had signed on in Dundee and Stromness, the *Ultima Thule* seemed curiously deserted as she made her way into the cold, grey gulf of the Davis Straits. Harry Wilkie's job, monotonous as it was, left

* Greener gun: a generic name for swivel harpoon guns mounted in the bows of whaleboats. Their effect was to fire a harpoon about 100ft (30m), an improvement on hand-thrown harpooning, which they augmented, but never replaced, in the Artic fishery. Greeners were made in Birmingham, though the first wholly effective gun of this type was built by Wallis of Hull. Guns of a similar pattern were produced in Dundee, Norway and the United States.

him time for little else but work and sleep as the ship bore north into increasingly heavy weather. The sickness that had gripped him on the Atlantic crossing did not return, but the constant fear that he might be gripped by pain drained his energy more than the toil of feeding a hungry fire on a constantly pitching deck. Harry seldom met Yule during the passage to the mouth of the Davis Straits. This was the specktioneer's busiest time: checking the whaleboats and equipment; preparing the killing lances and bomb darts;* packing powder into cartridges. From their first day out of Newfoundland, a constant lookout was kept from the masthead. Finner whales were rumoured to be about. Muffled to the eyes, Alexander Yule paced the quarterdeck with Captain Jamieson. They fell into deep and secret debate at any hour of day or night as the ship ploughed ever closer to the whaling grounds.

Let me show you this map from Scoresby. You'll appreciate the quality of engraving. It predates our voyage by seventy years, but in the Arctic, in the days when all the factories in the world could never warm the globe, when soot from Baxter's chimneys only blocked the sun from the yard of the Half-time School, certainties were engraved to last. It's still true. All the pack ice in the Davis Straits tends to move west. The east side clears first; so to get north early to where the whales might be found on the edge of the floe, you try to find a passage along the eastern or Greenland coast. Captain Jamieson had intended, as he made his way north, to fish the grounds between Resolution Island in latitude sixty-one degrees north and Disco Island, which lies off the coast of Greenland in latitude seventy degrees north. After Disco, the *Ultima Thule* and her sister ships had no option but to take to the pack and wear their way across the Straits locked in the ice till they reached clear water on the western side. But luck was not with them. Bad weather and scarcity of whales had limited sightings to two. Only once did Pinnacle Tam think it safe to lower the boats. Their crews spent four hours in heavy seas and returned frozen and demoralised with nothing to show but

* Bomb darts: explosive projectiles fired by a darting gun into captive whales to hasten their death. Bomb lances had a similar function, but were hand held, the charge being detonated on impact.

swamped boats and missing oars. In one boat, an Orkneyman called Norquoy suffered broken ribs when his oar parted at the gunwale and the broken end struck his chest. When the boats were at last secured to their davits, Jamieson had decided to abandon any hope of catching whales on the northward passage, and to make for the pack ice as quickly as possible in the hope of better fishing to come on the western side of the Straits.

Harry Wilkie had seen nothing of this drama. While his shipmates had been vainly trying to spot the ribbed back of a finner whale amid wicked, windswept waves, he and Tom Bell had fed the furnace deep in the hull of the wallowing ship. But later, in the forecastle, surrounded by silent, exhausted men who slept or stared blankly from the shadows of their bunks as their sodden clothing steamed before the stove, he realised the danger these men had faced and accepted and would face again.

When the *Ultima Thule* at last took the pack a little north of Disco, the ship's routine changed completely. In the grip of the ice, fishing was impossible until the west side of the straits was reached. In fact any thought of catching a whale was so utterly abandoned during this time that it was common to remove several whaleboats from their davits and stow them inboard, and to take out the whale-lines and other tackle from the remaining boats to lighten them in case the ship should be crushed in the ice and have to be evacuated in a hurry. To minimise the chances of disaster, the old whaling skippers always tried to enter the pack ice if not actually in company with, at least within sight of another ship, so that mutual assistance could be rendered if need be. This practice also bolstered the spirits of the crews, who felt they were not entirely deserted during the long days in the ice. So when the steamer *Esquimaux* broke free of the pack and slipped rapidly away over the western horizon, the older hands aboard the *Ultima Thule* began to grumble as only old seamen can about the devilish luck that had left them set in the ice while their rival steamed off to fresh fishing grounds. Despite the frequent snow squalls that beat upon the ship, despite the Arctic wind that swept streamers of powdered ice from the crests of the floe, Captain Jamieson was confident that three more days would see them clear of the ice and into clear water. To emphasise his optimism, he set an extra lookout in the forward crosstrees during daylight with orders to report the least sign of movement on the ice, whether it be a flash of darkness in the icefield signifying a lead to the floe's edge, or the sudden glimpse of an animal, a walrus or seal maybe, that might provide sport and profit for the despondent crew. The chief engineer was told to be ready to raise steam at one hour's notice, and, as expected, the sudden activity both above and below decks had a marked effect on morale. It was in this new spirit of anticipation, during a lull between squalls, when the lookout in the barrel on the mainmast, who had the advantage of a powerful telescope, shouted out through his speaking trumpet and pointed north-east with his signal pole. At once, those men who happened to be on deck scrambled into the rigging while the mate sent below for the captain and the specktioneer. By the time they arrived on deck, the lookout had clambered down from the barrel and was thumping his sealskin mittens against his chest in a cloud of icy powder. Yule was first on the scene.

'Well, Davie?'

'Twarthree seahorses on the floe maybe twa mile noreast.'

Jamieson emerged from the companionway in time to catch the Orkneyman's words.

'You're sure they're not old bull seals?'

'Ower big for that, Captain.' The captain and the specktioneer exchanged a glance, and while the old man returned below, Yule chose two men to accompany him on the hunt then followed the captain down the companionway. Jamieson was first back on deck in a long coat of seal fur and a knitted helmet that covered his ears. Regardless of this encumbrance, he climbed the ladder on the after side of the mast with ease and disappeared through the trap door in the bottom of the barrel. Yule had picked Dickson, an old Dundee harpooner with a keen eye for a gun-sight and Davie Groat, the lookout who had first spotted the walrus. They soon appeared wearing thigh-length oilskin waders, thick, woollen mufflers and such jerseys, pilot coats and jerkins as each felt necessary to face the cold on the ice. As well as his gun,

Dickson carried a sealpick to help him cross the treacherous floe. Round his waist he had coiled a foreganger: three fathoms of the finest white, untarred, hempen rope which was normally spliced between the hand harpoon and the whaleline. Dickson was canny. Dickson took no chances, which was why he was so old. Groat carried only his rifle and a slender pole topped by a small, triangular flag to mark their kill in case worsening weather forced them to abandon it on the ice. Yule also travelled light. In the little canvas rucksack slung low in the small of his back, he had packed oatcakes and six slices of salt pork along with extra cartridges. If the cook had not already drawn the galley fire, he would have had a flask of sweet tea as well. When Alexander Yule went on to the ice, he took care of himself.

It was just after six in the evening when the three men climbed down the ladder hanging against the timbers of the ships side and set off across the floe. The men on deck watched them for a while in the crisp, clear air, and smoked their pipes and spoke about walrus that had been caught in past seasons and walrus that had escaped. But the wind was so cold and the hunters' progress so desperately slow that, within the hour, the only eyes which followed them were those of the mate on the quarterdeck, the single lookout in the forward crosstrees and the old captain in the barrel on the mainmast, whose presence was signified only by an occasional glint of light when the sun caught the lens of his telescope.

The surface of an ice floe, particularly near the seaward edge, is one of the most dangerous expanses imaginable to cross. The ice, which has been forced by a season of gales and tide into craggy, angular ridges and deep snow-troughs, is often scattered with shallow pools of ice-cold water that look, in the refracted Arctic light, so convincingly like snow it is impossible to walk any distance without plunging into one, sometimes to the waist. Within an hour of leaving the ship, all three men were wet. They had expected this, and dressed accordingly, but the shear toil of removing thigh-high waders every couple of hundred yards to empty the water soon had its effect. Dickson, the old harpooner, and young Groat, who, despite plenty of stamina, lacked experience, gradually fell further and further behind Alexander Yule, who had a better feel for the ice and was less frequently obliged to wade cursing from a frozen pool. Maybe the prospect of a good bag of seahorses was enough to spur on the specktioneer. He understood their scarcity and elusiveness, and how time wasted crossing the ice could easily mean the difference between a well-judged shot and loosing off a bullet after a fleeing walrus.

When the next squall came, casting a bleak shadow over the glittering beds of ice, Dickson and Groat were still visible from the barrel of the *Ultima Thule*, and Yule had only just passed out of sight behind a distant ridge of ice. He must have been almost within rifle shot of the walrus, which the old captain could see hanging about at the edge of a lead through the ice, apparently oblivious to human presence, though the ship was upwind of them. The squall came between the ship and the hunters on the ice with uncanny speed. As the horizon turned to a belt of impenetrable grey, Jamieson climbed slowly to the deck. Another lookout went aloft at once, but as the captain passed the mate on his way to the warmth of the saloon, he said, 'We'll not see a thing for an hour at least. I dare say I heard a shot before I came down. Maybe two.'

'I canna say I made them out,' the mate replied, and huddled close in the lea of the companionway as the captain went below.

On the frozen waste, crouched in the shelter of a shelving ridge, the Orkneyman and the old harpooner had also heard two shots. Neither spoke. Neither tried to peer into the whirling wall of ice. But both knew Yule had got within rifle shot. They sheltered a full hour. When the wind dropped enough for them to stand up and look around, it was as if the rugged surface of the floe had been flattened out and smoothed off by the driven snow. The topmast of the ship was just a speck to the east, and though they could not see him, the lookout soon spotted their raised flag and pointed his signal pole in their direction. The mate scanned the floe, but could not see them from the quarterdeck. When Dickson and Groat at last found their bearings and set off in the direction from which they reckoned they had heard the shot, they found that, far from smoothing their way, the driven snow had merely drifted into the numerous crevasses in the ice, slowing their progress still further. Another hour passed. Neither spoke as they laboured up the last ridge, the older man just ahead of his companion. The walrus, which would no doubt have taken to the water when the squall struck, might have returned to the ice. There might be the chance of another shot. And Yule might well be lying in wait, ready to fire at the first movement in the snow. They crept forward gingerly: two black spots scarcely moving in the lens of the lookout's telescope. But when at last they reached the crest of the ridge and stood in a common cloud of frozen breath, there was not a walrus to be seen. Directly below them, on the glittering floe, lay the tiny black form of the specktioneer. Already, streamers of snow had drifted across his legs. He seemed to have mislaid his gun, though it might be hidden in the snow. They shouted, but neither was certain of a response to the dead echo of their voices. They didn't hurry. Dickson was cautious. Dickson took no chances. Though no walrus were to be seen, the men sensed there was something else besides them on the ice. The specktioneer had already sensed it. Why else would he lie so still? As they approached Yule's huddled form, Dickson and Groat let their eyes stray for just one second from the threatening ice-field. One glance was enough. There was no mistaking the tracks, already filling with powdered snow, that led from the crumpled figure on the ice. A single blow from a great ice bear had severed Yule's arm clean from his body and laid open the whole side of the specktioneer's chest. His poor, bursting heart was already beginning to cool amid a mess of shattered bone and torn pilot jacket.

Twenty minutes later, a party left the ship and set out across the ice. The lookout had seen the pennant being waved frantically far out on the floe where the walrus had been. The party was led by the mate, and consisted in the main of harpooners and boat steerers, who carried enough tackle to retrieve a number of walrus, and all the ship's remaining rifles save one in case they should meet more game on the ice. The man in the barrel kept them in view. Whenever they deviated from their course, he fired a shot to attract their attention and indicated with his pole whether they should bear left or right. As the party drew farther and further from the ship, the mate kept the lookout in view with his telescope until at last they spotted the tiny pennant before them on the horizon and struggled on to meet the sad little group on the ice. Harry Wilkie was on deck in the thin Arctic night by the time the search party returned to the *Ultima Thule*. As soon as they recrossed the distant ridge, the lookout had realised all was not well. Through his telescope, he had watched the tiny figures labouring across the ice, carrying between them a misshapen bundle lashed to Groat's flag pole. The burden that caused them to slip and stumble was not a walrus. The object so carefully being carried towards the *Ultima Thule* was not even a bull seal, for in the brassbound lens the lookout clearly saw it wore a pilot coat and thigh waders.

When they dumped Alexander Yule's remains on the frosty deck, the corpse was as stiff as if it had been taken from an ice-house. Harry Wilkie stood on the engine-room casing and looked over the heads of the silent men who gathered round the body, uncertain whether to stay, but unwilling to leave. Arrangements had already been made. By the light of a lamp in the tweendecks, the sailmaker was working with palm and needle on a strip cut from the least serviceable spare sail. No one thought to cover the remains of Alexander Yule, and as Harry looked down and saw the frozen face appear and disappear behind the uneasily shifting ring of legs, he felt a spasm as if all the pent-up vomit of the past months was about to break free. He jumped on to the deck and ran to the gunwale. When Harry at last opened his stinging eyes, the yellow splash had already frozen on the ice below. Nausea never quite left him for the rest of the voyage. As for the rest, they reacted to this forceful reminder of the precariousness of their existence according to their characters. Some muttered prayers. Others were silent. And those who most felt the loss of their shipmate, took on a mantle of exaggerated cruelty and speculated, with muffled jest, how the specktioneer had at last lost his touch. By the time Harry rejoined them, Yule's body had been firmly stitched into the sailcloth sheath after the effects had been removed from his pockets. If Harry had thought himself in any way a privileged friend of the specktioneer, he now saw that this had gone unnoticed in the eyes of the officers and men of the *Ultima Thule.* He stood aside as they hauled the stiff, canvas coffin across the deck and stowed it beneath a spare whaleboat until Pinnacle Tam decided on the burial arrangements.

In the forecastle, as the rescue party dried off and the off-duty sailors questioned them about the mishap on the ice, talk began about the specktioneer's bad luck. Old Dickson could not believe Yule had died simply through carelessness.

'If there was a bear on the ice,' he said, 'Yule would have found it long before the bear found him. Unless they were both so surprised tae see one another he didna hae time tae fire. Ye see, Alex Yule kennt the ice so well, he might just hae thoucht exactly the same as the old bear. When he sees the squall comin, he fires off a couple o rounds on the off chance o gettin a seahorse, then he heads for the best shelter around. But the old bear has already picked out that spot for himself, so when Alex fires, it's just enough tae wake him up. Yule must hae stepped richt on top o him. He widna stand a chance.'

In the saloon, the captain and the mate drank pinnacle tea and speculated.

'What I don't understand is why the bear was anywhere near Yule in the first place,' said Jamieson. 'We had the walrus in view for well over an hour before the weather closed in. That would be plenty time for a hungry bear to try at least one kill. But for some reason, he worked his way diagonally across the ice away from the walrus towards the ship. He must have bumped right into Yule in the squall. Quite a surprise for them both.'

'We'll hae a look for the bear the morn when it clears,' the mate said half-heartedly.

'I doubt you'll have to look in Baffin Land,' said the captain which, as it turned out, was not as far fetched as he thought. Twelve hours later, the ice around the *Ultima Thule* showed signs of becoming rotten. The order to raise steam and start the engine followed shortly. The big, two-bladed propeller churned beneath the stern, fracturing the ice and forcing a porridge of rotten ice-sludge followed by a cascade of bright, clear water through the fissures in the floe. With a shudder that travelled the length of her frame, the old ship thrust her stem against the floe and butted towards the rim of the ice-field. Just before noon, she finally broke free and headed up the west coast of the Davis Straits. The lumpy rafts of rotten ice became fewer and fewer in the clear, cold water. Just before supper, the lookout reported the hilly coast of Baffin Land with its fringe of land-ice within range of his telescope. They were just off Cape Christian, not far from Clyde Inlet, where a little community of Eskimos and traders had its base. As night approached, the *Ultima Thule* made fast to the land-ice at the mouth of the narrow, rocky bay. When the pale, Arctic night lightened marginally into dawn, three whaleboats were swung out from the ship's side and lowered into the still, black water. The first was to take the captain and the burial party to the shore. Jamieson, whose Christianity had never quite been able to reconcile burial at sea with the resurrection, had decided to deposit Alexander Yule's remains in the barren burial ground above the settlement. The other boats struck out along the edge of the land-ice east and west of the *Ultima Thule*. They were on the bran: on the lookout for whales. Just before the captain's boat pulled away, the second mate appeared at the top of the stoke-hole ladder and shouted, 'Wilkie. Get ready tae go ashore. The old man wants ye at the funeral.'

Harry climbed the iron ladder with trembling arms. He rested against the angular rim of the hatch and gulped cold air. For the time being, the nausea died down. Harry hurried to the forecastle and splashed water over his face. By the time he shinned awkwardly down the rope-ladder to the boat, they were impatient to cast off. The boat lurched as he stepped on to the unfamiliar gunnel, and he was bundled into the bottom of the long, narrow boat as it sliced through the spray towards the shore. Beneath the thwarts lay the canvas bundle that contained the remains of Alexander Yule. A stain from the water in the bottom of the boat spread gradually up the side of the sailcloth cylinder, and as the boat rolled, the bundle swayed from side to side and pressed against the legs of the oarsmen. Harry Wilkie wedged his knee against the sailcloth shroud to try to keep it still.

The silent crew were nearing the western side of Clyde Inlet when an explosion out towards Cape Christian made everyone look up. One of the whaleboats had fired its Greener gun. It was just visible, rising and falling in the swell at the mouth of the inlet. Twenty fathoms ahead of it, half-hidden in the drifting foam, the great, flat flukes of a right whale rose, thrashed the spray, then plunged beneath the surface. The boat-steerer in the captain's boat signalled for the men to back their oars and keep the vessel steady so the old man could get a better view. Already, the men in the fast boat had raised their bailing piggin* on a pole to show they needed more whale-line. The second whaleboat was closing fast to help, and just out of sight round the headland, the mate, who had been left in charge of the ship, was hurriedly launching two more boats filled with the remaining whalemen. Slowly Captain Jamieson drew his pale eyes from the struggle unfolding before him to the pathetic bundle at his feet.

'Pull awa boys,' he said quietly. 'The fish can wait for a wee while yet.'

And as the whaleboat took to the shingle between the pitted lumps of land-ice, and the seamen jumped ashore to make fast, the dull blast of a darting gun sounded from the open sea.

* Bailing piggin: a small, one- or two-handled, open-topped cask used to remove excess water from whaleboats, pour water on whale-lines heated by fritction when fast to a fleeing whale and, in this case, as a rudimentary signalling device.

Chapter 25

NO, MY dear. There's no doubt whatsoever. Do you imagine I'd tell such a story without a hint of corroboration? Sadly, I missed out on the logbook of the *Ultima Thule*. I heard it was in Canada, and that it might be sold in a job lot of Newfoundland memorabilia; but by the time word reached me, the auction was over and it was firmly in the hands of the Arctic Institute at McGill Queen's. Here's their response to my inquiry, and a photostat of the relevant pages noting the death of 'Alxdr. Yule, Specktioneer, killed on ice by bear'; and 'Alxdr. Yule buried at Clyde Inlet'. The worthy professor, with whom I have developed a sporadic long-distance rapport, took an interest. He asked some students on a field trip to look out for the grave. Results were disappointing. Time and the unforgiving, icebound land had obliterated the whole graveyard, far less the plot where Yule was laid to rest. We must look elsewhere to find the mark he left on the world.

And Harry Wilkie? How did he react to the tragedy? With shock and with a sense of guilt that deepened as they spent week upon week in the northern sea. His depression lasted the rest of the voyage and I'm sure that was why he never again signed on a whaling ship.

You see, Harry Wilkie blamed himself. After they had sewn up the body, the men stood around on deck and wondered out loud what had made the bear set on the specktioneer when there were plenty of walrus to take its attention. Harry stood white and shaken in their midst. He remembered that just after the three hunters had set off, the galley boy had appeared at the top of the stokehole ladder with a bucket of swill in each hand. He said the cook had drawn the galley fire, so he couldn't burn it there, and Pinnacle Tam was against dumping rubbish on the ice for fear of attracting foxes. Tom Bell, the senior fireman, would not let the lad put his swill into the furnace in case it stopped up the firebars. They had to be ready to get up steam at a moment's notice. Harry thought he was being awkward. Bell soon went on deck to see the walrus, and when he was gone, Harry and the galley boy threw the rubbish on to the back of the fire and dropped the fire door so nobody could see it till it had burned away. It never crossed his mind that the wind might blow the smoke towards a hungry bear which happened to be watching the walrus with equal longing. Though his shipmates couldn't fathom what had distracted the bear, Harry was convinced it had been drawn towards the *Ultima Thule* instead of its natural prey by the smell of burning herring bones and salt pork fat drifting across the ice from her funnel. Pretty tempting for a hungry bear, you'll agree. He must have smelled it even in the blizzard and just kept coming towards the source of the scent. If he had been anywhere nearby before the squall started, Yule would surely have seen him. For though the coat of a polar bear may look white in a zoo or in the water, on the ice it is definitely yellow and anyone who knew about hunting could have spotted it. The specktioneer must have walked right into him in the snow.

Quite right, of course. The bear was never found, so I've absolutely no proof that it was male. Forgive me the incorrectness which I'm sure your article will put right; but in my mind it was a lone male on the edge of the floe that put paid to Alexander Yule.

Oh yes. Forbes knew all about Yule's untimely demise on the ice, but it left him cold. At least the silent, stalking ice-bear failed to inspire him in the way its European cousin had, whirling in a tangle of coloured washing. Too much white, maybe.

What about Ethel? Did Harry break the news to her?

You must remember the voyage was only two-thirds over when Alexander Yule was killed. The *Ultima Thule* made still further up the Straits on the Baffin Island side and even got a few whales, but the weather was always against her. Back in Dundee, Harry heard an old boy who had sailed on the *Nova Zembla* for years say that the weather in the season of 1900 was the worst any of the old hands could remember. When Harry stepped down from the cab and lifted his cabin trunk across the threshold of his parents' house, Ethel had already lost her husband, and the child was well on the way. Under the circumstances, Harry avoided upsetting her any more. He simply said they'd put Yule ashore in Canada and that he wouldn't be coming back. After the child was born and she seemed to have settled down, he told her what had happened. But Ethel didn't seem to care. Maybe she said, 'I might have guessed.' Nothing much more. The fine sealskins Yule had put aside for her were bundled up with his things and disappeared into the hands of the executors. Harry had a few skins of his own. He gave them all to Ethel, but she never had a winter coat made up. The skins hung around the house for years until my great grandmother finally took the huff and sold them to a man who came round the doors just before the Great War. She died not long after that.

But I must tell you about Forbes. You disguise your impatience well, though I see my ramblings annoy you so near the end of our story. When you replay the tape in the quiet of your room, you'll see the relevance of my half-imagined Arctic tales. Anyway, Forbes arrived at last in a brand-new, hired Range Rover packed with overnight bags, much-labelled metal cases of video equipment, lifejackets, yachting wellies, travelling rugs and the fair Inez, whom we'd last seen in Brown's Hotel. She shivered when the chill breath of the Tay entered their mobile cocoon. The run north had taken many hours. As Forbes paced about the driveway and stretched his arms and played the part of someone who has driven hundreds of miles, the women greeted one another like old friends. The door of the Range Rover was open. I noticed the seal-pick on the floor beneath the passenger seat exactly as someone might have discarded a shooting stick or golf umbrella. Forbes caught my glance.

'Familiarisation, old chap. I've been putting in a bit of practice on the road north. Getting the feel of things.' I imagined him in a layby, or more likely in the carpark of some stylish restaurant, wielding the pick like someone working on his swing. Forbes was impressed by the boat. He walked round and round the huge grey shape in the gathering dusk, running his hands over the cylindrical walls of the hull, heaving on the grab-ropes looped along the boat's side. We left the video gear in the car. It was well concealed. I could lock the gates to the drive and it would be pointless unloading it only to load up again next morning. For Forbes was keen on an early start. I couldn't imagine why there were so many boxes. For the first time, I began to doubt my ability to record Forbes's outrageous performance. I even doubted the capacity of the boat. But after dinner, when I spread charts on the table and he sat where you are sitting now and nodded his head and didn't once object to any of my proposals, my confidence returned. Forbes peered at the banks and shoals and the indigo blobs like dot-less exclamation marks that showed the lights around the mouth of the Tay. Forbes watched my nail as I traced the various options we had of reaching our goal. Then I put my finger on the spot and said,

'Have you ever been inspired by this particular chunk of half-tide rock? Southey certainly was, with his rhyme of the abbot and the rover; and even the eminently logical Stevenson must have been inspired to raise his lighthouse on such a dangerous reef.'

Forbes sat in your chair, one elbow on the table in a patch of light from the lamp.

'The Inchcape Rock,' he said. His voice sounded incredulous, almost shocked.

'I thought your spectacular event should happen in a spectacular place.'

Forbes removed his glasses and passed a hand across his brow.

'It's a dangerous reef.'

'That depends on weather and tide; and remember, the boat draws hardly anything. If we're careful we can land.'

'But the lighthouse. We'd be seen.'

'The Bell Rock has been automatic for more than a year. If we're unlucky and maintenance men are visiting, we'll see their boat before they see us, otherwise there will be nothing but birds and seals.'

'Wedderburn on Inchcape.'

'Wedderburn on the Bell Rock?'

'It doesn't have the same ring.'

Forbes's mind was made up. He wanted instant action.

'Let's do it tomorrow.'

'Steady on. I want some practice with your London box of tricks, and I must check the tides. We can't just jump into the boat and set off.'

Downstairs, we found Inez had let the cat out of the bag. Louise looked at Forbes with a mixture of admiration and disbelief. The fact that I had been chosen to commit Forbes's murderous antics to videotape amused her greatly. What she really felt about our plan was less obvious, but we were going to have an audience from then on.

And so it was a little convoy that arrived at Muirhead's shed next morning: my Mercedes towing the boat on its trailer and the Range Rover, whose owners had wisely avoided fitting a towbar, bringing up the rear. Inez still looked distinctly chilly. She went off with Louise to look at the harbour. If Muirhead recognised Forbes Wedderburn, he didn't let it show. We waited the obligatory five minutes until he finished filing something at his bench, lit a cigarette and glanced in our direction. But when I mentioned the Inchcape Rock, when I revealed our destination and asked when we should leave to get there at low tide, even Muirhead was surprised. He pursed his lips. He scratched his head. He thumbed an oil-smeared booklet of tide tables. To reach the rock when the tide was at its lowest, we'd have to leave harbour when there was virtually no water. Not even enough to float our rubber boat. So we'd have anchor it in the bay, or put it on a mooring like the lifeboat and paddle out in a dingy. But what about all the equipment? A night in a locked car was one thing, but in a rubber boat in Broughty Bay? And an extra boat moored off, even for one night, would attract the sort of people who frequent harbours and must know everything that's going on. Forbes was wary of revealing too much. Muirhead was determined to know. Why the Bell Rock? Why low tide? I told him half the truth.

'We want to video the seals. The longer the rock's uncovered the better.'

'You'll find seals nearer than that. What's wrong with Fife Ness?'

Forbes put in his twopenceworth.

'Inchcape Rock at low tide,' he said, as if repeating an incantation. 'The seclusion. The associations. That's where we're going.'

Muirhead sensed Forbes's determination. Perhaps he was impressed. There was no chart in his shed, but he found a road map of the east coast and spread it among the debris on his bench.

'Carnoustie,' he said. 'You might gain an hour or so if you launch off the beach. The trailer will be fine in salt water, but you'd maybe better practise once or twice.'

While the trailer might be fine, the Mercedes might not. Images came to mind of spinning tyres and wheels sinking to the axles before an advancing tide. But Forbes had taken the bait. We hurried out of the shed, and while he rounded up the women standing white-faced by the harbour's edge, I had a quick and terse word with Mr Muirhead.

'If you think I'm taking that thing on to a beach . . .'

'Just a thought, Mr Dow. If I were you, I'd leave from here. Put the boat right at the end of the pier, so you're the first one to float. Okay, you lose an hour.'

We drove north-east. Louise had climbed into the Range Rover with Inez. Forbes, who was leading, tried to reach the coast down tracks which were either blocked by the railway or led into the firing range at Barrie Buddon. I stayed on the main road and waited for his inevitable, frustrated return. We reached Carnoustie, and doubled back on to the shore road. Rollers broke on the deserted beach. Gulls were almost stationary in the wind.

'If you think I'm taking this thing on to the sand . . .' I said when Forbes appeared at my car door. He was already talking into the wind as I let down the electric window.

'Okay, okay. But let's practise. You must try out the gyro-mount.'

We all climbed out and stood in the wind. Forbes lifted boxes from the Range Rover. I was surprised when Inez crouched down and unfastened the catches. Most of the equipment, it seemed, belonged to her. Inez was a photographer, didn't we know? Forbes wanted a record of our preparations.

What's that, my dear? Yes, her surname was Christiani. Is she really so well known? But in your line of work, I suppose it's likely you'd have met. Call her when you get back to London. Corroboration of Forbes's plan from such a famous source will be invaluable. But let me tell you what happened at Carnoustie. Forbes and Inez assembled the gyro-mount and strapped it over my shoulders. Soon I was festooned in power packs and cables and counterweights. The camera was clamped to the mounting, I adjusted the viewfinder and set off along the track. And no matter how much I lurched and stumbled, no matter how I tried to skew the picture, the mount absorbed the impact and presented a steady image. I struggled on to the beach and focused on the waves. I bobbed and dipped to imitate the motion of a boat, but even my wildest movements could not unsettle the amazing device. When at last I returned to the cars, I found Louise alone in the Mercedes. Her mood had changed. With some annoyance she helped me off with the equipment ('Shouldn't you be able to do this for yourself?') and said Forbes and Inez had gone off alone to take some pictures. When I suggested we find them, she shook her head, climbed back into the car and turned up the stereo. I set off alone along the road that skirted the bay. Soon it was little more than a track. I had walked to the point where the road curved inland, leaving between it and the coastline a series of grassy mounds on which a handful of sheep were grazing when I heard voices on the wind. With some difficulty in my sailing wellies, I crossed the hummocky ground to the crest of one of the mounds. Below me, on the grassy slope between the hillock and the sea, was one of the most peculiar sights I have seen. Oblivious to my presence, Forbes and Inez were gamboling about in the dunes. Over and over again, Forbes raised the seal-pick and brought it slicing down on to a tussock of bent grass. Like a dancer in some modern ballet, Inez skipped and leaped round Forbes as he devastated the tussock, catching the action through her motorised shutter. Suddenly, she'd crouch beside one of her boxes, choose another camera or lens, then start again. Grass blew about wildly. Inez tripped and stumbled over the tussocks and Forbes sweated and grew redder and redder in the face. No wonder. He was wearing one of Muirhead's survival suits which he must have taken from the boot of my car. Forbes was clad from head to foot in fluorescent orange nylon, which appeared to double his girth and make physical exertion well nigh impossible. I started down the slope. My smooth soles compelled me to run to keep my footing. Forbes stopped thrashing about when he saw me coming. Inez let her Rolliflex drop on her chest as I slithered to a halt on the moist grass. Forbes anticipated my question.

'Stills,' he said. 'Low-angle shots. Only the sky as a background. We'll use them in posters.'

'But why are you that peculiar shape? You look just like the Michelin Man.' Forbes's florid face glared from its day-glo cowl.

'You said we'd need these suits for safety.' He fiddled with a nozzle that projected from the collar of the remarkable garment. 'Don't you know the top part inflates? The instructions say where there's a risk of danger the suit should be at least partially inflated.'

'I think the other one's a wee bit roomier,' I ventured helpfully. 'I've tried them both, you see.'

'But it's covered in logos,' he said. 'I'm not doing this to advertise oil.' And Forbes dropped the seal-pick and folded his arms across his bulging chest. As he pressed, the air escaped through the valve in a long, plaintive fart.

Chapter 26

I'M AI [illegible] her did Forb [illegible] e lid of one of h [illegible] tory in London [illegible] orbes a brave ar [illegible] e were tidebou [illegible] nd sun move ir [illegible] t their highest [illegible] hipped across th [illegible] a week would n [illegible] elieved but tried [illegible] re were commit [illegible] iss our triumpha [illegible] 'd even set foot on Inchcape Rock.

A couple of days after our escapade among the dunes, we left Broughty Ferry harbour on a tide so high you could almost step from the quay to the boat without a ladder. Forbes clung behind me like a pillion-rider in his orange suit as we made a wide sweep into the estuary. If he tried to talk, his words were lost in wind and spray. I felt his anxious hands grasping my shoulders. But as I brought the boat round and planed back towards the castle and the harbour mouth he let go. I craned round in surprise and found him astride the seat, clasping the grab-rail with one hand and with the other brandishing the seal-pick above his head. His face was wind-red, his glasses opaque with spray but his expression was ecstatic. I cut the speed, and as we swept between the granite piers I saw Inez with her camera at the edge of the quay, so close she might have fallen into the water. Forbes's triumphal return is on film. No doubt your editor can negotiate favourable terms. Inez didn't seem the sort who'd sell out to the tabloids. And after all, Forbes alive or dead is of only peripheral interest.

An interesting question. Inez phoned a week later to see how we'd got on. Louise broke the news. Of course she was in shock herself and apparently a little abrupt. We rather expected Inez to appear when the death was confirmed, but as you know, she's stayed away. Maybe she has other commitments. Maybe she'll show up at the funeral, though heaven knows when that will be. Ah yes, my dear. I quite understand your wanting to call your office before it closes. Use your mobile if you prefer, but you're welcome to our telephone. Good idea. Have a breath of air in the garden and I'll see Louise about tea. I hope you can stay this evening. I'm feeling much better now. The toothache in my toes has quite died down. You have a soothing effect, you know, or is it talking into your little black microphone that brings me peace of body as well as peace of mind?

How did we fill our tidebound, windswept days? We practised. We argued. We played cards. Forbes spent hours on the phone to the people who were going to edit whatever I managed to video on the rock. How could a non-existent tape take so much hot air? Forbes was becoming twitchy. Animals floating in formaldehyde were old hat, but there were rumours of worse excesses on the border where art meets anatomy. Real attention grabbers. He was afraid of being upstaged, of someone letting the cat out of the bag. He wouldn't even go into town for fear of meeting someone who might ask what he was up to.

For my part, I soon discovered the limitations of the gyro-mount. It was impossible to wear it and drive the boat at the same time. And try putting it on with the boat wallowing in the waves. I almost went over the side, mount and all. We tried to find a solution. When Forbes took the helm, he drove the boat like a car. He was incapable of keeping her head into the sea. We bobbed around like a cork with waves splashing over the gunwale. Eventually we decided to play things by ear.

'You'll just have to busk it on the day,' said Forbes. 'If we're both able to land, put on your kit on the rock. If not, shoot hand-held from the boat.'

A tide of despair washed over me. I imagined blurred, useless images. I told Forbes to find a professional cameraman. The tutor from the college would do. We were so close to shooting there was no chance of the secret getting out.

'Don't tell him what you're doing till we're out there.'

Forbes was appalled. He rushed to put his finger in the dyke, to stem the leak of confidence. Didn't I know what this meant to him? It was as much my idea as his. More! Hadn't I suggested the seal-pick? He found the weapon and put it in my hand. We were in it together. Shouldn't I take some of the credit? He'd even add my name to the title. How about that? Then he looked me in the eye through his tinted lenses and said, 'I expected the blood of a specktioneer, not a linen merchant.'

Oh yes, my dear. He piled on the agony. He pulled out all the stops. He hardly let me out of his sight until at last, late one night under Muirhead's sceptical eye, we tied the boat to the furthest rings in the harbour mouth and let it settle with the tide. Next morning at ten, we reckoned, we should just be able to reach it from the lowest rungs of the ladder. Forbes heaved on the mooring lines one last time. We turned and sauntered inevitably to the pub, which was full and almost closing. Time for one drink. I half-expected Forbes to bang the counter and propose a toast, but we drank in silence, soon broken by the landlord's electric bell, as if exhausted by the days of waiting.

We awoke to grey drizzle. Louise had laid breakfast in the conservatory. Forbes chewed bacon and watched the dripping leaves beyond the panes.

'It should clear. I heard the shipping forecast. The glass is rising at Fife Ness.' Impressed, Forbes beamed and offered me a place at my own table. Louise was on edge. She'd already said she'd rather not come. ('What's the point of waiting at the harbour?') We told her we'd be back by three and to stay near a phone, though I'd no idea if Forbes's mobile would work so much farther out to sea than Muirhead expected us to go. She waved us off in her dressing gown. More than she does when I go to the office. We took the Range Rover and drove against the thinning traffic towards Broughty Ferry. The drizzle was now little more than sea fog. Of course we were too early. The boat was still firmly on the bottom. Forbes changed into his survival suit, then took it off again as a watery sun burned through the mist.

'I don't want to cook in this damned thing just yet.'

We sat in the car and watched the deserted harbour. Even Muirhead's shed was locked and abandoned; unusual at that hour. I switched on the radio. When Forbes shot out his hand to turn it off before the sound had gelled to music or speech, I got out and walked away. I pulled the lines. The boat was just afloat. I turned to tell Forbes, to announce the inevitable, and saw our Mercedes turning past the bollards on to the quayside. Louise jumped out. She hurried towards the Range Rover, but then spotted me and changed direction. She was in jeans and a jersey, the first things that had come to hand, and ran with her arms clasped in front. There was a little package in her hand.

'A biker brought it from the office,' she said, gathering her breath. 'I thought I'd try to catch you.'

I tore away the courier's label to find an A4 envelope in mock-vellum. The stamps were French. There was a discreet ligature of A and V embossed at the lower corner, and alongside the carefully-penned address, my secretary had scribbled, 'This came first post marked personal. Thought it might be urgent.'

There was the sound of a closing door. Forbes was walking down the pier. Louise shivered in the sea air and clasped herself more tightly. I made a show of inspecting the ropes, then put my arm round her and led her towards Forbes. Before he could see that the boat was afloat, I shouted, 'Not long now. Fifteen minutes should do it.' Forbes stopped and turned back with us towards the cars. He eyed Louise and the envelope. I said, 'Something from work. Probably needs a signature. Why don't you get changed?'

Forbes said, 'Why don't you help me into this rubber monstrosity?' And Louise slipped from my grasp and followed him towards his car. I climbed into the Mercedes and read what I had almost given up hope of receiving.

Here are some photostats. You may see the original, but I dare say you'd rather I read the words into your wee machine. It's in English. No need to pardon my French.

Chapter 27

Maître Adolphe Vuillaume
281b Boulevard St Germain
Paris 7

Gilbert Dow Esq.

My Dear Gilbert,

At last I can reply to your fascinating letter. I apologise for the delay. For six weeks Geneviève and I have been in Nice, where her mother is seriously ill. A problem with the digestive system which needs constant medication. Happily Mme Vernet is a little improved and we returned to Paris last month. Your letter was awaiting me.

How curious and sad a story you tell. I had no idea your grandfather died in our city. As soon as commitments allowed, I showed the details to an old acquaintance who is employed in the records department of the *Préfecture de Police*. Within a few days, he verified that in April 1900 a British citizen named Jock Dow had indeed died in a traffic accident in the Square Montholon. Next of kin was listed as Ethel Dow, née Wilkie, of Dundee, Scotland, c/o Hôtel Beau Séjour, Bd Poissonnière. There was registration of death and a document recording the release of the remains from the city mortuary. No further details were to be found. It was so long ago. Many old documents were disposed of or lost during the war. But my friend, whose retirement is almost due, gave me a clue. In those days, routine reports of traffic accidents would not have been filed at the *Préfecture* but at the local station to which the *agent de police* was attached. After the passing of some time, they were either destroyed or removed for storage to the *mairie* of the *arrondissement* in which the accident took place.

During the next few days, a case concerning illegal fishing took me to Fécamp on the Normandy coast. A tedious dispute in which our case was lost from the start, but which dragged on day after day. When I returned, I visited the *mairie* of the ninth *arrondissement* in Rue Drouot. The building has hardly changed in a hundred years. There is something to be said for our leisurely attitude to municipal modernisation. I admit my enquiries were greeted at first with incredulity, and when I persisted, with truculence. No such record existed. But the building was so old. I was not convinced. There was still a chance. Then I remembered Gervaise Cavaignac is deputy for this district. A quick call, a few moments' time and *voilà*, I may search where I like. The conservator who comes with me is old. We find nothing. But at last he remembers some files in the mansard, right under the roof. And here they are. All the depositions of little crimes, little fights, traffic offences from long before the Great War. So much work. So much dust.

I made arrangements for Giradoux, an apprentice in our practice who is ponderous but dedicated, to examine the documents. It took almost a week. At last he found it. 'Fatal Accident at Intersection of Rue Baudin and Square Montholon, Saturday, 12 April 1900.' It was fortunate he recognised the document. For many years now Rue Baudin has been called Rue Pierre-Semard. The present Rue Baudin is located in Levallois-Perret, which is many kilometres from the ninth *arrondissement*. This at first confused Giradoux.

I had the original document photocopied. It is now very faint, being hand written in cheap ink, but at least it was kept from the light. Also there are many quaint phrases you might find difficult to understand. To explain these abbreviations and terminologies I have had a translation made which I enclose with the copies.

May I hope this serves to help your researches, and that it is not too long before Geneviève and I have the pleasure of meeting you and Louise again.

Your friend,
A. V.

How did I know him? A chance meeting years ago. I was in the chair of the local Law Society when a symposium took place in St Andrews. The Auld Alliance. French and Scots Law Compared. The aim was to find parallels in the systems. The result was to match handicaps on the Old Course. Adolphe and I were immune to golf. We went to Edinburgh. While Louise helped Mme Vuillaume spend her holiday allowance, I showed Adolphe the Advocates' Library and one or two of the more choice New Town bars. We've kept in touch. Let me pour you a whisky before I go on. I never could read screeds of type without getting a dry mouth.

So here is the translation in double-spacing on French legal bond which I read alone in my car as Louise zipped and velcroed Forbes Wedderburn into a fluorescent suit on the quayside at Broughty Ferry.

12 Apr. 1900 Accident Death
Deposition of Police Agent Fermier R. no. 211
08.05 (I was) on duty at corner of Rue de la Fayette and Rue du Faubourg Poissonnière when passers-by informed me of an accident in Square Montholon. I proceeded to Square Montholon, where I found a small crowd surrounding a water wagon (property of the *Ville de Paris*) which was jammed at an angle against the railings of the square. Several of the iron railings were broken and between the railings and the wheels of the wagon was wedged the body of a man. The railings had penetrated his back and the wheels had passed over his abdomen. I performed the usual procedure to check for signs of life, but without doubt, the mortal flame had been extinguished. One of the horses was also badly injured, having been cut in the belly by the railing. I placed

my cape over the dead man and went to the police post at Poissonnière to call assistance.

08.10 The driver of the water wagon requested permission to release his injured horse from the traces. I granted permission and told him to stay nearby to give his statement. A. R. Ladeuil, *rentier*, of 26 Rue Baudin informed me that the dead man had been in the company of a woman. She had narrowly escaped injury and had been taken to the Café St Bertrand in a condition of collapse. M. Ladeuil offered his statement as a witness.

08.15 Agents Matieu and Ferrari arrived from Poissonnière. The crowd was dispersed and further witnesses sought. I went to the Café St Bertrand. The proprietrix showed me a woman lying on a bench inside the café. She told me the woman was a foreigner. The woman seemed to be senseless. I asked her several times for her name, but she did not reply. I instructed that a doctor should be called and returned to the scene of the accident.

08.25 Brigadier Kestner of the ninth *arrondissement* came to the scene and took charge. He instructed me to take down the depositions of M. Ladeuil and M. Duval (the driver of the water wagon).

I append these depositions to this report together with details of damage to municipal property viz.: six iron railings, one water wagon and one draught horse.

08.30 The Brigadier judged the injured horse was beyond help and Agent Ferrari shot it.

08.35 I supervised the removal of the dead man from the roadway to a vehicle of the City Mortuary which had been summoned by Agent Matieu.

08.40 I questioned MM Ladeuil and Duval.

09.15 I resumed thoroughfare duty in Rue de la Fayette.

Signed, Robert Fermier *Agent de Police*, no. 211

12 April 1900

Here are the photocopies of the witness statements. How's your French? I find the documents have a quaint charm, but then I have more than a passing interest in legal ephemera. No doubt they were taken down in indellible pencil and transcribed in ink when the redoubtable Agent Fermier finished his beat. I'll read you the translation.

12 Apr. 1900 Deposition of M. Auguste Ladeuil,* rentier, *26 Rue Baudin Paris 9

Born Auxerre, Yonne, 27/6/24

About eight o'clock (08.00) I was on my way back to my apartment in the Rue Baudin with milk from the dairy in Rue de la Fayette and sundry other small purchases. Since my wife died, I have always done my shopping at an early hour. Normally I walk up the pavement on the east side of Square Montholon which takes me straight to Rue Baudin, but today I remembered I had promised to play *boules* with friends at ten. Our first game of the year. We play in the little garden in Square Montholon and I wanted to make sure it was not too muddy. There had been a lot of rain overnight.

I was about to cross from the pavement to the middle of the square when I heard a shocking noise from Rue Baudin. People at the Café St Bertrand were jumping to their feet and crowding towards the corner. I too hurried to the end of the street. A water wagon had gone out of control in Rue Baudin and was careering down the hill. As it passed under the bridge that carries Rue Bellefons across Rue Baudin, the driver jumped from the box and landed on the cobbles. It was then I noticed a young couple about to cross the street in front of the wagon. I thought they must be deaf not to hear the terrible noise and everyone screaming. They were looking the wrong way. Then all at once the young woman turned and threw herself out of the path of the horses. She landed on the pavement almost at my feet. The man also saw the danger but he did not move. Perhaps he was petrified by fear. I have seen that, you know, on the barricades in seventy-one. Just before the horses ran over him, he did a peculiar thing. He raised his hat and bowed towards them. At least that's how it seemed to me. Then it was all over. I could not see the man. He was beneath the wagon. A horse started to scream. Its belly was ripped open. Water was spraying from the wagon and mixing with the blood. A terrible sight. The young woman was lying on the pavement. She must have fainted, for I'm sure the wagon did not strike her. I said they should take her to the café, and eventually two workmen carried her there.

12 Apr. 1900 Deposition of M. Gaston Duval, driver, 217 Rue de Belleville Paris 19
Born Charenton, Paris 1/9/48

It is my duty every morning except Sunday to water the streets in the eastern part of the ninth *arrondissement*. At about seven forty-five (07.45) I refilled my tank from the pump near the Gare du Nord. Then I drove down the Rue de Maubeuge and turned down Rue Baudin. The street slopes steeply and I applied the brake as I always do. At the top of the hill I turned on the water sprinkler. About half way down, the horses were suddenly startled and bolted with the wagon. It was impossible to stop them. I drove a gun team with McMahon at Sedan, so I should know. I just tried to save myself. I narrowly escaped with my life. And now the wagon is wrecked and one of my horses is dead. Who'll carry the can for that? Both my legs must be bruised. Can I claim compensation?

Supplementary Statement from Police Agent Fermier R. no. 211
Response to questions regarding fatal accident.

M. Auguste Ladeuil.

Agent 211: Did you notice where the man and woman involved in the accident came from or where they were going?

Ladeuil: I have no idea. A cab was leaving the other end of the square. They may have come from there, but I really can't say.

Agent 211: Have you any idea what caused the horses to bolt in Rue Baudin?

Ladeuil: As I have said, I did not know what was going on until I saw the commotion at the Café St Bertrand. By the time I looked up the hill, the wagon had run away and the driver was about to jump for his life.

M. Gaston Duval

Agent 211: Have your horses ever given trouble before?

Duval: Never. Nothing like this. They've been with me for four years. They're always blinkered and accustomed to the traffic. They're never out of the city. I am a good driver. I've driven this wagon for fifteen years. Before that I was a driver in the field artillery. There a man really learns to drive, I can tell you.

Agent 211: Can you say what frightened the horses?

Duval: You bet I can. It was on the iron bridge that crosses Rue Baudin. I saw it from the top of the street. When it reared up, I thought it might jump right over the parapet. No wonder the horses bolted.

Agent 211: What did you see on the bridge?

Duval: A bear, of course. The one that's been dancing for centimes in the Place de la Fayette. I'd swear the keeper made it rear up on purpose. They're damned Bosche, you know.

Agent 211: Before the horses bolted, did you see the man who was killed or the woman who survived?

Duval: I only saw them after I had jumped from the wagon. There was time to escape. The woman rushed out of the way, but the man just stood there. He even took off his hat.

Agent 211: He was petrified by the stampeding horses?

Duval: Perhaps. But to me he seemed not to notice the horses at all. He was watching the bear and smiling even as he fell under the wheels.

One last thing, my dear. Typewritten and bearing the arms of the Office of the Examining Magistrate. It's just a memo. The sort of thing such people generate by the dozen every day. I'm surprised it has survived.

21 May 1900

Fatal Accident in Square Montholon: 12 April 1900

Deceased: Jock Dow, businessman, of Dundee, Scotland

I have read the report of Agent Fermier passed to me by Brigadier Kestner of the *ninth Arrondissement* and that of Sergeant Baptiste of the Highways Squad who traced the owner of the bear referred to in the deposition of Duval G. viz: Dau of Koenigsberg, a German citizen. Though Dau admits he was in the approximate area around the time of the accident, he cannot remember exactly where. No witness other than Duval can be found to confirm that the bear was in Rue Bellefons on the bridge which crosses Rue Baudin. Dau's papers were in order, but he was warned to obey the Highways and Public Order Act. He stated that he intended leaving Paris that day.

As there is no proof of any offence, no further action will be taken. I have informed the British Consul that the case is one of accidental death.

la Croix, Examining Magistrate.

I doubt if it ever dawned on M. la Croix that the victim and the bear-keeper had similar names. Such coincidences happen all the time. I was still staring at the last page when Louise knocked on the car window. Forbes was heading down the quayside, fluorescent and forlorn, lugging the camera gear to the top of the ladder. Louise caught my expression.

'Something important?'

'Something I'd half-expected, or rather the answer to something that has puzzled me for years.'

'You look as if you've seen a ghost.'

'The Ghost wasn't involved. Only the bear.'

Louise watched anxiously from the warmth of the car as I struggled into my suit. She didn't offer to help, but when I followed Forbes to the ladder and held the mooring rope taught as he clambered over the edge of the quay, she appeared at my side and quite unexpectedly kissed me. If Forbes saw this touching tableau from the deck of the boat, he said nothing. But when we'd stowed the gear and I was about to start the outboards, he looked up and held his arms aloft like a portly tenor saluting from a precarious stage.

'We owe you so much,' he yelled. 'Tonight we're going on the town.' Whether Louise heard the invitation I can't say, but when I dropped the rope and opened the throttle, I saw the concern on her face through the haze of petrol fumes. She didn't wave and watched motionless till we passed through the harbour mouth.

What's that? Don't worry. One tape will be enough. Tomorrow you'll check out and head south to unravel the secrets of your miniature cassettes. I wish you luck. And as this will be our last evening together for a while, let's take a glass.

Chapter 28

I SCARCELY GLANCED behind, but felt Forbes settle astride the seat and the grip of his fingers round my waist. Waves broke across our bow, then slipped away as we began to plane towards the river mouth. I remember feeling very cold, colder even than when Muirhead had first sped me towards the sand bar earlier in the year. The river was deserted. Sooner than I'd ever have thought, we reached the buoy where once the Abertay Lightship marked the northern limit of the Tay and Broughty Lifeboat went down with all hands when she broke adrift. We'd tied down our cargo in the bow, beneath a rubberised tarpaulin of which Jock Dow would have been proud. Spray foamed over the lumpy shapes of the camera and gyro-mount but not over the seal-pick. Not over the hand-fashioned club with which Forbes was about to stun the art world. Forbes wouldn't part with it, and now I felt the shaft and angled head against my spine where he had wedged the club between our bodies. With every bump of the boat, despite the padding of my suit, Muirhead's handiwork drove against my kidneys till I twisted round and yelled into the face that beamed over my shoulder:

'Take that fucking thing out of my back!'

It's not a word heard often on my lips. Still, I'm sure its appearance so late in your tapes won't be a problem for your editors. *Tempo* is peppered with the word, as verb and adjective, deployed by artists keen to bring the common touch to their opinions. Anyway, that's what I said. 'Take that fucking thing out of my back!' And in the instant before I turned to keep the boat's head on course, I saw Forbes's eyes darken and a look cross his face of sheer disdain.

Suddenly the lighthouse stood above the crest of the waves. From the speeding boat, so close to the surface, it was no taller than a cigarette, but I was proud to have found it so easily and felt Forbes's grip tighten as he caught sight of it too. It took ages for the rock to appear. I cut the revs and watched as Stevenson's tapered column of keyed stone became more distinct. It stood in a snowstorm of seabirds, like a Christmas novelty. As we approached I stood and scanned the waves for signs of other life: a maintenance tender, maybe, or creel-boat hauling lobster pots at the base of the rock. The Bell Rock was deserted. The glazed slits in the tower looked blindly down, but still we were observed. How could fluorescent orange escape five thousand glittering aerial eyes? How could twin Evinrudes, though cut to scarce a gurgle, elude four hundred auditory meatuses on the long, broken finger of reef? I felt Forbes unstraddling the seat. He lurched past across the swaying deck and stood, legs splayed, in the bow. Wedderburn at Inchcape.

Anxiously I looked for a landing place where Forbes or I could jump with a line and tether the boat. To catch a foothold on the slimy stone seemed near impossible, then I saw, some way to the right, a patch of shelving rock on which we might be able to run the prow of our boat just long enough for one to step ashore. As I opened the throttle and lined up the boat and waved to Forbes to take the mooring line, the surface of the reef seemed to move. Two hundred basking seals rose and craned their fat necks and gazed through globular eyes at the intrusive grey shape that rose on the swell then surged ahead and slithered alongside them on the rock. Forbes stumbled ashore. The nearer seals were already taking to the water. He cast about for something to secure the rope, but as he made up his mind to loop the line round a spike of jagged rock, the swell caught the boat once more and swept her even further up the shelf of rock. I struggled to tilt the propellers clear of danger. When I turned, the line was fast and Forbes was advancing on the wary animals, pick raised just like the wire spook he'd made to bash the life out of a stuffed sealskin in Hampstead.

I don't know how I got the gear ashore. By the time I'd carried it clear of the waves and set enough line to keep the boat safe, Forbes had scared every seal from the vicinity. Their blunt snouts bobbed accusingly in the swell. Our choices were to wait quietly in the hope they might return, or to make our way further down the reef, away from the lighthouse, where another hundred seals lay if not in ignorance, then in no fear of the intruders that had disturbed their neighbours. I told Forbes this while I unpacked the loaded camera. As we were on dry land, however insubstantial, I left the gyro-mount in its case. The clouds were clearing now. I knelt on the rocks as I had seen Inez do among the sand dunes and shot a few moments of Forbes against the sky. But on Inchcape Rock, Forbes Wedderburn wanted no tricks of the trade, no cunning angles to disguise the lack of targets for his club.

Forbes set off down the reef. He skidded on wet birdlime, then righted himself, the seal-pick held before him like Blondin's pole. I followed, and briefly held his plump, swaying figure in the viewfinder as if Forbes were an animal that should be recorded for posterity. On safer ground, he turned. Again I caught the anger in his eye. This wasn't the picture he'd hoped to show the world on shocking, wall-sized screens. Forbes was after blood, but as he stalked towards the hundred shapeless backs, the seals stirred one by one and rolled into the waves. When almost half the herd had left the rock, I realised he'd never make it. Forbes walked towards me holding out the club. Slowly he raised the pick and, taking it by the metal tines, held the handle invitingly. I laid the camera on the rock, and as I took the seal pick and felt its weight and grasped its worn shaft, Forbes said, 'This isn't in my blood. Why not see if it's in yours?'

Oh yes, my dear. It was. Where Forbes had caused dismay and languid flight, I met curiosity. Bearded muzzles rose at my approach. Some even thrust against me like earless dogs greeting a welcome stranger. I swung the seal-pick, and when it hit the mark and did its sudden, lethal work, stepped across the twitching corpse and swung again. I needed no practice with tussocks in the dunes. I had the right tool for the job, and used it as effortlessly as a rake on my own lawn. The deadly tine pierced skulls so neatly. Not a sound escaped, except an occasional gasp of fishy breath. There was hardly a trickle of blood. I stepped along the fringe of the docile herd, picking my victims one by one. As for Forbes, he might not have been there, my attention was so focused on the task. I supposed, now that our roles were reversed, that he'd have picked up the camera. But Forbes had no wish to tape his stolen thunder. I must have killed six or more when there was a roar that stopped the seal-pick in mid stroke and sent my grey companions scrambling to the sea. Of course he knew just enough to handle the boat. I'd even shown him how to start the outboards and set the throttle. I thought he might be hoping to film me from the water, but then I saw the camera exactly where I'd laid it on the rock and realised the truth. I didn't shout or wave. I stood with warm corpses at my feet and watched the low grey shape head towards the horizon and the mouth of the Tay.

Oh no, my dear, my memory's quite clear. But when the cold set in I seemed to lose my grasp on time. Forbes had the mobile phone. I knew he'd not get help. At first I thought I'd head along the reef towards the light and climb its base beyond reach of the tide. It seemed so simple. I left my dead companions and climbed over rocks humped like upturned boats and slick with slime, but then I found the neck I'd shinned across to reach the pod of seals was gone beneath the swell. I had no choice. Launch into the rising tide in hope of finding a handhold on the other side, or pick somewhere on the outcrop which might not be entirely submerged. In my life-saving suit, I scrambled upwards till I found a small plateau no more than three yards long with stones piled like a pulpit at one end. The empty mussel shells and skin of birdlime seemed not to have been shifted by the last tide. I set my back against the rock and then passed out, for my next impression was of a lifeless, whiskered face nudging my frozen cheek. The water was at my chest. As the dull-eyed head with the red hole punched in its brow drifted away, I let go the seal-pick

(I'd left the camera to its fate long ago) and edged higher into my cleft of stone.

The tide rose in slow, tantalising waves which foamed on the half-submerged finger of rock. But where I was wedged in the angle of weed-slimed granite, it formed a treacherous, inky swell, which one moment lifted me clean off my feet till my fingernails were all that held me to the rock, the next set me down so suddenly I was almost sucked from my perch. I was very cold. My clawing hands lost all sensation. My nails broke and peeled from the flesh, and I looked on with no more concern than I would watch of an untwining leaf or an insect shedding its carapace. There was no pain, not even any blood, for each successive wave washed clean the wounds before blood could seep from the torn skin. My concentration focused utterly on clinging to the patch of rock. All thoughts of crossing the gap to scale the black foundation of the lighthouse dissolved. My movements seemed to need less effort as time passed, though now I know my ebbing strength was matched by failing consciousness. The cold played tricks with my mind. Once, when my eyes had almost closed and I was on the brink of icy suspension, I caught a fetid whiff and saw through salt-stung lids that the waves had a brownish sheen and a granular texture that dripped and clung to the slime and turned the foam at the water's edge the colour of infant spew. I shut my mouth, but who can survive a ducking with clenched jaws? As my lungs filled with rancid air, a wave washed in a mouthful of the yellow chaff that seemed to cover the whole surface of the sea. At that moment or the next, the cold that had numbed me beyond sleep drew my mind into a void in which Louise, in whalebone and stockings, stood over a fan which raised her skirt in rhythm with the tide while Forbes, still buoyant in his suit, would offer me a long, cool drink but leave it just out of reach to take a call on his mobile phone.

My next impression was of open sea, clear of the foul swell, but dotted with black, barking snouts that nuzzled towards me. I floated upwards and saw an inch before my face, and then a yard, and then another inch, an iron ring, or rather a staple driven into the rock to take a long-corroded ring to moor Stevenson's barge when he built the blank-walled tower on Inchcape Rock. I caught the worn loop and held it as my final grasp on life. Then, in a moment of absolute clarity which even now seems a beacon in a mist of confusion, I unfastened the velcro strap that closed the left cuff of my survival suit and tied it through the ring. My makeshift tether held. For once I could relax my grip and sink and float in the numbing swell. How long I hung from the rock I can't tell. Sitting here, nursing my wounds, trying to account for every minute, my guess is that I floated for four hours. And then I heard him. At first a disgruntled grumble, then the full-throated bellow of a brown bear driven to distraction by screaming washerwomen. Water splashed and flew all over from unattended faucets. Foaming suds cascaded over the stones. The roar of the bear filled my head till I opened my eyes and saw him twisting and whirling before me, his gigantic frame plastered from head to toe in sodden orange petticoats. I tried to escape, to follow the fleeing washerwomen into the sunlight, but I was tethered by the wrist and could not even look away as the bear called Kaspar lunged towards me. I saw his brown face. I saw the coal-black eyes above the muzzle which enclosed his snout, then his great paws clasped me. We wrestled, but I had no strength and soon he swung me off my feet clean into the air. Over the rock. Over the lonely lighthouse towards a yawning washhouse door, where arms stretched out to wrest me from his grasp.

When next I looked around, or peered between caked lids, not moving, not giving anything away, my head was vibrating gently against a concave plastic window. I was wrapped in a silver blanket, strapped in a steel-framed seat in what seemed not unlike a shaking, noisy van. The negro winchman, hanging from a grab-strap like an aerial commuter, leaned across and placed his pale palm on my brow. He grinned and his lips moved behind the microphone mask clipped across his mouth. I can't remember what he said, except for the words 'Boulmer' and 'Anybody else?' Much later, I heard from an anxious Coast Guard that an amateur ornithologist, who happened to be aboard the sludge ship *Gardyloo* as it discharged Edinburgh's compacted effluent within sight of the Bell Rock, spotted my fluorescent shape among the angry seabirds. The lifeboat put to sea, and soon found our boat upturned on the sandbank I showed you from this very window.

At home, in the gazebo where old Paton would watch for ships, Louise saw the lifeboat leave and nervously lifted the telephone and set in train another search. But in the helicopter, I ignored the winchman's repeated questions, set my head against the cool plastic and watched trails of moisture dance across its curve. I saw a smudge of coastline. I saw the shining, empty river mouth but not the lifeboat nor the upturned hull of our RHIB. Radio voices echoed in the throbbing airborne box. The winchman balanced with his knees against my seat. He shook my shoulder. His mike-mask hung unhooked on his chest. He wore a pencil moustache just like Cab Calloway. You won't remember him. But this Cab didn't want to jump and jive.

'There were two. Right? Two of you. In a boat.' This Cab held two fingers before my eyes as if I'd been concussed and yelled above the static and the engine. His eyes went blank. I felt the pressure of his knees withdraw. A message must have reached him in the chipped white dome that bore the disappointing label 'Smith'. He shot a sceptical if not a hostile glance. 'You're going to hospital. Then we can refuel and search for your chum.'

I did not even move my head. I saw the castle, guarding its shameful treasures; I saw the harbour, and white cars with blue lights winking helplessly at the end of the pier. I saw my own roof amidst the trees and the gazebo where old Paton would watch for jute ships and where Louise had seen the lifeboat heading for the bar. Was she still watching now? I saw the railway running straight as a die towards the congested sweep of road where once there was a bridge and before the bridge a Blondin Car that slipped from its cable. And Stannergate, and Craigie (where now there were too many red-tile roofs to hide a ghost and too many fences to leap, even with spring-heeled boots) passed out of sight beneath the shuddering plastic. And then the shining network of the city. The curve of Crescent Street, but no trace of Baxter's Half-time School, where, in the morning, thirty-two sleepy eyes and in the afternoon forty exhausted eyes watched Ethel Wilkie's chalk squeak eagerly across the board. I saw the roofs of Dens Mills, sheltering in storeyed compartments rich with period charm a new breed of people who never sighed on passing through the gate, slept easily where great machines had stood and dreamed of property prices and IKEA. I saw the great, grey roof of the Bell Mill, where the Craigie Ghost had climbed in his Inverness cape, and through rain-smeared perspex, the tower where a young man with a stolen name had invented Tayline and almost come to grief in an accident that had never been explained.

And then we soared and banked. We were not heading for the airport, nor the infirmary, in whose jagged shadow a municipal wash-house once stood, but for Ninewells, whose shadow fell only on spacious grounds with easy access from the air. Over a black rim of hill, the townscape of Lochee slanted till it seemed that Cox's stack was slanting too. And then the little window went dark with the mass of the hill. The airframe shook. The pilot slowed and dropped the nose to line up his approach. The downdraught changed and swept the rain-tracks from my plastic bubble till the only silver tracks I saw were those that crossed and circled the ancient mound. And in its lee, quite hidden from the ground, invisible save from the air, I saw four black indentations where once a rotting jawbone vault had stood and where everything may or may not have begun beneath the Law.

The winchman tugged the belt that held me in my cot. He unclipped his mask, and as he turned to take his seat, yelled out the comment he must have made so many times.

'You're a lucky man.'